North of the Border

T. Allen Winn

Pp
PROSEPRESS
www.prosepress.biz

North of the Border
Copyright © 2013
T. Allen Winn

Published by ProsePress
Pawleys Island, South Carolina 29585
www.Prosepress.biz

Comments: Contact T. Allen Winn at
TALLENWINN@mail.com

Comments can also be found on
T. Allen Winn's Face Book

ISBN: 978-0-9893063-0-0

Cover Design : OBD Art and Illustration
Contact: proseNcons@live.com

<u>Novels by T. Allen Winn</u>

The Caregiver's Son,
Outside the Window Looking In

Trudy Wagner Detective Thrillers
Road Rage
North of the Border

The Bully Series
Dark Thirty

<u>Soon to be published</u>

The Perfect Spook House
Abbeville, South Carolina, Halloween 1968, eleven 11th graders vent by exploring old deserted houses, something they've done countless times. Picking the wrong house on the Cedar Springs Road forever changes their lives. Nineteen years later, they're still searching for answers. Reminiscing is not for the weak hearted but the truth can set you free or can it? Sometimes it is best to leave the past where it belongs.

Foot
Mid eighteen hundreds, Washington State Mountains, trapper Bad Nose Ed Carlson leads a handful of hopefuls to a new life.
The Spokane Tribe's warns stay clear of the great northern woods. It is home of the S'cwene'y'ti, the giant hairy men. Patrons of the wagon train rival the unknown. Mountain men fear nothing. B. N. battles legend and his fellow man the only way he knows how, head on and he never looses but he had never met Big Foot.

Sea, Sand and Secrets
Dead Men Tell No Tales

Mar, La arena y los secretos
Los muertos no hablan

ACKNOWLEDGEMENTS

Nothing is ever possible without the support and encouragement of family and friends.

I especially owe my beloved wife, Judy, for her many hours of assistance in my pursuit of this annoying hobby, and special thanks to Danny Singleton, no relation to Hank.

Finding success is when those same family and friends still support and encourage you after they have read your first one.

North of the Border features 'You can be in my next novel' contest winner, Marian Bond Samion. You decide if she should be a reoccurring character.

He who profits by a crime
commits it.

Seneca, Roman philosopher

Jorge Cruz, deep in thought, almost didn't notice the white Mustang convertible with its hood up, pulled on the shoulder of highway 90. The young lady never waved him down, just sat there in the driver's seat with her head buried in the steering wheel. He glanced at his dash clock and it was a quarter past midnight. This stretch of the highway, dark and desolate, was no place for a woman alone.

He spotted an old pulpwood road in his high beams and eased in and turned around to see if he could assist. Pulling off the shoulder directly in front of the white convertible, the raised hood blocked his view of the lady sitting behind the wheel.

Leaving his old Buick running, headlights down on low beam, he opened the creaking door and headed toward the woman in distress. The lady stepped out of the driver's side and smiled, looking relieved to have someone stop to help her. Jorge noticed she wore a white polka dotted mini skirt, sheer black blouse, and knee high black leather boots. Her huge breasts pressed braless against the fabric, exposing more of her than he felt comfortable seeing. His first impression was that she had to either be a local stripper or a prostitute. That was not his concern. She required assistance. He would not judge her.

"What's the problem?"

"If I knew that I wouldn't be sitting here now would I?" She smiled, answering him in an almost angelic yet sarcastic tone.

"That was a stupid question on my part," Jorge apologized in his broken English accent.

"You are Hispanic?"

"Does that concern you if I am?"

"I didn't mean it as an insult. I have this thing for languages. It's almost a curse. I have to guess the origin when I hear an accent."

"No offense taken. I'm originally from Mexico. I hope that is not a problem?"

"On the contrary...I had you pegged for Mexican. I simply love your culture. Do you think you can help me?"

"I'm no mechanic, but let's see what I can do. What did your automobile do to bring you to a stop?"

"It just sort of chug-a-lugged, and then the engine died. The gas gage indicates I have at least a half tank of gas so I'm not sure what happened. My baby has never stranded me before."

"Let me take a peek under there," said Jorge, peering under the hood.

Leaning forward, he checked the battery cables, jiggled the spark plug wires, opened several caps, checking fluid levels, and pretended that he knew more than he really did about the mechanics of an automobile engine. If he couldn't fix it, which he had no reason to believe he could, he would offer her a ride; probably not the safest thing for a woman alone to accept a ride from a stranger. It just struck him. He had not introduced himself to her and didn't know her name, either. How rude he had been.

Jorge never saw her making her move. The syringe penetrated his neck like a bee sting. He instinctively grabbed his neck and clutched the female hand holding the needle. How had he been so stupid? The Good Samaritan made eye contact with the lady in distress questioning her intentions then collapsed on the ground.

She closed the hood on her White Mustang and made a quick phone call on her cell phone. She needed to dispose of the Buick as quickly as possible. She tugged on the limp and lifeless body of Jorge Cruz, maneuvering him into the passenger side of her vehicle.

She checked the ID from his wallet. "Yep, this was him, and right on schedule." It paid to do one's homework she thought.

Horry County Police Department
Near the South Carolina Grand Strand

Constable Woody Anderson had been summoned to Sheriff Hank Singleton's office. This always made Woody nervous when the big guy formally requested his presence. Woody had just received troubling information and wasn't in the best of moods, and he felt things were only about to become much worse.

Hank stood and shook Woody's hand then said, "Woodrow, you look a tad down. What seems be the problem, tough case?"

"Janice's cousin Marian Bond is coming to town this weekend from Gatlinburg, Tennessee, extending her honeymoon to the grand strand. I say, Bond, but she just recently got married again. I can't remember her new name this time. It begins with an S, something like Salmon or Samson, Simian or something like that. I've never met the groom. She will be living in Butler, Tennessee with him after they wrap up this honeymoon stop, so she says. Marian was originally from Abbeville, South Carolina, a little town nestled in the Piedmont, near the upstate area, about four and half hours from here. You might remember it. It was the place they filmed parts of the movie, *Sleeping with the Enemy*, with *Julia Roberts*. Anyway, she'll want me to play tourist with her. You know how I hate that crap."

"Come on Woodrow, it won't be that bad. Look at it this way; you'll be doing it for Janice, rest her soul."

"Oh it will be that bad. She's already sent me a partial list of places she wants to go. I can just see them sitting on that motorcycle at Hard Rock Café up at Broadway at the Beach, the perfect tourist photo op. I'll have to drag the rug rats along too; they eat this stuff up, and especially any chance to go to the Pavilion, unless I can corral Lullabelle or the mother-in-law into babysitting."

"It could be worse; you could be the one mounting the motorcycle, smiling for the camera. Besides, your chaps deserve a little downtime with their daddy, now and then."

"I draw the line on being in any of those gosh awful touristy pictures. Maybe you could have me pull a double shift this weekend. I could tell them you were short handed or something. "

"Woodrow, I'm not going to that, and you know it. This is Janice's family. You just need to man up and do what's right."

"Maybe I should locate that bastard, Lance Rocker and let him be their tour guide. He'd probably enjoy ruining another marriage."

"You know you don't mean that. Okay, humor me, son. Where do the newlyweds want you to take them?"

"It's not that big of a deal. I'll survive. I didn't come here to air my grievances. You asked me here. What's up, boss?"

"It's time for me to take it easy and pass the baton," stated the mountain of a man, Sheriff Hank Singleton. "Woodrow, I'm a dinosaur and too set in my ways. Besides, the old ticker isn't what it used to be. It would be unjust for me to stay out my term."

"Just like that, you're rolling over. You're just going to hand it over to someone else and walk away?"

"Woodrow, look at me. I'm an old fat fart with a diagnosed heart condition, and it's time for me to call in the dogs. I'm damned fortunate I survived that serial killer ordeal a few years ago. Lance Rocker lobbied for my resignation back then. Lucky for me he moved on to the big time, got the hell out of town with that big TV show deal, and things finally died down."

"Come on Hank, you still have some good years left in you."

"Woodrow, to be honest, I'm tired of doing this. I'm just plain burned out on law enforcement. I'm ready to kick back and do a little fishing, a little hunting, and maybe just plant me a row or two of okra and a few tomato plants. I'm glad you've been promoted to Constable. You deserve it. You've earned it."

"I guess I can sort of understand. We've all come a long way. I really had to work to overcome Janice's death. I, for one, am glad Rocker has moved on to greener pastures too. I hate that bastard for screwing my wife, and I still hold him partly responsible for her death. Not having to deal with him probably saved his life and me a term in prison. Good riddance, I say."

"I would feel the same way if I were in your shoes. You and Wagner did a fine job. You brought down Joseph Preston, putting to bed all those road rage murders, and you even nailed Tim Ford. Ford is still locked away and should never see the light of day."

"That was indeed a defining moment for Horry County law enforcement, and kudos to you for allowing Wagner to form that CSI unit."

"She just confirmed why I hired her. I still have a tough time swallowing Preston's rampage, though. That troubled soul killed a hell of lot of motorists, just to avenge his folk's deaths."

"I just wish we could have brought him to justice. The damn coward had to put a bullet through his brain."

"It saved the taxpayer, Woodrow."

"So when does your retirement go into effect?"

"End of the month, just three short weeks," replied the grinning mountain of a man with a slick shaved head, now standing up from behind his desk. "It'll be just enough time for me to teach new arrival, Sheriff Burton, the ropes."

"So tell me about this fellow Burton."

"She's not a feller."

"Not again...don't you believe in hiring men anymore, Hank?"

"Dag-nabbit, Woodrow, she's qualified and was available."

"It's not going to be the same reporting to a skirt."

"Now don't prejudge, Woodrow. Samantha Burton had quite an impressive career down in Charleston."

"Samantha Burton, I'm sorry chief, she just doesn't sound like sheriff material to me. For some reason I have this vivid picture of *Bewitched*!" Woody tried to twitch his nose like the television witch.

"Give her a chance, Woodrow. You felt the same way toward Wagner, if memory serves me right. On paper she looks like she can hold her own in this position."

He shrugged. "I suppose I really don't have a choice, do I?"

"Nope, that's a fact. How do you think Wagner will deal with reporting to a woman?"

"Why don't you ask her, sir?" She responded, standing in the doorway. "And my last name is now Pierce, remember."

"I reckon I just did," answered a scrambling Hank Singleton. "Good morning, Detective Pierce."

"So you're really going to do it, sir, just up and retire?"

"That's my plan and I'm recommending this Burton to replace me, at least until the next election. The Mayor has bought in on it, so I reckon I still carry a little weight around here."

"We need more women in this department. I'd say we're on the right track," stated an exuberant Trudy Wagner Pierce. "No offense Sheriff!"

"Watch what you wish for, Detective Wagner. I mean Pierce. She's a tough piece of work, and she has a reputation for kicking female butts."

"I have a big one to kick, sir, and always welcome a challenge."

"This is going to be just great. This department is going to hell in a handbasket."

"Come on Woodrow," advised Hank. "That's an inappropriate comment even for you."

"Sorry Hank, I sort of liked things before the female invasion."

"Not to worry, Sheriff, she'll wear him down like I did. He's not as tough as he acts."

"See what I mean, Hank."

"Enough, do I have to remind you that you're supposed to be professionals? Can we just change the subject? Y'all really ought to get out there and fight some criminals and make Horry County a safer place."

"We can do that, Hank," answered Woody, winking at Trudy.

"Pierce, we have a missing person," advised Hank. "Go by the Pentecostal Church in North Myrtle Beach, and talk to Raeford McCrery. He's the preacher there. It seems that his associate pastor is missing. He hasn't shown up for several days. The good preacher said he hasn't been seen in a couple of days."

"Will do, sir," replied the blue eyed detective, still fit. Her six foot one frame remained lean and hard at one hundred forty pounds. Now twenty nine, she no longer wore her blonde hair cropped short. Brady Pierce, her husband, had convinced her to let it grow out shoulder length. "What do you have on your agenda, Constable Anderson?"

"Homicide, domestic dispute down in Surf Side, and I'm doing the follow-up."

"Who bit the big one, a man or woman?"

"Neither," Woody replied, shaking his head in disgust. " A nine month old girl; the father just got tired of her crying and smothered her with a pillow, best we can tell while the mom stood by and did nothing to prevent it."

"Pathetic," chimed in Hank. "I hate it when innocent chaps are victims. It's just a crying shame."

"What's really pathetic is the mother. She's not fingering the father. They're claiming they just found the baby dead in its crib. Coroner says different. Worse still, they were manufacturing methamphetamine in their home."

"Keep me posted, officers. Now go do your duty," said Hank, his nearly three hundred pounds supported by a mountainous frame would have made him look like Big Foot, except his hairless head would not support the Sasquatch theory.

Woody in contrast was eight inches shorter. He no longer sported a mustache and side burns. He was now clean shaven and twenty pounds lighter, and he still remained a pit bull. His hair once jet black, was now peppered with gray, compliments of the road rage murders and the loss of his wife, Janice. She had died at the hands of the serial killer after having had a one night stand with newsman, Lance Rocker. Preston, the road rage killer, had attempted to pen the murder on Rocker.

The road rage serial killer case had shaken the beach community but had no long term effects on tourism; rather the opposite. Lance Rocker had penned a book on the case. It had landed number one on the best seller list for almost sixteen weeks. The book launched his lucrative television career, and he now hosted a weekly investigative reporter show on the Crime Channel. No longer a thorn in the Horry County Police department's side, he had relocated to Atlanta.

The beach community had eventually returned to normal. Sure, it still had its fair share of crimes, but nothing to the magnitude of the Road Rage Murders. Transients, especially during the peak tourist season, brought with them numerous home break-ins, assaults and shoplifting. There were still the occasional murders but most were domestic or gang related, and not the work of a deranged serial killer

Pentecostal Holiness Church
North Myrtle Beach

Detective Sylvester Stone, a member of Trudy's CSI unit, met her at the church. Nicknamed Sly for the Family Stone Band, he stood an inch taller than Trudy, and like her, he too was a fitness nut. He had a chiseled and toned physique, with not one ounce of body fat on his thirty three year old frame. He sported a neatly trimmed, full beard, one inch afro and his skin color revealed his pure African heritage, black as pitch. Sly was respected and liked by everyone in the department and the community. He was a local.

"Thanks for meeting me here," welcomed Trudy, patting him on his broad muscular shoulders.

Sly, rubbing his chin asked, "My gut tells me this might have the potential to be Hispanic gang related?"

"Let's hear what the reverend has to say and then we'll decide."

Reverend Raeford McCrery greeted them at the church's main entrance. The southern born and bread preacher, age sixty five, slender build, *Ichabod Crane* in appearance, measured in at six foot three. He spoke like a true gentleman, directly out of a scene from *Gone with the Wind*.

After formal introductions had been completed, Trudy asked "Reverend McCrery, when did you first become concerned about your associate pastor's disappearance?"

"Please call me Preacher," offered the smiling southerner. "It rolls off you tongue much better than all the reverend stuff and saves time and effort, don't you think?"

Trudy nodded. She liked this man already. "Preacher, please catch us up to speed then."

"Jorge has always been prompt. He usually beats me to the church and takes care of all the daily formalities. I've never known him to be sick or absent."

Sly interrupted, "And that would be Jorge ...?"

"Sorry, Jorge Cruz, a fine young lad, he is. He'll be twenty eight next month, but he looks ten years younger. He's been my associate pastor for almost two years now. He really strives to one day have a church of his own, and let me tell you, he is a shoein for one. We have a large Hispanic following here because of Jorge."

"Is Mister Cruz a citizen of the United States?"

"Not yet, Detective Pierce, but his paperwork is in order if that's what you are asking. He's not an illegal, I assure you."

Sly asked, "When did you first miss him?"

"He didn't make either of the services Sunday, morning or night, and I phoned his apartment off and on throughout the day. I even drove by there Sunday afternoon between services. His car was not there. I knocked and tried the door. It was locked."

"So he's been missing for two days then," stated Sly, scribbling in his notebook.

"Yes, that's right. I would have reported it before now, but I had a funeral out of town, and I just got back late last night. I drove to his place again this morning after I still couldn't reach him. I talked to some of his neighbors. None have seen him since Saturday. That's just not like Jorge. I've been praying for his safe return, but I fear something terrible has happened."

"Do you have a photograph of him?"

"Yes ma'am, let's go to my office. I have one of him and me, and his Sunday School class on my desk. He serves as our youth minister. The kids just love him."

Walking to the office the two officers continued to pick the minister for any additional information, but there simply wasn't much there. Jorge Cruz was respected and liked by all. That was obvious. He had no known enemies nor had any immediate family in this country. He lived alone. He drove a late model Buick Skylark with South Carolina plates. There wasn't much to go on yet.

Upon leaving, Trudy asked Sly, "What do you think?"

"He could be here on the up and up, and then again I've seen too many cases where the papers were forged. On the surface the guy sounds legit. I'll put out some feelers in the Hispanic community and see what turns up."

"Put out an APB on the car once you know the particulars. Other than that, I'm not sure we can do anything else for now."

"Yeah, a missing Hispanic immigrant won't exactly stir much interest I'm afraid. It's sad but this is a sore spot for most in the community. Many locals unfortunately think all are illegal. They blame them for taking jobs."

Trudy nodded. "I'm going to break for lunch. I'm supposed to meet Brady, so I'll see you back at the station afterwards."

"Tell him hello for me," smiled Sly, walking toward his cruiser.

Surfside Beach
Seaside Trailer Park

Woody Anderson had just wrapped up his preliminary investigation, and all pointed toward obvious child neglect and repeated abuse. One neighbor stated she had seen them mistreating the dead infant's three year old brother. Woody shook his head, unable to fathom how an adult could witness such behavior and not report it. The infant might still be alive if she had stepped forward.

The couple had apparently been operating the meth lab for several months according to several of the neighbors. One had witnessed suspicious activity and plenty of people traffic. Unbelievable how the neighbors had decided to stay out of it and just looked the other way; what was wrong with these people, wondered Woody.

Woody despised those who would harm or abuse children. He could only imagine what he would do to someone who had the gall to harm any of his. Thank goodness for his mother-in-law and Lullabelle. They had stepped in and filled the void left by Janice's death.

Loretta, Janice's mom and Lullabelle, the black woman who had helped care for Amy Wagner, now swapped out keeping the kids while Woody worked. Lullabelle had been a Godsend for Trudy, dealing with her sick mama. She had been wonderful with the elder Wagner.

Woody had been a workaholic when Janice was alive, but now he cherished his time off with his children. He no longer volunteered for extra duty and avoided double shifts when possible. Being a Constable had its perks. His kids were his top priority. He had learned his lesson, having lost them once to social services, when he had been consumed by Janice's death and her affair with Rocker. It would never happen again.

Opting to lunch at the area's Waffle House, Woody's meal was disrupted by an unexpected visit from Scat Crowder, his old high school buddy. Good old Scat was the alleged right hand man to Brock Boudreaux, local leader for the re-emerging Ku Klux Klan chapter. Scat had drifted to the dark side soon after they had graduated. He oozed of the badass biker image, tattooed from head to foot and had a shaved skinhead. All he needed was a white rope and hood. He had quite an impressive rap sheet to boot.

Fortunately, Woody had never had to personally arrest his old friend. It pained him to see Scat like this. Before they had graduated, Scat had received several football college scholarship offers, and he had chosen to attend the University of South Carolina. Bad judgment had prevailed. Scat had chosen to run with the wrong crowd. He had gotten busted for DUI, and been arrested for receiving stolen merchandise. The coach promptly kicked him off the football team his very first year.

Poor Scat had not coped well with college life and his newfound freedom away from home. He had elevated his bad boy reputation after returning to the beach. Woody had always believed Scat was just one incident away from doing hard time, if he didn't get himself killed first.

"Officer Woody, how's it hanging?"

"A little to the left, Scat, and are you keeping your butt out of trouble? Or, I guess I should say, at least not getting caught in the act?"

"I see you haven't lost your edge, even with wearing that damn cop's uniform squeezing the life out of you. So, Captain America, are you keeping the roadways safe from another wild maniac?"

"And are you still licking Boudreaux's butt squeaky clean?"

"What trash talking from one of our county's finest. Brock Boudreaux does more for this community financially than the governor."

"Yep, he's got plenty of the big dogs in his back pocket, that's for sure. And he's got flunkies like you to do his dirty work, so he keeps his nose clean. Just how many more times are you going to take the fall for him, Scat?"

"Such unfounded accusations, and I thought we were all innocent, until proven guilty."

"Your record stands for itself. There's not an innocent bone in your body, and you know it. What happened to you, Scat? You had so much promise. You could have done anything with your life, and now look at you."

"My life is just wonderful and none of your damn business, thank you very much. Look at me. I'm riding a brand new Harley. I have my own place right on the beach. I've got women stumbling over one another, just begging to jump my bones. I have an endless cash flow and pretty much do any damn thing I want. I believe I'm doing a hell of a lot better than you, my old bosom buddy."

"Do me a favor, Scat. Don't do something stupid on my watch. I'd rather not be the one to take you down."

"Come on buddy, you're making me sound like some sort of ruthless criminal. Now isn't that some sort of profiling you're laying on me?"

"If the profile fits..."

The middle aged waitress, with breasts just bursting to escape her uniform, walked up to take Woody's order. "Hey honey, give him anything he wants," winked Scat, slipping a twenty dollar bill between her cleavage, then two fingered another five bill in her waist band. "Here's a little extra for you."

She smiled and pinched Scat hard on his cheek. She was familiar with his tactics and his bed. She would tolerate either when the price was right and so far he had made it worth her time. She had done worse than Scat, more times than she cared to count.

"See you later Mister Po-lice man. Good luck on catching the bad guys."

"Got my eye on them as you speak, and thanks for the lunch offer, but I don't wallow with pigs."

"Suit yourself, officer. Honey, you just keep it and you can work it off later."

"Sure thing," she responded, blowing him a kiss as he headed for the door then whispering, "What a prick, but one with a bankroll."

Woody sipped his glass of sweet tea waiting for his meal to arrive. He dreaded Hank Singleton's retirement. He didn't relish having to break in a new sheriff at this point in his career, a woman at that. Looking on the bright side, she was at least home grown, originally from Walterboro, South Carolina, and she did bring with her some sheriff experience.

Other than that, he didn't know what to expect. He dreaded the worst. Most females holding positions of authority came with something to prove, a chip typically on their shoulders and he expected she would not surprise him in that aspect. He vowed he would not be an ass kisser. He would do his job like he always had, and if she didn't like it, then screw her. He smiled, thinking he sounded like he was the one with a chip. The top heavy waitress delivered his patty melt and fries. He attempted to enjoy his meal.

K&W Cafeteria
Myrtle Beach

Trudy sat across the table from Brady, finishing up her all veggie lunch platter. Trudy turned up her nose. Brady had opted for disgusting calf's liver smothered in onions. She would find it tough to kiss him before she went back on duty. She still found it hard to believe that they had been married just a little over a year now.

She had come so close to losing him at the hands of Preston, the Road Rage serial killer. Brady's quick thinking and smooth talking had shamed Joseph Preston into thinking he had crossed his own line, causing the accident that had taken out those vehicles at the Willbrook and the highway 17 intersection in Litchfield.

Preston had always selected his victims from those committing road rage maneuvers on the highways against him. He had ironically found himself in the reversed role, driving badly, running a red light, causing the accident. He served justice by taking his own life with the gun he had just been waving in Brady's face.

Brady, her rock, had spent the last moments with her dying mother when she should have been there. Some caregiver she had been. Her career had always come first. She had avoided her responsibility for her mom like the plague. Alzheimer's had just scared the crap out of her, and denial had served her purpose better than facing the inevitable consequences.

The ordeal did have one silver lining. It had brought her and her sister closer. After the dust had settled, and their mom's modest estate had closed and been disbursed, they had somehow buried the hatchet. Allison had been her bridesmaid.

Trudy had just returned from her niece's birthday party in Atlanta last weekend. The Wagner girls were playing nicely.

Even though she loved Allison, she had placed Brady at the top of her priority list followed by her career. Some old habits are tough to break. She wondered how long that would last. She did love Brady with all her heart, something she once thought she couldn't do. He did make her life complete, and she couldn't image a life without him.

She stared into those pools of inviting brown eyes still finding it hard to believe that he was eighteen years, her senior. If not for the gray on the sides of that full head of brown hair, his age would have remained a mystery to most. At six foot two, just one inch taller than her, he still wore the same neatly trimmed beard and was solid as a rock, carrying his one hundred eighty five pounds like a Greek God, at least in her eyes.

His Golfing Merchandise business continued to flourish. How could it not with all the courses here in the Myrtle Beach area. His trademark golf knickers were still a hot item. He now had four stores and a successful on line catalog website.

She knew he wanted kids but she wasn't quite ready to make that leap right now. Maybe in a couple of years she would give in to him, but not yet. She had just gotten her new CSI unit up and rolling. They had to prove themselves worthy to ensure the county budgeted for their continued existence.

She had a solid team, hand picked by her. Tim Burroughs, the computer geek was still with her after the road rage frenzy. He excelled as an information resource and had turned out to be a damn good detective.

Trudy had exiled that nutty Professor Swanson, the Lance Rocker and Tim Ford informant, replacing him with Doctor Dallas Solomon. She was a psychologist, plain Jane, average height and build, in her early forties, could have been the school librarian. She wore tiny black rim glasses and her premature streaked gray hair in a pony tail. Unlike her predecessor, she was completely trustworthy and professional. Better still, she never claimed to have ever known Mickey Spillane.

Trudy had recruited a colleague from her old Ohio precinct to join her as their forensics expert, Kirk Cardoon, nicknamed Captain from *Star Trek* fame. The name suited him well because he indeed was a closet Trekkie. Kirk had been one of her few and loyal friends there. She had a crush on him once, but she had never acted on her feelings. Better than average looks, thick wavy black hair, gorgeous emerald green eyes and hard body mounted on a six three frame, eye candy for sure, but no longer an attraction or distraction to her. She had Brady now, end of story.

Sly rounded out her little merry band. The team hadn't been really challenged yet but she would put them up against any unit, even at this stage. She wished she'd had their support during the road rage fiasco.

"Are you going to join me here or you just going to stay there in la-la land?"

"What...can't a girl fantasize about her husband?"

"So you're a girl now? You usually remind me you're 100% homegrown woman. What's really up with you?"

"Nothing, Circus Boy, you know me, I sometimes bring work along for the ride."

"Big case?"

"A missing pastor...he's Hispanic and could have just headed back home for all we know. The real kicker is Hank just informed Woody and me that he plans to retire."

"The old buzzard can't be serious. I thought he was married to his job."

"He was but I guess the heart problems, compounded by the road rage case, have just taken their toll. I think he is sincerely ready for this."

"I guess next you're going to tell me you're planning to run for Sheriff."

"No, he's bringing in an interim replacement to finish out his term, then I suppose there will be an election later in the year, but that's months away."

"So how long before you throw your hat into the ring?"

"Honestly, I haven't really given it any thought. He just laid it on us today and besides, I like what I'm doing with my new unit."

"Who's the replacement, anyone we know?"

"Female, an officer Burton from Charleston...the sheriff says she has an impressive record."

"You, working for a woman; now that ought to be worth the price of admission," answered a grinning Brady, reaching for his glass of water.

Before he could lift the glass to his lips, his hand suffered an odd tremor, the ice jiggling loudly. He set the glass down, hopefully without Trudy noticing. This had been the third time in less than a week that he had experienced something similar. He thought he probably should schedule a doctor's appointment, just to be on the safe side.

"Well, I guess I better report back to duty. What's on your agenda this afternoon?"

"I'm supposed to meet with Coastal Carolina about them possibly using logo knickers for the golf team. If it catches on then I might just have an opportunity to pitch it to Carolina or even Clemson."

"If I know you, and I certainly do, it's in the bag. See you tonight." She kissed him and copped a little feel underneath the tablecloth.

"Tonight," he responded. "Grilling and drilling on me."

"You're on, Circus Boy, under the big top. Good luck with your meeting at CCU."

"I'll win them over with my marketing strategy as always."

"As always," she repeated.

Horry County Police Department
Hank Singleton's Office

Hank read the investigating officer's account of the incident and it troubled his soul. The county certainly didn't deserve this sort of activity. The beach community being a tourist attraction, already lured the cream of the crop riffraff, thieves, drug entrepreneurs, cons and prostitutes. Keeping the streets safe had become an ongoing battle and now this.

"Gangs," Hank spoke out loud. "We don't need any damn gangs here." Oh how he wished the department was budgeted for a task force, a team that could head this off at the pass and educate the people on potential gang related impact. He chuckled to himself, thinking a consulting opportunity might just be in his future after he retires.

Hank was certainly not naïve to the fact that gangs were operating in and around the Grand Strand. He just dreaded how it could devastate the tourism and lives of the full time residents. Florence and Marion counties had seen their fair share of gang activity, with the likes of the Valtos Locos and the Sur-13s, two of the more predominant forces out there.

The arresting officers had picked up two Sur-13s members on suspicion of kidnapping and possibly murdering a Valtos Locos member. A body had yet to be located to validate the accusation. All remained circumstantial, with the original witnesses retracting their initial statements, now saying they had not seen the abduction. The eye witnesses obviously had been intimidated or threatened. Hank expected the case to be dropped.

"Hey short timer, that's some frown you have on that mug of yours," commented Woody, passing by Hank's door.

"Come on in, Woodrow," motioned Hank, leaning back in his chair and rubbing his slick head.

"I hate it when you call me Woodrow in that tone. I've either done something terribly wrong, or you're about to drop another bomb on me. Which is it this time?"

"I've got a little side project for you Constable."

"Something tells me I'm not going to like this..."

Horry County Police Department
Conference Room B

Trudy, standing in front of a blank whiteboard, asked, "So what do we have so far?"

"Not much I'm afraid," answered Sly. "I attempted to question a few more of Cruz's neighbors, and they're more or less hushmouthed. Where he resided is predominately a little Hispanic community, and they shy away from any dialogue with the police. If we did a thorough search, I don't think we'd find too many legal citizens there. Cruz may just be the exception, if what the preacher believes is on the up and up."

Dallas leaned back in her chair and said, "So they told you nothing?"

"Nothing except that he's a good guy and a man of the cloth, but we already knew that."

Trudy chimed in, "And we haven't turned up anything on his vehicle?"

"No sightings," reported detective Tim Burroughs. "Just like Jorge Cruz, it has vanished."

"I got the warrant like you requested, and we searched his premises, but nothing seemed out of place," added Captain Kirk. "He lived a meager existence, no frills, pretty much a neat freak. We observed no signs of a struggle. He left no notes, poof, he's just gone. There were fresh food items in the refrigerator and pantry. We found a checkbook and extra check booklets in a drawer in the kitchen. The most recent check was dated the day he disappeared and supported the grocery purchase."

Trudy said, "So it appears he had no intention of leaving, at least not on his own."

"It would seem so," replied Sly.

"Still no family connections?" inquired Trudy.

"Well, Sylvester did find some letters Mister Cruz had received from a Miguel Cruz in Matamoras, Mexico. I traced the address, and the gentleman could be his brother from the best I can tell. There's no phone number but I have contacted the authorities and am patiently waiting for their feedback on the matter," reported Tim.

Trudy had noted the meager pieces of information on the whiteboard. There wasn't much to go on and she really didn't expect any major development. She dismissed the team, advising them to focus on a recent robbery and one murder still on the books.

Woody caught up with her by the coffee pot. "Well, Detective Pierce, what intriguing case are you and your illustrious CSI team working on this afternoon?"

"Not much," she shrugged, "Just that missing associate pastor, no real leads or clues about his disappearance. Best guess, it wasn't voluntary. What about you? How's that domestic homicide going?"

"Well, when the dust settles, I suspect we'll have a couple of worthless parents behind bars, and another kid in foster care, a cute little boy."

"What a shame," commented Trudy, shaking her head in disgust.

"Hank just blindsided me with another assignment. It seems we have elevated gang activity in the county, and he wants me to birddog it, when I have extra time. He's asked me to research a couple of the noted gangs and do some community PR."

"Tell you what; I'll hook you up with Detective Stone. He's an expert on gangs. He may be able to shed a little light on it and assist you with your community service."

"That would be great, thanks. How was lunch with knicker-boy?"

"Okay I guess..."

"Want to talk about it?" Woody detected some concern in her response.

"I don't know. He just seemed a little distracted like something might have been bothering him. It's probably nothing but my paranoia. He accused me of acting the same way."

Woody nodded, not knowing what to add. "Well, I don't know about you but I think I'm going to call it a day."

"You've certainly done a 180 with your work ethics."

Woody smiled. "Yep, I reckon I have. Life's lessons sort of put things in perspective sometimes if you just listen to them."

"You still miss her, don't you? Don't you think it's about time you...?"

Woody interrupted. "Now don't you start pulling that matchmaker crap again. I still haven't forgotten that last blind date you lined up for me."

"Carol was a charming lady."

"Right, I don't think I ever saw her actually take a breath. She talked so much my ears rang for days. I know everything about her now, from her earliest childhood experiences to her last yeast infection."

"She's a very liberated woman, and these are liberating times."

"Call me old fashioned, but I get a little nervous on a first date when I'm asked what my favorite sexual positions are and her telling me how much she enjoyed oral sex, giving and receiving it."

"I still can't believe you didn't bed Carol. That's exactly what you needed. I never intended you to fall in love with her."

"Thanks but no thanks. She was like a damned info-commercial for sexual fulfillment. I expected her to say *"But wait, try me now and receive a set of Ginsue Knives free."*

"You didn't need a new set of knives?"

"See you tomorrow," said Woody, throwing up his hands and exiting the hallway.

I just bet Barbara would be perfect for Woody, she thought. I'll work on that next.

11:30 PM
El Hombre Mexican Cantina and Grill

Tomás and his friend Lupe exited the bar, singing a catchy homeland tune. Lupe glanced at his watch and reminded Tomás that they were supposed to be at the construction site by 5 AM. Both men were in the country illegally and needed the job. Tomás knelt down and grabbed the bottle of Tequila concealed in the potted shrub next to the door and offered Lupe a pull.

Lupe waved him off, saying he had drank way too much already. Tomás then offered him a ride, but Lupe pointed to his bicycle propped against the wall on the north side of the building. Clumsily sliding into the driver's side of his rusted out pickup, Tomás managed to locate his keys, and after several attempts successfully hit the ignition switch, and fired up the smoking truck.

Spinning in the gravel, he fish tailed out of the parking lot right into the path of the approaching police car. Lupe had already slipped around the back of the building and never witnessed the blue light special.

He tried to mount his bike but could never negotiate swinging his left leg over the middle bar. Losing his balance on the third attempt, he crashed on his side, pulling the bike on top of him.

"It sure looks like you could use some assistance," spoke an angelic voice from behind.

Lupe closed one eye to obtain a better look. The senorita with long beautiful legs stood spread eagle, offering him a hand. He accepted, and she pulled him to his feet. He wobbled on unsteady legs. The kind lady offered him a drink, brown bagging the bottle.

Not wishing to be rude, he unscrewed the cap and took a sip. She encouraged him to take another swallow of the Mescal and he obliged. All went fuzzy and he could no longer keep his balance. The lady locked arms under his elbow and led him to her car. She eased him onto the backseat of her sports car.

Luckily, he understood and spoke English. She told him she would put his bike in the back. He tried to thank her but couldn't speak. He couldn't move, either. He willed his arm up to check the time on his watch but his arm just lay limp by his side. She closed the door, and he sensed movement as the vehicle drove off, taking him to her place for a night of romance. He hoped he could make his 5 AM because he really needed the work. He couldn't wait to tell Tomás what had happened. Funny, he hadn't recalled her loading his bike.

Tomás had problems of his own. He sat cuffed in the back of the police car. He had no license or identification, only twenty three bucks and some change, and the half bottle of Tequila. He spoke very little English. He would not make his 5 AM appointment, either. He was destined for lock-up.

He feared what the authorities would do with him once they confirmed he did not belong in this country. Why worry, he thought. This was his forth time entering the United States illegally. If sent back, a fifth trip crossing the border would be a piece of cake. He knew the routine far too well. His only regret, his friend, Lupe, would not know what had happened to him. He didn't realize what a lucky man he was tonight to have been arrested.

Lunchtime, Horry County
Boathouse on the Intercostals Waterways

"Woody how about us grabbing a bite of lunch at the Boat House? I'm buying," said Trudy, giving her ex-partner a call on the radio.

"It sounds good to me, if you don't mind a little extra company, partner."

"New love interest," asked Trudy.

"Nah, Janice's cousin and her husband just arrived from Tennessee. They're newlyweds. I have forced family fun on my agenda, unfortunately."

"Newlyweds and they want to spend time with you?"

"Believe me; I think three's a crowd too. Besides, I think this is her third or fourth lap in the marital pool."

"Janice would probably appreciate you doing it, don't you think?"

"Stifle your guilt laden lecture. Hank has already beaten you to it. I'm going to have to grin and bear it, and play tourist. If you still want to do lunch, I'll meet you there in thirty minutes, or I should rephrase that; we'll meet you there."

"I can't wait."

Trudy arrived early and had secured a table for four. She had time to do a little thinking while waiting their arrival. She would miss Hank Singleton. He had paved her way and had given her the perfect opportunity to organize the CSI team, and all that after the road rage debacle. Trudy intended to a make this successful, and had the perfect team to make it happen.

She spotted Woody first, and then a second car pulling into the parking place beside him. The female wore a Kevin Harvick tee-shirt. Must be them, she surmised. Yep, it was them. Woody was chatting and pointing the way. Trudy wished he would at least give them a token smile, but instead she could read the dread on his face, even from this distance.

"Marian and Blaise Samion, this is Detective Trudy Wagner, I mean Pierce."

"Call me Trudy, pleasure to meet you. Woody tells me you're still honeymooning."

"Yes, we were actually married in Gatlinburg earlier this week, just the sweetest and most romantic little ceremony in a Smokey Mountain log cabin. Blaise went out and picked wild flowers for decorations and we were surrounded by a few family and friends. He had never been to Myrtle Beach before, being from Florida and all, so we thought we'd come here before heading back to Butler. That's in Tennessee, too."

"Well I hope you enjoy your visit. Where are you staying?"

"We're staying right on the ocean front at Royal Gardens, a neat little one bedroom condo. It's sure better than the place I stayed at here in '81'. I was between marriages, and I came here with a girlfriend. We didn't have much money and pooled our resources and rented the cheapest place we could find. Let me tell you, you get what you pay for. That place had the biggest roaches I had ever seen in my life."

"We call them Palmetto bugs," interrupted Woody.

"Anyway, like I was saying, I was divorced and was cutting loose a little bit, but when we were here, it was a rainy stay, and Harriet wasn't much for the bar scene and I was no night owl, so we ended up playing indoor Putt-Putt, more our speed, I reckon."

This gal was a talker, thought Trudy. "Things have changed a lot since then; I mean with the beach and everything."

Marian nodded, and then continued, "I had just met this guy at Starnes, a Greenwood club, that's in South Carolina too, before we came to the beach that time. He was from North Carolina. Every time I would walk by him that night while at Starnes, he would smile and speak to me. After a few drinks, I got the nerve to ask him why the heck he kept staring at me. He told me I was really cute. You know how they get when they have those beer goggles."

Trudy nodded, thinking she doesn't take many breaths, and is providing way too much information. What the heck, sit back and enjoy the free lunch break entertainment. She glanced over at Woody and he was rolling his eyes, obviously dreading her stay. Trudy almost kicked him under the table, but figured this was really none of her business.

"The very next day, he came into the store where I worked. I just so happened to be pulling security duty watching for shoplifters, when I spotted him instead on one of the cameras. Let me tell you, I almost broke my neck getting out there to see him."

"Was he shoplifting?" asked Woody.

"No, silly, he wasn't shoplifting. Harriet and I already had the Myrtle Beach trip planned, so I didn't get a chance to start a serious relationship. Get this; I did leave him there dog sitting my dog; how precious was that? He called me at the beach and I aired the dirty laundry, telling him what a terrible time we were having. That's when he told me he loved me. Do you know how long it had been since I had heard those words? I just melted. Six months later we were married and then moved to Kentucky."

"Marian, I'm sure Trudy doesn't want to hear all of your little escapades, and do you think this is the sort of thing your hubby is interested in knowing."

"Woody, Blaise and I have no secrets, do we honey?"

Blaise smiled and rubbed Marian's shoulder. She squeezed his arm and made goo-goo eyes at him. Woody felt like he was about to puke, and wanted to be anywhere but here. *Okay, they're newlyweds, I get it.*

"Anyway, we later moved to Monroe, N.C. We were close to Myrtle Beach and came here about every other weekend. Those trips went downhill fast. My husband would go off, leaving me in the room, while he was out screwing around with whatever little hot thing he could find. He was a real good looking hair model and could get girls with the drop of a hat. I was blinded for the longest because he fooled me by keeping me on a pedestal, giving me everything I could ever want. Our trips here soon ended up just being his trips here, without me. In 1990 we called it quits, after I finally wised up and I moved to Banner Elk, said to heck with him and then I met Blaise."

"A match made in heaven," mumbled Woody.

"Well that was quite the adventure," said Trudy.

"Some people think I'm one of those cougars. I'm 58 and Blaise is 44. So maybe I am, but what does it really matter, if it works for us, right? I was married the first time right out of high school, in '74, and that one lasted about four years. Boy, I sure hated high school. I'd much rather be out making money, working, instead of studying and all that crap. You have to do what you feel like you have to do, right? Anyway, I think I've finally done it right this time, with Blaise."

Blaise was certainly a man of few words, thought Trudy; or then again, when does he really have a chance to jump in. "We should probably order."

"Yeah, before the lunch specials expire, "added Woody.

"You must live an exciting life here at the beach, Trudy. I remember reading about that road rage killing spree mess. Was that guy crazy or what? Aren't you the one he kidnapped? I'd just freak out if someone kidnapped me."

"Marian, we can't discuss police matters," interrupted Woody, not wanting to venture there, just in case Lance Rocker's name surfaced.

"That guy killed Janice, didn't he? I couldn't believe it when I heard she had been murdered. Woody, I'm sorry. I guess this is difficult for you still, isn't it?"

"It is and I think we should drop the subject, okay?"

"Are you working on any blockbuster cases, now? I bet it was hard to top that one. He was a killing machine. Can you imagine all the body bags? People do drive crazy around here. We were cutoff more times than I can count. I could have gone road rage several times. I don't mean I would have killed anybody, but boy I was pissed, and I wasn't even driving. So, do you have an important case or what?"

"Marian, we can't talk shop talk," fumed Woody.

"All right, I get it; hush, hush. I'll change the subject. Woody, will you be able to take us to Hard Rock tonight. I told Blaise about Broadway at the Beach and he really wants to have his picture taken on that Harley over there, so he can send it to some friends in Orlando. That would just be hoot. He wants to buy us a Harley. I could be his biker babe, his hot chick, riding the hog, I just love it."

Just shoot me, thought Woody. He stared across the table at Trudy, pleading for help. Trudy just smiled and winked. Woody kicked her under the table and she almost yelled out loud. Rubbing her shin, she gave him *the look*, the go to hell look, and then said, "I bet Woody would love to have his picture taken on that motorcycle too, if the truth be known."

Trudy may have pushed it too far. After all, Woody was armed and could be dangerous. Just the same, she had thoroughly enjoyed lunch.

"We sure hope to see you again before we leave," said Marian.

"Hell, she can join us at Hard Rock," added Woody.

"Sorry, I have a hectic schedule over the next few days but you kids enjoy. You too, Constable."

"It was our pleasure, Trudy. Drop by if you're ever in the vicinity of Butler. It's not Myrtle Beach but we'll show you a good time."

5:45 AM
Fox Hollow Subdivision
Aynor Construction Company

Juniper Burdette cursed and spat tobacco juice on the pile of red dyed cypress mulch. Two of the Mexicans he had hired were no shows. The trouble with employing illegals, no one to complain to if they did you wrong. A black man like him just couldn't get ahead no matter how hard he tried.

He shook his head, very peculiar; seven had gone missing on him in the past six weeks. He hadn't read about any raids or fed busts so he couldn't quite figure why this had become an issue all of a sudden. Up until recently he had pretty good luck using them and they worked hard, earned every cent of their pay.

Faced with the deadline ahead he would have no choice but to contact the temporary services and pay primo rates for additional help. A tough pill to swallow after skirting outside the law and avoiding all the other expenses associated with the labor regulations.

Juniper had asked the other three Mexicans working for him if they knew where the two missing hombres were, but they just shrugged. He had to hand it to them. They were loyal to their kind and never ratted out anybody. He couldn't say that for other people of color, including his own.

North Myrtle Beach
CSI Unit

The Caucasian male, possibly in his early twenties, lay covered in the street with a blanket, ambulance on the scene. The man had been struck by oncoming traffic on Business 17 while attempting to cross the busy intersection, near The Crazy Horse Gentleman's Club.

Witnesses said what started as a foot chase, had ended up with one pursuer taking to a vehicle and chasing the man into the highway. There, he had been stuck and killed by a family from Ontario, Canada driving a motor home. Several eye witnesses identified the pursuers as dark skinned, very mean looking, Hispanic types.

Further questioning by detectives Tim Burroughs and Sylvester Stone indicated that the descriptions of the two men chasing the victim matched members of the Valtos Locos. Based on the color of their clothing and one tattoo spotted on the arm of the man on foot, there was no mistaking their identities?

A search of the stiff's pockets had uncovered he had over fifteen hundred dollars in cash and an assortment of prepackaged drugs. The motive most likely had been a robbery attempt, possibly a territorial dispute.

"Gang related for sure," commented Sly. "And we're seeing more evidence every day of them getting a foothold here at the beach."

"We have a make and model on the car but no license number," stated Tim. "I called it in, just in case we get lucky before they get completely out of the area."

"My best guess, they're still in the area. This is probably their turf, so I suspect they have the car in a garage, or stashed behind an apartment. They'll turn back up but not before they paint and completely modify that vehicle."

"We have a positive ID on the kid," said Tim, taking a deep breath. "Stewart Patrick, sixteen years old, his driver's permit indicates he lives west, just three blocks away. He would have been seventeen tomorrow, some birthday party, ugh."

"Promises of easy money and fast cash get them every time. Here's the hook, track marks down the inside of both his arms. He was a seller and a user at such a young age."

"I mowed lawns at that age to get my extra cash, and it would have taken me a zillion years of mowing to have earned the wad we found in his pocket."

"Tim, you were raised right, my friend, as was I."

"Boy, I dread telling the parents."

"In most cases like this, the parents couldn't care less unless he was a source of revenue for them. Let's wrap this up so that the transport can move the body to the coroner."

Oliver's Luncheonette
Conway

"Doggone it, you just had to ruin my lunch didn't you?" snapped Hank, talking on his cell phone. "So you say he has a permit. Yeah, I know. I'll take care of it, Mayor. No, I'll see to it. I promise, there won't be any trouble. Yes sir, will do. I'm on it, I said. Yes sir, I got it. You have a good day too...*you old fart*," said Hank, after ending the call.

"What was that all about," asked Burgess Thomson, a local scrap metal dealer, partaking of vittles with Hank Singleton.

"It was the Mayor. He's all riled up because Brock Boudreaux has gotten himself a permit to hold a rally this coming Saturday. He was already pissed anyway because Brock and his hooded pals wanted to adopt a section of highway 9. It seems they wanted to be recognized for picking up litter. That one will end up in court for sure. The county will never stand for the Klan's name being on a highway sign. "

"That old Cajun boy just can't turn loose of that KKK crap, can he?" replied Burgess. "He should have stayed down yonder in the bayou where he belonged."

"He's probably lived here longer now than he ever did there. He's got what, three, maybe four pawn shops in the area. I reckon I've known him almost thirty years and he's not that much younger than me, fifty five or six. He's one hell of a smooth talker. He can con the fangs off a snake. Those he can't con, he buys off."

"We catch enough crap about flying the confederate flag on the State Capital grounds. We don't need him stirring the pot," grumbled Burgess. "Where is he planning on having his rally?"

"Center stage at the Pavilion, where he can get the most attention and a larger audience," fumed Hank, cracking his big old hairy knuckles. "He probably has thirty or forty folks in that chapter of his, small by comparison when the Klan dominated the south."

"You would think we would have outgrown this crap by now," said Burgess, removing his old faded Ford cap and running his hand through his thinning hair.

"Not as long as we have fellers like Brock and his counterparts at the NAACP. That's all they live for and where they pull in the big bucks," explained Hank. "Without controversy, there's no reason for either chapter, so their job is to always make sure that neither whites nor blacks forget the slavery thing and the confederacy. Blacks blame the south for slavery, and the south blames the Yankees for setting them free. Both just want to stir the pot as much as they can. It's big business."

"It's all just a bunch of crap, Hank. We're all Americans, end of story."

"Funny thing," said Hank, standing up now. "If both groups did their research properly, they'd know that more slaves were brought here flying the United States Flag than the confederate one and the North was as much to blame as the South, if not more."

"Like you said Hank, if the truth be known, both organizations would be out of business, and that's not lucrative for either one of them."

"Well, long as they keep it all peaceful and don't start any rock throwing, we'll survive it, I suppose. I certainly don't need a mess like that on my watch when I'm trying to exit gracefully."

"Sheriff, there ain't a graceful bone in that big ole fat ass of yours," laughed Burgess, replacing his cap on his head.

"Takes one to know one, doesn't it? See you here tomorrow, Burgess, same time, same table."

"You got it Hank," replied Burgess, also a creature of habit. "And we're going to miss you being our sheriff. Put your money away. This one's on me."

Hank smiled and nodded. He had mixed emotions, but he was ready for retirement. He had earned it. Let somebody else worry about gangs and the such.

Cash and Carry Pawn Shop
Socastee, Thursday, 9 AM

Brock Boudreaux, sporting his trade mark rebel flag tattoo on his right forearm, flipped over the sign on the pawn shop's front door, signaling he was now open for business. His store manager had taken a couple of days off for vacation so Brock now substituted until his manager returned. He actually enjoyed doing this occasionally to release the pressures of the daily grind.

Brock still had a thick Cajun accent when he needed it, damn proud of his Louisiana heritage, definitely a throw back of times long forgotten. A third generation Klansman, it had been his birthright to carry on the family tradition, and he loved every second of it.

His thick bristly beard, hanging six inches below his chin, streaked in gray, served perfectly to accent his uniform when he participated in civil war re-enactments, his cherished hobby. He strived for authenticity when paying homage to the South on the battlefields, his uniform, weapons, and accessories perfectly replicated those worn by the mighty warriors of that time.

He insisted that all members of his KKK chapter join him in these re-enactments. He specifically included this requirement in the bylaws. Brock often daydreamed of living back then, convinced he could have impacted the outcome of the hard fought war. The South would have won under his leadership.

The front doorbell rang, the sensor indicating he had his first customer of the day. He engaged his patented wholesome meet and greet game face and he turned from the counter to gaze on three greasy headed, dark skinned Mexicans. They were clutching an assortment of power tools in their arms, most likely stolen from a construction site.

Smiling he asked, "Speak English?"

One nodded, "How much?" as they all placed the tools onto the counter.

Continuing to smile his best con, Brock assessed the tooling and quoted them a very unfair price. He despised Mexicans, even more than he hated blacks, but they were some of his best customers. He never passed up an opportunity to stick it to them on both ends of the deal, buying and selling. They took his offer and his money and soon exited his premises. He cursed them under his breath.

He immediately disinfected the power tools, and then washed his hands several times after handling them to remove the stench of their breed. His upcoming rally would offer his concerns for the new invasive species of America, and he would offer suggestions for their extermination.

The sensor warned him of another visitor. Expecting to see more of their kind, he clenched his fist then opened them, placing both hands on the counter palms down and put on his happy face.

"Slumming today," said Scat Crowder, grinning, resembling the Cheshire Cat.

"Coo-yôn, dôn mess wit me dis morning!" snapped Brock putting on the thick Louisianan tongue.

"And don't call me a fool, how about it," spouted Scat, putting his finger in Brock's face. "Why don't you drop that bayou mumbo jumbo and talk like a Carolinian?"

Taking a deep breath and losing as much of his accent as possible he responded, "I had tree, I mean three of those little illegal bastards in here, and dey brung me dis here bunch of lifted tools. Socostee is overrun wit dim now days."

"What you bitching about? You make a good living off them, don't you?"

"Nuff I suppose, but we don't need dim here screwing up our country, taking our jobs and marrying our women folk."

"What you going to do about it? Kill all of them," asked Scat. "They're like roaches, there's another thousand for everyone you grind under your shoe."

"One less though," he smiled. "Watch da sto while I hit da batroom."

"To the batroom, Robin," mocked Scat in his best Adam West *Batman* voice. "Sure thing, take your time. By the way, I almost forgot. I've got that new batch of Uzis you were wanting stashed away at our usual hiding place. You let me know when you're ready to move them."

"Good job pod nah, I will call dim what want da merchandise and we set up a handoff."

While Brock did make a decent living operating his four pawn shops, the big bucks rolled in via his sales of illegal weapons and explosives. The consumer recognized his ability to deliver what they needed, when they needed it, at a fair cost, no questions asked, and no trail or evidence of the transactions, a win-win for everyone. His business thrived on repeat customers.

"Ah now dat show feels more better," he said, dropping a log in the toilet. He couldn't wait until his rally down at the Myrtle Beach Pavilion. The South would rise again under his leadership, once he got rid of all these relocating Yankees. There were more people from New Jersey here at the beach, than real South Carolinians. Flushing, he cursed their existence.

Mammy's Kitchen
Noon

Woody sighed, attempting to enjoy his lunch, relieved to know Marian and her hubby were headed back to the Volunteer State today. He had already said his goodbyes last night after supper at Creek Ratz's on the Inlet marsh walk. He hoped the two would have a blissfully long life together and never set foot in Myrtle Beach again. As much as Marian liked coming to the beach, he doubted he would get his wish. Big dog on the radio, Woody wondered what he wanted this time.

"Woodrow, please report to my office, immediately, do you copy?

"I copy, Sheriff, this sounds urgent. What's the problem?"

"Just get your butt in here, ASAP, and I'll explain when you arrive."

This didn't sound good. Woody was leery of Hank's tone. ASAP, he had said and he didn't want to talk about it on the radio. Woody recapped any recent arrests and none came to mind that could be problematic. Oh well, he may as well see why the big ole bear sounded like someone had pissed in his cornflakes. Ten minutes later he stood in Sheriff Singleton's doorway. Two people were sitting in chairs directly in front of Hank's desk. Oddly, they looked familiar.

"Woodrow, your…Janice's relatives have gotten themselves in a little bind."

"Oh man, Marian, what the hell did you do? You were supposed to be leaving town today."

"We were I assure you. We stopped at one of those Wings to buy some last minute souvenirs. Did you know you could buy five tee-shirts for ten dollars there? They have those cute hermit crabs with the painted shells too. My nephew would just love one of those."

"Marian, just get on with it, what happened at the tourist trap?"

"We had bought the souvenirs, when this guy came over and asked us could we jump off his truck. Blaise said sure, because we had jumper cables. You never know when you might need a favor. We pulled our car over to where he was parked. Let me tell you, this fellow was in some hurry and couldn't wait to get that truck started. Blaise got him going and he gave him a twenty for his trouble. "

"Sheriff, can you fill in the blanks and get this over with, please?"

"They came in here and turned themselves in, Woodrow. Mrs. Samion had me call you after explaining the relationship. It seems they unknowingly jumped off the getaway car for the guy who had just robbed the Bank of America next door. They were spouting they had aided and abetted, or at least were accomplices; and they think they received stolen money."

"How did you even know you had jump started a bank robber's truck," asked Woody.

"A customer ran over to us from the bank and told us he had just robbed it. He was at the drive through and saw the whole thing. We figured we better come here and throw ourselves on the mercy of the court, before we crossed the state line and become federal fugitives. "

"Woodrow, we've taken their statements and they are free to go, but she insisted I let you know what had happened."

"I didn't want rumor to spread that we were involved. This is where you live, Woody. We don't want people around here to think you were associated with bank robbers. It could ruin your reputation and might end your law enforcement career. Janice would turn over in her grave if that happened, and we were the cause of it. We gave the Sheriff the twenty. We don't want any part of dirty money."

"Janice would be proud of your actions, but you heard the Sheriff; you're free to go. I'd suggest you be on your way before the paparazzi comes looking for you and ruins all of our reputations."

"Thank you Woody, for being so understanding in the face of an honest mistake. We would never help anyone rob a bank."

"Have a safe trip back to Butler."

"We're going to stop in Abbeville on the way. Blaise has never been to Abbeville either. You know they made that movie with Julie Roberts there. We're going to stay at the Belmont but we won't be jumping off any more cars. I'm not even going to let Blaise help anyone with a flat."

Let's hope his stay there will go smoother than here, thought Woody. He shrugged at Hank, what could he say, and then escorted them from the station, making sure he saw them on their way. He wondered if there was an expiration date on in-laws.

Pierce, she would have a field day with this once she got a whiff, and be assured, ole Hank would tell her the entire tale. Worst still, she has those photographs of me with my butt parked on that stupid Harley at Hard Rock; what the hell was I thinking? What a way to start off a Monday morning. I hope my chaps don't inherit these genes.

Horry County Police Department
Conference Room B
Thursday 3:15 PM

Trudy asked, "No new leads on the Stewart Patrick case?" "No, we haven't located the automobile seen chasing the kid and the parents were of no help," advised Sly. "They claimed they didn't know he had a drug problem or that he was selling them."

Dallas added, "I accompanied Sly to their residence, and based on their mannerisms and facial expressions, I can almost guarantee they were lying on both counts."

"Officially, this goes down as just an unfortunate accident. Even if we located the alleged pursuers, we can't really implicate them. The kid ran out into traffic, got minced, end of story," added Captain Kirk, the forensics expert.

"Do we have anything on the missing associate pastor?"

"No new leads," answered Tim Burroughs. "The car hasn't turned up nor has any sign of Jorge Cruz. Captain Kirk and I checked back with Preacher McCrery, and he hasn't seen any sign of him either."

"We're not a very effective unit are we?" Trudy took a sip of coffee, making a face because it was cold.

"You can't get blood from a turnip," replied Sly.

"Sly, when you have a chance, how about dropping by and talking to Constable Anderson. He's investigating gang activity, and he could use your insight."

"Will do..."

"Otherwise, have a good night, folks," said Trudy, closing out another day.

Trudy returned to her office to file some long over due paperwork. She couldn't dismiss the suspicion that Brady was hiding something from her. He couldn't lie like she could, and she smelled a rat. Just what could be his little secret? Surely he wasn't being unfaithful or anything like that. They didn't skip too many nights without some sort of sexual interlude, and she was sure he still enjoyed it as much as she.

She would figure it out sooner or later. After all, she was the detective in the family, and she did have a reputation to uphold. No crime went unsolved on her watch. The phone rang. She picked it up.

"Detective Pierce, CSI unit, how may I help you?"

She could hear breathing on the other end, but the caller remained silent.

"Detective Pierce, how may I help you?" She repeated, and the breathing sounded louder, more labored.

"Brady, is that you? Are you pulling your little perverted, obscene caller routine again? You know I love that game and you talking dirty to me, but not on my official line while I'm at work."

In a thick tongued, English speaking, Hispanic female voice, the caller finally responded. "Help, my husband, he is missing. I don't know what to do. We are almost out of food. The children are hungry. Please...help me."

"Caller, can you please identify yourself?"

"He is missing. Please, help us...the children"

"I can't help you if you don't tell me who you are and where you are," Trudy desperately tried to pick the information from her. "I can send officers to assist if you tell me where you are."

Click, the line went dead. The caller had hung up. Trudy sat there, staring at the phone, clutching it in a death grip, unable to do anything to help the distraught woman. Finally she placed the phone back on her desk. She waited, thinking the caller would try again, but she didn't. Frustrated, she called it a night and headed home, unable to do any more.

La Palma Grocery
10:30 PM Thursday

Fifteen year old Pablo left the store carrying three bags of groceries, his arm looped though two of the plastic bags, and the third clutched against his chest. He was large for his age and more resembled an eighteen or nineteen year old. His mother had sent him to the market. He now had almost six blocks to walk on his return trip.

The Mustang slows, and then the driver pulls onto the curbing. There is only one street light and no houses. A very beautiful woman motioned Pablo over, offering him a ride.

He had never ridden in a convertible sports car before. She had such a friendly face, he thought, and he has so far to walk. Pablo figures why should he be a pack mule when he can travel in luxury? The woman is kind enough to offer him a ride. He would be so foolish not to accept.

She opened the passenger side and told him to place the groceries in the back seat. He complied. She smelled nice. Her dress was hiked up so high he could see her lacey black panties underneath. He tried not to stare but could not help it. He made eye contact with the woman. She had caught him looking.

She smiled and then placed her hand on his upper leg and squeezed it, signaling him it was okay to look. She then caressed his hand, and then placed his hands on her panties. Her womanhood was so fiery hot that he now became aroused.

She engaged the mechanism that closed the convertible's top. He was perspiring profusely now, wondering what the pretty lady had in mind. She told him to find good music on the radio, and he began fumbling with the dials.

Distracted, he never saw her reach inside her purse and retrieve the syringe. She smiled and he smiled back. He can't wait to tell his friends about her, and mentally thanks his mother for sending him to the store.

The Mustang pulled back into the street just before meeting the utility service van. The van's driver noticed the beauty behind the wheel as they passed, wondering what she was doing driving alone here on a very dangerous side of town. He watched her in his rearview mirror as she drove from view.

A woman sitting in a rocker on the front porch eyed the passing sports car, wondering why it was taking her son so long at the grocery. Poor Pablo's face rested in the pretty lady's lap; out cold, his fantasy had expired.

The Pierce Beachfront Residence
Litchfield Beach
2:15 AM Friday

Brady, still awake, stares at the ceiling. He listens to the ocean waves crashing on shore, synchronized with the nasally breathing from Trudy. She is curled against his right shoulder. He stresses about his doctor's appointment scheduled for Friday morning, still seven hours away.

He has felt so fatigued lately, and the hand tremors have increased. Brady has found it extremely difficult to conceal them from her. He decides he must be feeling the arrival of old age because his joints and muscles have seemed so stiff lately. He dreads the thoughts of arthritis, confident that's what the doctor will surely tell him.

Trudy stirs and turns on her other side and subconsciously backs up against him with her bare butt, cold to the touch. Both of them prefer the freedom of nudity in bed. Unladylike, she cuts one in her sleep, loud and foul. He fans the covers and smiles, thinking women don't think they are capable of such manly things, but most can hold their own, even if they don't care to admit it.

Brady, unable to shut his mind down, decides to get up and pour himself a brandy. He relieves his bladder first, before heading to the bar. Picking up the bottle, the shakes overtake him. He has to hold the bottle with both hands, and even then, he misses the glass, spilling a jigger's worth of the brown liquor on the bar.

Wiping it up with a napkin, clutching his glass firmly, he walks out onto the balcony, his naked body almost glowing in the moonlight. The warm summer breeze greets him. He can almost taste the salt spray in the air. He watches the ebbing tide and the twinkling of stars and the almost full moon reflecting on the ocean's surface.

The brandy goes down smooth, warming his throat and chest. Glass empty, he turns to go mix a second one, and discovers an equally glowing nude body blocking the entranceway. "Is this a private party, or can anyone join in on the festivities?"

"Sorry, did I disturb your sleep?"

"Not until I almost backed off your side of the bed trying to locate my usual snuggle zone. It's not like you to be up and about in the middle of the night. What's eating you?"

"Forget about me, what you say I have you? You look quite appetizing there in the moonlight."

"You are a smooth one aren't you, Circus Boy? I must say, you don't look quite Ringling Brother's enough without your colorful knickers. On second thought, I might just have to dub you the elephant man. That trunk of yours seems to have a life of its own, and it beckons me to do its bidding."

Doing his best elephant trumpet call, Brady managed to hands free raise his half hard penis a couple of times, mocking an elephant's swaying trunk. The circus had definitely come to town, or in this case, to the balcony.

They returned to bed shortly past 4 AM where Trudy collapsed back into sandman land, with Brady still staring at the ceiling long after she had crashed and burned. Sleep would not come easy for him. He eventually turned on his side, curled up behind Trudy, and watched the digital clock on the night stand as it advanced slowly but surely toward its 7 AM pre-set alarm time.

Horry County Police Station
7:15 AM

"Thanks for meeting me here before our shift begins," Woody told Sly.

"Glad to help. I'm pretty much in here about this time every morning anyway. I hit the gym before five, then shower and head in."

"I used to arrive early myself, but with the kids and being on my own, it's tough to do. You can keep the gym. It would just screw up my manly figure, and I worked too hard to get my body in this shape," Woody smiled, rubbing his slightly overhanging belly.

"So where would you like to start?"

"*Gangs 101*, I suppose, and then which games we might expect to contend with around here. Sheriff has me on a twofold issue; snoop for activity and help educate the community."

"Gang facts...where do I start? We can't get too deep in the time we have allotted, so why don't I just give you my perspective?"

"Works for me..."

"First off, I think it's just a misconception that Hispanic Immigrants are responsible for more crimes. There's no data to support that theory. Gangs are but a small percentage of illegal activity but they do contribute to much of the crime. Ironically, illegal Immigrants are more apt to be robbed and victimized by the gangs."

"Why would they rob their own people?"

"Simple, the victims won't report the crimes because they are in this country illegally, and they horde their cash where they live."

"They're easy marks."

"Exactly, there's no loyalty among thieves as it goes. We've spotted two primary Hispanic gangs in this area, the Valtos Locos and the Sur-13s. The Valtos Locos are the more prominent. Sur-13s have been seen passing through and might be scoping out the area. The two gangs do not get along. We probably have better than 150 gang members in Horry County. They all recruit from the same general teenage demographics, and commit the same gamut of vandalism, assaults and burglaries. Most of the time they pull these off without being caught."

"From preying on their own..."

"Primarily," confirmed Sly. "We also have the racial element present, and they, too, prey on the illegal immigrants for the same reason as the gangs."

"Are you talking Klan?"

"Brock Boudreaux specifically and he takes advantage of their thievery at his pawnshop. Worse still, I smell trouble brewing with that little rally he's planning tomorrow."

"Scat Crowder, one of my old high school buddies, is Boudreaux's right hand man. He's a badass wannabe. I've heard Brock could have as many as fifty followers. Do you think they will clash with the Valtos Locos?"

"Not likely. Today's Klan shies away from those types of situations. The Valtos Locos will avoid them too, unless they're personally attacked. They won't step up and protect the unfortunate, common illegal population. It's not about politics to gangs."

"Isn't that the way?"

"We believe that the kid, Stewart Patrick, who was killed running into traffic, may have been drug related. It possibly involved a turf battle with the Valtos," added Sly.

"White kid killed by Hispanics, you would think that would be the perfect recipe for the Klan's involvement," commented Woody.

"And it could possibly spur a confrontation with the likes of someone like Boudreaux, attempting to snag the limelight, but then again, *Klan 101* is a whole different session. Here's my journal. Keep it as long as you like. It may help explain things, my theories anyway."

Woody opened it and saw that it was a chronicle of incidences. "What's this, your own personal diary?"

"Sort of...I've always been fascinated with the subject, so it documents articles and incidences concerning gang activity over the past eight years from police reports and news articles. It has helped me develop my theories and identify patterns."

"Thanks, Detective Stone. I'll get this back to you when I'm finished."

"No rush, that's just volume I. I dabble with writing on the side too, and this makes for good fiction writing."

"Detective stories?"

"That and life's lessons, but I don't have any published yet. I do send short stories to the local detention center. It gives the prisoners something to read, and I do get some feedback."

"The prisoners do your book reviews."

"Sort of, I suppose."

"I would like to read some of your work sometime."

"Finish the journal first, and then we'll see."

Horry County Police Department
8 AM Morning Debriefing

"Good morning Horry County's finest. Allow me to introduce to you, interim Police Chief, Samantha R. Burton, my eventual replacement," stated Hank Singleton. "Over the next three weeks she will have the opportunity to meet each and every one of you and familiarize herself with your existing duties. Once I'm out of the picture, she will have the luxury of customizing those duties to satisfy her needs for the department. Until then, boys and girls you're still under my watch, beck and call, so business as usual."

"Good morning officers," spoke up Co-Sheriff Burton. "I have indeed heard numerous wonderful things about this department and your achievements, and I personally look forward to becoming part of this exceptional community. As some of you may already know, I am a native of the Palmetto State, having been born in Walterboro, where most of my family still resides."

Trudy eyed her new boss, as only a woman could do. Over the next five minutes she spouted off her resume, her background, credentials, and personal accomplishments. Trudy pegged her for being in her late twenties, maybe early thirties, a very attractive and intelligent, light skinned Afro-American, five nine or ten, a hundred thirty or forty pounds, top heavy but with an attractive, hourglass figure, flowing black, silky, medium length hair, impeccable taste in clothes, shoes and jewelry. She was definitely a looker and would most certainly elevate the department's testosterone levels.

She perceived this woman to be a force to be reckoned with, and Trudy could typically read people. She sensed that the new sheriff carried a chip on her shoulder, with a spattering of arrogance. She oozed pride and professionalism, but also displayed a whiff of low self esteem, probably indicating she had fought hard to get where she was.

On the surface, Trudy sort of liked what she saw, but her instinct warned her that troubled waters could be ahead. She visualized a tough transition for the department after its long reign under Sheriff Hank Singleton's leadership and work ethics. She vowed she would make the best of it and embrace the opportunity. Trudy hoped the new sheriff took the same route.

After the formalities had been completed, Hank reviewed open cases and new assignments. Trudy smiled, watching Hank do a little showboating with a much more formal presentation than usual. He was not going to be outdone by his successor.

After the dog and pony show had subsided, Hank motioned Trudy to join them in his office. She had mixed emotions about being singled out for this invitation, but reluctantly complied.

"Sheriff Burton asked to meet you," began Hank, making the formal introduction. "I'll give you two a little privacy. Call me when you're finished, Sheriff Burton."

"Pleasure to meet you Sheriff Burton," said Trudy, extending her hand.

"Call me Sam," she said, with a pearly white smile and a firm hand shake.

Trudy was not comfortable with this protocol, too personal to suit her taste, so she avoided addressing her as Sam. She tried to end each sentence with ma'am.

"Sheriff Singleton tells me you're the lead for the newly formed CSI unit. I've been privy to your resume, very impressive and that Road Rage case; excellent work, Detective Pierce."

"Thank you."

"If I can be frank, it appears we've traveled down a similar path, you and I. Discrimination and prejudicial thinking has frequently stymied our careers. The gender and race card can often raise its ugly head to prevent the advancement of individuals such as we, don't you agree?"

Trudy hadn't seen this one coming. She had badly misjudged her characterization of the new sheriff. She had pegged her as tough, no nonsense and strictly by the book, but not racial. This certainly posed a new twist, one she wasn't prepared to deal with or comment on. She measured her response very carefully, sensing this could be some sort of trap or test.

"Police work is a tough vocation. It has always been a predominately male-ruled world, much like many other jobs. I stand on principle and my ability to perform my job. I've always believed that if I am not worthy of the position, then I shouldn't be considered for it."

"So you don't think you've been passed over for previous positions because you have no penis between your legs?"

Angered by the question, but again attempting to carefully weigh her answer, she replied, "No ma'am, I prefer to be judged on my performance and credentials." *The only penis that I am concerned about is the one between my husband's legs and how often it ends up between mine, thought Trudy.*

"You're a tough one aren't you, Detective Pierce? Something tells me you haven't been completely honest with me. You too cautiously articulate your bullshit responses. Maybe you're just in denial, or possibly think I'm testing you, but you know what I am talking about because you've definitely been there."

Trudy didn't utter a word, but maintained controlled eye contact with her superior. She already missed Hank Singleton, and envisioned a tough and uncomfortable road ahead.

"Detective Pierce, regardless of what you are thinking right now, we will become very close and you will be my eyes and ears for this department. You will keep me posted on any behavior that disrespects this department, and let's just call it intolerable prejudices by the male species on my watch. Do you understand what I am saying?"

"You are my superior and I will support you within the confines of the law, but I will not be your snitch, do you understand what I am saying, Sheriff Burton?"

Sam smiled, "Once Sheriff Singleton has exited the premises, you will be on my clock, and I will expect you do as I request."

"Sheriff Burton, you do realize you're asking to become one of the people you hate the most, ma'am."

"We must stick together to advance both our careers. Do I make myself clear, detective?"

"May I be dismissed now, ma'am?"

Sam stepped forward, inches away, face to face, and placed both hands on Trudy's shoulders, "Trust me, we will see the world eye to eye on this Detective Pierce. You and I will become valuable allies, possibly even best friends. By the way, this conversation never took place, and I so look forward to working with you."

Trudy clinched her jaw and her right fist, fighting off the urge to deck her, just like she had cold cocked Tim Ford, during his murder confession of Ed Bradshaw. She knew if she crossed that line, it would be a career ending KO. While nothing would please her more, she loved her job too much and would not jeopardize it for the likes of this bitch. She backed away until she relinquished her hold on her shoulders, turned and walked from the office.

Hank met her in the hallway. "Well I hope things went well between you two. She's a piece of work and a valuable asset to the department's future."

"Yes sir. She is indeed a piece of work." *And an ass...* Trudy mustered up a false smile and nodded as she passed. Her presence would definitely impact the department's future if she didn't expose her for who she really was. She had to think long and hard about it.

The Pierce Beachfront Residence, Litchfield
Friday 8:40 PM

The remainder of Trudy's day had been uneventful by comparison. She had arrived home to chilled wine and steaks marinating, ready for the grill. Brady had apparently sensed she needed serious tender loving care and, after finishing off the better part of a second bottle, they retired to the master bedroom to allow him to complete his pampering of her.

Basking in the afterglow, she recapped her day, the arrival of super bitch. Brady listened patiently, periodically kissing her neck and shoulder, caressing her privates, and pondering his own news. Finally after rattling off for the better part of an hour, she turned and kissed him saying, "I'm quite the motor mouth tonight, aren't I? Sorry."

"We all have to vent."

"I haven't even asked how your day went, have I?"

"Well, you did have valid issues, didn't you?"

"So just what did you do today, Circus Boy?"

He got right to the point. "I had a doctor's appointment this morning."

"I didn't realize it was time for your annual physical. I thought we said we would schedule our appointments together."

"I didn't go to our usual physician. My appointment was with a Neurologist." Cutting to the chase, while he had the courage, he continued, "They think I have early stages of Parkinson. Sounds like I'm piling on, I know."

She caressed his face and kissed him long and hard before asking, "What made you suspect something was wrong? You haven't said anything to me."

"I've been experiencing these bouts of uncontrollable shaking and very painful stiffness. The doctor explained both are classic symptoms of the disease. They did some tests and should be able to confirm it for sure next week."

"Maybe it's something else."

"The doctor doesn't think so. The tests are a mere formality. He is almost 100% sure."

"So what does all this mean for you, for us? Will you be taking some sort of medication or treatments?"

"I'm not sure. There is no cure. It's a progressive disease. It affects people differently. Further testing should provide us with answers. The doctor gave me some pamphlets. He recommended a couple of websites that might help us understand the ramifications. He said they should answer some of our questions until my next appointment."

Trudy suddenly had flashbacks of her mother and the Alzheimer's. She shivered, wondered how Parkinson's would screw up their lives. It sounded selfish and obviously was, but she wasn't quite prepared to become a caregiver a second time, not so soon. She had certainly launched into a gloom and doom mood. That wasn't fair to her or Brady. She had to rebound and do it quickly before he noticed.

Too late, she could see it in his eyes. He had picked up on her negative vibes. She wouldn't be able to lie her way out of this one, so thought it best to put her concerns and worse fears on the table. It was just after ten when she began doing just that. She struggled to tell him how she felt.

A quarter past ten, with darkness as a cloak, a hungry predator never sleeps. Top down, the warm Atlantic breeze flooding her senses, the white Mustang once again prowled the outskirts of a well known Hispanic community. Her target had already been identified earlier in the day. Medical records never lie. His indicated he had to be an illegal, so she decided to move swiftly.

Music blared from the back yard of the duplex, festive and invigorating. From her vantage point, she surmised that the risk was much too great to snatch up her quarry right now. Too many witnesses populated the backyard haven, drinking, singing, and dancing the night away. Any one of them could probably serve her purpose, but how could she cull one from the herd?

Twenty precious minutes had ticked off the clock as she made her fourth pass by the house. Determining that she might begin raising suspicions, she decided to forgo a rendezvous tonight. She knew where he lived. He would be there when the time was right.

Just as she approached the intersection three blocks away, she spotted a likely candidate, so all might not be lost yet. Under closer observation, the brown bag toting, obese stranger looked older than she preferred. She decided to give him a pass too and made a left turn. The stumbling drunk never took notice of her as she drove by. He would have been easy prey if she had chosen to take him. He was a lucky hombre tonight.

Two more blocks, and almost out of the neighborhood she spotted him, her original mark. How fortunate. He had not yet arrived at the house. His soiled clothes indicated he had been working late. He had probably just exited the bus at the stop half a block away. She could still see the bus's tail lights, confirming she was right.

Approaching his location, she intentionally sputtered the Mustang to an abrupt stop, perpendicular to his location. She pounded the steering wheel, unleashing a series of unladylike profanities. Acting was a very important part of laying the trap. Without hesitation, he walked over to the woman in distress. She looked up and smiled.

Less than seven minutes later she drove off, poor Pedro, motionless and unconscious under the blanket in the back seat. Mission accomplished.

It didn't go off completely without a hitch. There had been a witness this time...a very careless mistake.

Myrtle Beach Pavilion
10 AM the Ku Klux Klan Rally

Trudy and her complete team, assigned undercover duty, discreetly blended in as tourist keeping a weary eye on the assembling Klansmen, specifically Brock Boudreaux and Scat Crowder. So far, less than a dozen true-blue KKK true-blood had shown up. Trudy took this as a positive sign that the Klan was no real threat in the area.

She had a tough time focusing on the event, her brain swirled with the revelations of the previous day, Brady and the one wishing to be addressed as Sam. She found herself once again juggling too many critical priorities. Brady still occupied the number one slot.

Unlike the undercover CSI unit, Woody, along with half a dozen more officers, strolled around in full uniform, making their presence known to the Klansman and curiosity seekers. He had expected to see a gathering of hooded KKK participants with their identities concealed. Instead the Klan did not obscure their faces, but wore the traditional silky white robes and pointed hats.

He counted nine of them so far. Scat and Brock were center stage. Woody personally recognized two others. The rally was set to begin at 11 AM, 45 minutes from now. He intentionally avoided any contact with the undercover officers to protect their identities.

Detective Sylvester Stone ambled near by, completely intrigued by the event. So far he had spotted no obvious Hispanic or Afro-American presence, other than a couple of stray black tourist with their kids riding the rides and enjoying the carnival atmosphere the Pavilion had to offer.

Detective Dallas Solomon pretended to be watching one of the vendors, drawing caricatures of two young girls sporting skimpy bikinis, while she conducted her own character profiles. She scrutinized those walking about the Pavilion.

Captain Kirk Cardoon wandered near by, eating roasted peanuts and sipping an orange soda, taking his role as a tourist way too seriously. Decked out in plaid shorts, a Gilligan hat, and an *I Love Beach Music* tee-shirt, he looked almost too touristy. He even stopped and played a ring toss game, almost winning a little fuzzy bear.

Detective Tim Burroughs watched the roller coaster, entertained by the screaming riders. He never liked carnival rides. They seemed such a waste of time and money. A geek with a pocket protector would think like that. He would have been a shoe-in for the supporting cast of *Revenge of the Nerds*.

Trudy first spotted the white stretch limo near the ocean side entrance. Like clowns pouring from one of those miniature circus cars, Trudy counted fifteen robed Klansmen, one wearing the robe of an Imperial Wizard. Brock had called in all his favors and intended to milk the moment.

A Channel 12 news crew prepared to film the rally. It didn't seem quite the same, not seeing Lance Rocker primping and preparing for the shoot. Her watch indicated fifteen minutes until show time. She hoped this went smoothly.

On the fifth and top level of the Pavilion parking deck, just across the street from the Pavilion, interim Sheriff, Sam Burton, dressed in shorts and a midriff blouse, watched the unfolding saga through binoculars. She had decided to assess her new troops in action.

There was no room in her town for the KKK. She would make it a priority to remove the garbage from her streets, once that fat-ass country bumpkin of a sheriff retired. Three weeks felt like an eternity.

Show time, Brock Boudreaux at center stage, stepped up to the podium. He began with the usual Klan rhetoric. After their brief fascination with the group's wardrobe, and realizing they were not part of the park's entertainment, the audience of mostly tourist appeared undisturbed and uninspired by his speech. The Pavilion's rides and midway games quickly recaptured their attention.

Brock introduced The Imperial Wizard and more of the same ensued. Unless you were a member of the chapter or a neo-Nazi, a skinhead or into white supremacy, the spill verged on appalling with all the hatred spewed.

Trudy thought, what a shameful display of mankind stood before her. The Imperial Wizard painted on his canvas a non-convincing artist's rendition of America headed for the toilet. Trudy shook her head as Brock verbally attacked Afro-Americans, Jews and other minorities. She marveled at how one group could ooze so much hatred.

After about fifteen minutes, the Imperial Wizard turned the microphone back over to Brock, and that's when the other shoe dropped. The real reason for the rally became vividly clear.

He began by stating he believed illegal aliens undermined the economic fabric of our country. He said these same illegal trespassers were taking sub-prime loans from the whites, and were responsible for higher taxes, the destruction of our schools and hospitals, loss of American jobs, and a negative cultural revolution.

Why should our children be forced to learn their language, he asked. Why must our ATM machines ask if you speak Spanish or English? Why must every aspect of our lives be a translation for one race? Regrettably, Trudy had to agree with some of these talking points. His spewing had now perked the interest of a gathering crowd of tourists.

Brock drove the message home. He brought up the recent Stewart Patrick accident, calling it murder at the hands of dirty, filthy, illegal Mexican gangs. He portrayed Stewart Patrick as an innocent young white boy, dying at the hands of monsters that did not deserve to be in our country, and did not follow our laws or beliefs.

Trudy shook her head in disbelief. The bastard never mentioned the kid's own drug abuse problems and the fact that he was a pusher. Yes, he had most likely been the target of gang related activity, but he had not been murdered. Mission accomplished. Brock had snagged the growing crowd's interest. This wasn't good, thought Trudy.

Sly didn't like the direction this was heading either, after just recently telling Woody that the Klan and Hispanic gangs rarely crossed serious paths. He scanned the Pavilion visitors, looking for any signs of the Valtos Locos or the Sur-13s; so far so good.

Whoops and howls echoed from the ever growing group of onlookers, expressing their sentiments of innocent young children being slaughtered at the hands of these troublesome, illegal aliens. Strategically planted Klansman among them egged on this process. The television cameras captured bonus coverage; just what they had hoped to record.

From her bird's eye view, Sam didn't like what she was now witnessing. The rally was coming unraveled, and the KKK was achieving exactly what they had hoped to accomplish. Whispering, she encouraged her officers to intervene but none did. What were they waiting for, an all out riot?

Instigated by the disguised Klansman, the crowd of less that thirty people now reached a feverish pitch and began turning and scanning their surroundings for any signs of dark skinned Hispanic or Latin types. One such person performed janitorial duties for the park, a clawed pickup device and trash bag in hand; he snagged up food wrappers and other discarded trash items.

Two men, each presumed to be Klansman, approached the unaware worker and scooped him up by both elbows and marched him toward the stage. The confused man, in maybe his late forties, didn't have a clue what might be in store for him.

Woody, closest to the stage, attempted to head them off, but a well placed foot tripped him. He sprawled to the asphalt surface, landing hard on his knees and palms, leaving his mark with peeled, bloodied skin. Sly saw what had happened and signaled for the rest of the CSI unit to close ranks.

After allowing the helpless janitor through, other Klansman blocked off the stage, standing shoulder to shoulder to restrict access. The perplexed janitor was lifted onto the stage by Scat. Brock began shouting and pointing to the Hispanic, blaming his kind for the young boy's murder. The crowd now in a feeding frenzy, demanded restitution and revenge.

Trudy scampered up the back of the platform followed by Kirk. She placed her hand over the microphone and gave Brock a tongue lashing while Captain removed the poor man from Scat's clutches. The Klansmen were very well disciplined and avoided any physical retaliation, for they did not wish to be portrayed as the bad guys. Instead, the police force served as the scapegoat for the crowd's anger.

Numerous bottles were tossed at the stage, one striking the janitor on the forehead and a second hitting Kirk on his cheek. The uniformed officers and remainder of the CSI team slowly but surely restored order and dispersed the crowd.

When the dust had settled, Brock, Scat and several of their cohorts had been taken down to the station and reprimanded. Sheriff Singleton contemplated arresting the lot for inciting a riot and encouraging a lynching. He thought better of it. It would just bring more media attention to the incident, and give the Klan exactly what they wanted. None were booked.

When hearing of the sheriff's actions or lack thereof, it infuriated Sam. She could not believe that the old fart had ignored his duty. He should have locked them all behind bars. This would change on her watch.

She envisioned Hank Singleton standing in front of a burning cross, sporting a white hood, convinced he too must be a member of the loyal order; the way of the good old southern, white boys. In three weeks that would change; possibly sooner, if she could discredit and disgrace the sheriff into an earlier retirement.

Sheriff Singleton's Office
4:15 PM

"Worse than I expected," spouted Hank, addressing his frustration to his captive audience of Woody and Trudy. "I really thought Brock had better sense than to pull that sort of crap."

"He had to put on a show for that Grand Wizard character," Woody reminded him.

"And luckily no one was seriously hurt, sir" added Trudy.

"The poor Pavilion employee was legit," stated Woody. "He's been in this country for almost twenty years and has his citizenship. He did it the right way."

"I hate stereotyping. I should have locked them all up and thrown away the key!"

"So why didn't you, sir?"

"Pierce, I could see it in his smirking bigoted face. That's exactly what Brock Boudreaux wanted; free publicity, a sure fire way to reel in more recruits."

"You're probably right on that account, boss."

"By the way, while all this was going on, we received an anonymous call from a female that she had witnessed what she thought was some sort of abduction last night."

Trudy rubbed the back of her neck. "A kidnapping last night and she's just reporting it now?"

"The dispatcher said she sounded Hispanic, and gave the name of the missing as one Pedro Rodriquez. Guess what? We have no such resident listed as living at the address she gave us."

"Which means he is an illegal," finished Woody.

"It gets even better," stated Hank, rubbing his face with his big old bear paws. "The caller said that the best she could tell from her vantage point, the alleged kidnapper was a Caucasian female, driving a white sports car. She said the white woman somehow disabled Mister Rodriquez and stuffed him in her back seat."

"You think this could be Klan related? It may be retaliation for the Stewart incident?"

"Yeah, Pierce, I had considered that angle and wondered if it could have been in retaliation for that Patrick boy's death."

"I wouldn't put it past them," added Woody.

"I sent officers to the address the caller provided, but as soon as the cruiser pulled up in front of the house, the occupants scattered like roaches scurrying when the light is switched on. They found the house deserted when they entered, most rooms without significant furniture, over a dozen makeshift cots, numerous coolers, and two Coleman gas stoves. I suspect we've seen that lead go cold because I don't expect any of them to return, fearing we were there to arrest and deport them."

"You're probably right on that one, sir."

"How's your Captain Cardoon?"

"Kirk, seven stitches, but he'll live to fight another day," she replied. "And the Pavilion employee, Juan something or other was patched up and released too."

"Perez, his name was Juan Perez," added Woody.

"Right," Trudy thanked him. "It's been a long day."

"By the way storm troopers," said Hank, standing and cracking his knuckles. "Sheriff Burton will be shadowing me starting Monday morning, so please try to be on your best behavior."

Sam, Trudy thought; what a wonderful way to begin the week. Almost tempted to tell Hank about her little conversation, but she thought better since he had hand picked her for his position. Hopefully, her temperament and obnoxious approach to policing would surface before the changing of the guard transpired.

On to her next greatest adventure she thought; Brady and his potential illness. She felt she was reliving her Mom's ordeal. Well, maybe a second chance at making things right would be the charm. She certainly had screwed the other one up by deserting her Mom as she wilted away on her death bed.

This whole Klan and Hispanic gang thing troubled her too. She had a bad feeling that a storm of Hurricane force approached, and the situation was far from over. Her gut instinct seldom betrayed her. She hoped this would be a first time, and her gut would be wrong, but she had serious doubts.

"One more thing," spoke up Hank, jolting Trudy from her dream state. "Residents of Little River area have reportedly received unsolicited invites to join the Ku Klux Klan. The Sun News is reporting that one of the people who received the flyer was a black girl; the KKK Director responded to the allegation saying 'If a black person got it, it's just a mistake. We're not trying to recruit blacks.' Now doesn't that just beat all? These boys are just too damn arrogant for my taste. The flyers are not illegal, but I had them logged into evidence. Keep your eyes open out there and your guard up. This mess is stewing like frogmore stew in a crock pot."

"We will, sir. There is no room in the sand box for the white hoods and the gangs." Trudy returned her thoughts to the new sheriff, thinking she might be worse than the Klan and Gangs combined.

"This is no longer our little ocean and sand tourist trap. Evil needs its fun in the sun too, I reckon. I'm just glad it won't be on my watch. The timing for me couldn't be better."

But what does that say for the rest of our sorry souls, thought Trudy. Ohio looked better everyday. The southern belle needed a vacation away from the ocean breeze and salty air. Who was she fooling? Brady would never consider leaving the Grand Strand. Deep down, she couldn't blame him. She had sand between her toes too, and still didn't look half bad in a bikini.

Duty called, so the beach would have to wait. Monday, the devil would be shadowing Hank. She owed it to the community to keep an eye on Sam. She had a bad feeling about how this might play out. Enough she thought. *I will not allow my work to consume me. I have my priorities in order this time. I am not going to screw this up again. I miss you, mom, and I am so sorry. I should have never left your side. You taught me better, and I let us both down.*

The Woodrow Anderson Residence
Saturday 8:45 PM

Woody had decided to take his mother-in-law up on the offer to keep the rugrats overnight. He had dismissed Lullabelle. He sat in his favorite cushiony chair, feet propped up on the vinyl ottoman, sipping his second ice cold glass of sweet tea, while paging through Sly's journal. It seemed like appropriate reading after today's events.

Sly had jotted down some particularly interesting statistics. Twelve Americans are murdered every day by illegal aliens. Thirteen are killed by drunk illegal alien drivers every day and another eight American children are victims of sexual abuse by illegal aliens every day. In quotations he had written "you do the math."

Reading on; illegal immigrants represent about 4.9 percent of the nation's labor force and work in construction, grounds maintenance, painters, maids and dishwashers. In quotations, "How many of these have killed Americans?"

As a side note and unrelated to gangs, Sly had recorded the impact on South Carolina from this illegal work force. The demand for workers had increased during construction surges. Competition with illegal Hispanic immigrants adversely affects black South Carolinians more directly than whites, possibly because of educational attainment.

Sly, being black himself had written: I'm surprised there hasn't been more of an organized uprising from the Afro-American community against the exploding Hispanic population, a black KKK equivalent. If the illegal population goes unchecked, and no valid attempt is made to prevent these illegal entries, soon both the black and white Americans will some day discover they are at the bottom of the food chain, and coexist as a minority.

Sly certainly spun his own personal, yet interesting perspective on illegal aliens. It made Woody sit back and view things differently.

He had documented countless cases of gang related crimes, page after page after page, and had spun his opinions of the crimes, those that had committed them and those whom had fallen victim to them. More pages documented Hispanic gangs attacking illegal Hispanic families, and robbing them of their hard earned money and possessions. What could they do about it? They couldn't report these to the police, fearful they would be deported themselves.

Stories of senseless murders, beheadings, massive burial site discoveries, rapes and robberies sent Woody's head spinning. The shear viciousness of these gangs overwhelmed even a seasoned officer. The present day Klan almost appeared amateurish by comparison.

He had read enough. He closed the journal and poured another glass of tea. He then closed his eyes for a couple of minutes and tried to leave the carnage behind. His thoughts turned to Janice, his nightmare continued.

"Why in the name of God do I insist on living here?" he questioned out loud. "Because it's the only place I've ever known. Where else could I possibly go where the demons wouldn't track me down?"

The Captain's Sea House
Myrtle Beach, Sunday Brunch

The mayor, hosting a neighborly meet and greet brunch for interim Sheriff, Samantha Burton, had invited prominent town council members. Hank had bowed out; telling Mayor Belcher the event should be for the new sheriff. He didn't want to cause any distractions by being there. The mayor had agreed.

"Lovely setting," remarked Samantha Burton, taking note that the restaurant bordered the beach with a wonderful view of the Atlantic Ocean. "Thank you, Mayor Belcher for the warm welcome."

"This is one of my favorite places. I thought it appropriate that you should meet some of our fine people on the council before you begin your interim stint. Some could be good to have in your pocket come the next election, if you catch what I'm saying."

"I agree. You can't have too many friends, now can you?"

"Allow me to introduce Bob Voile. Mister V is a history teacher at Carolina Forest High School". Bob, of Swedish ancestry, stood five-ten, average build and sported his trademark attribute, thick, wavy, blondish hair, compliments of his heritage.

"An honor to meet you, sir," said Sam, pouring on the charm. Prim and proper, he wowed Sam, captivating her with his encyclopedic approach to the world, especially wars and the strategic angles of battles.

Mayor Belcher finally had to drag her away, telling Mister V that he couldn't monopolize the guest of honor. He motioned over Doctor Lincoln T. Hawthorne, owner and operator of a local health clinic. Forty one years old, very distinguished, an inch shy of six feet, with auburn hair, and a neatly trimmed matching mustache. His family had been a cornerstone of the county for generations.

"I find your loyalty and dedication to the less fortunate very intriguing and refreshingly genuine," Sam played the game well.

"Yes, Lincoln could have practiced medicine most anywhere, but he chose to run this clinic of his and treat the underprivileged and less fortunate minorities," added Mayor Belcher. "You'll find no finer family on the Grand Strand, I assure you."

"Pay our Mayor no mind, my dear," expressed Lincoln. "He is simply playing his little role as a suck-up and courting me for more contributions and support for his next run for office. Sorry, I can't help myself. I jest to get a rise from him and it always works delightfully."

"You two must be such close friends to be able to egg one another on like that," chuckled Sam.

"We do go way back, and I truly support our good mayor. He and I see the significant issues eye to eye, most of the time."

"Tell me more about your clinic," coached Sam, sensing she needed this doctor in her pocket too.

"Nothing much to tell, dear, it's a small clinic on the south end of the strand, just off 17 before you enter Georgetown County. As the Mayor has already described, we cater to the less fortunate. Many are Hispanic or African-American, with a spattering of less fortunate whites and transients. Besides my sister, who serves as both receptionist and nurse, we recruit young interns eager to learn the trade and make a difference."

"Sounds so fascinating, I would love to visit sometime," she painted it on thickly.

"You are welcome anytime, my dear sheriff-elect. Here, take my card. Once you have yourself settled in, I'll personally give you the grand tour."

"Thank you Doctor Hawthorne."

"Please, call me Lincoln," he replied, caressing her hand.

"And you may call me Sam," she said, locked in eye contact.

"I'll have to tell you like I did Bob," broke in the Mayor. "We must share our guest with the other dignitaries."

"Certainly," smiled Lincoln. "If you need anything my dear, please don't hesitate to ask."

Sam sensed she had struck gold with this Lincoln gentleman and would milk him for all he's worth when the time was right. She spent the next couple of hours mingling with the remainder of what the council had to offer. None stood out like Doctor Lincoln Hawthorne.

Brookgreen Gardens
Georgetown County, 2:30 PM Sunday

"I just love picnicking here, Brady. Thank you for bringing me again."

"Well, it's just been one week since we were last here. I didn't want you to suffer withdrawal symptoms."

"It's just the perfect blend of culture and nature. Just look around Brady; all these exquisite statues accented with wildlife. I can just get lost here."

"And forget about the real world," finished Brady. "What's really on your mind my dear wife?"

"You, you're my real world and I'm nothing without you!"

"So I've moved up in the pecking order," he laughed. "I figured you were being troubled by a new case."

"Not this time, I have my priorities straight, I assure you, and you're number one on my list," she said, rolling toward him on the blanket and smothering him with kisses.

"Watch it or you'll get us kicked out of here," he warned her, rolling on top and pressing his erection against her flat belly.

"There goes our membership. Seriously, how are you really feeling?"

"Tremors are getting more frequent, and I can't say I'm not worried, but we'll get through this thing."

"Together," Trudy replied, brushing the back of her hand against his cheek.

"How's it going with the sheriff-in-waiting?"

"She's probably basking in the limelight at the Sea Captain's House. The Mayor was rolling out the red carpet for her today. I trust her about as far as I can toss her. I already miss Hank. I should give her the benefit of the doubt, but unfortunately, doubt is all I have.'

"Do you really think she is going to be a disruptive force?"

"I think she will be a corruptive force. She's a black woman with a cross to bear. In some ways I think she could be as bad as that Brock character. Time will tell. You shouldn't have gotten me fired up."

"My bad, I should have kept to the script and let this be all about us."

"What say we stroll down to the zoo? I just love watching those otters."

"And I just love watching you."

"And I just love you period, and you're right, together we can lick anything."

"And we will, Brady."

Brock Boudreaux residence
5 PM Sunday

"Brock, you've been mighty damned quite this afternoon," commented Scat. "That usually means a world of hurt is about to come down on somebody."

Brock took another swallow of Jack but said nothing. He sloshed the ice around, clanging it in the glass. He took a pull off his cigar, blowing an impressive smoke ring but remained silent. Scat didn't like what he saw in Brock's eyes. He had never seen Brock like this before, and it scared the crap out of him and he didn't scare easily.

Brock's deck overlooked a natural swamp, fully equipped with swamp critters, including numerous gators, one almost twelve feet long. Brock bought this acreage at a bargain, no one else saw the beauty in living on a swamp. He said it reminded him of home. Scat saw no beauty in it either, constantly swatting gnats and mosquitoes. He definitely had no fondness for gators or snakes.

Brock still said nothing. He drank, he smoked and he drank some more. Scat had always been amazed by how much bourbon he could put away and never appear drunk. Scat knew he would have been shit-faced about now if he had downed what his boss had consumed.

Having to take a piss, Scat walked down the deck steps and out to the end of the dock. Unzipping, he aimed his golden stream at a medium sized gator resting in the shade just below the dock. The gator submerged to escape Scat's target practice. He chuckled, zipped up and took another swig from his longneck beer. Glancing back to the deck, he noticed Brock had disappeared.

Wasting no time, Scat made his way back to the deck and could see Brock inside the glassed-in combination den and bar, engaged in deep discussion on the phone. He couldn't hear the conversation, but the intense look on his boss's face said it all. Yep, things were about to be kicked up a notch or two. Scat could just feel it in the air.

He so envied Brock Boudreaux. The man had style. He had never forgotten his roots from his early upbringing in the Louisiana bayou, but yet he could hobknob with the rich and famous, using that Cajun charm to his advantage. In Scat's eyes, the Klan had no better spokesperson and representative than old Brock.

Scat himself had made quite a lucrative career out of doing Brock's bidding; the shadier and more corrupt side, ensuring his boss's hands remained clean and unblemished of any wrong doings. Woody had been right on those facts. He both cherished and enjoyed his role and had become damned good at it.

Homegrown in Horry County, Scat knew the lay of the land and who to trust and who to avoid. He knew how to play the game and use the pawns at his beck and call. Scat looked and played the good old boy, bad-ass, redneck part but was the opposite of his presumed stereotype. He too could turn it on and off like a light switch and play to his audience.

Finally Brock returned to the deck, still puffing his cigar, with a fresh drink of Jack in hand. He smiled, clinching the stogie in his teeth. As only a Cajun could say it, Brock finally spoke, "Nuff is a nuff. Da Calvary is on da way. We show dem and we show dem coo-yôn how dey must repek dis Klan."

Scat nodded, translating that Brock had said something like enough is enough and the fools were going to respect the Klan one way or the other. He raised his almost empty longneck and made a toast, "To the Klan, boss."

Brock clanged his glass against the beer bottle. "What time it is?"

"Almost six..."

Speaking in French now, Brock cried out in a good old Cajun yell, "Laisser les bons temps rouler." Let the good times roll!

Horry County Police Department
7 AM Monday

"Good morning Sheriff Singleton," said Sam.

"Just call me, Hank. We're on even ground here."

"Then you can call me Sam."

"Hank and Sam, fine, good old American sounding names," chuckled Hank.

Humoring the overweight short timer she said, "Sounds like we could do our own morning talk radio show."

"Or comic strip or even a morning cartoon show," Hank added, feeling his oats this morning.

"So where do we begin?" Sam was ready to cut the crap and get on with it.

"Let's go debrief the troops then," responded Hank, never suspecting her distaste for him.

"Are we going to review how badly things transpired at that Ku Klux Klan rally?"

Hank frowned at that remark.

"Sorry, I didn't mean to sound out of line. I caught it on the news. I did take the liberty to review that report on your desk, before you arrived."

"You're a real go getter, aren't you Sam?"

"Pays to do the homework and this could have the makings of something nasty, if I can be so bold to say. We certainly don't want this to turn into a full blown riot, now do we?"

"Not to worry, we can handle this, and lot more," defended Hank, not appreciating her comment or her tone. "This isn't Mayberry by a long shot."

"I didn't mean to imply that. I'm sure your officers are professionals in every way and are up for any task."

"We're a tourist town. We're accustomed to dealing with unusual circumstances."

"Like those road rage murders," she zinged him, knowing how poorly they had been handled, and then had been covered up.

"That was a difficult case," again Hank attempted to defend the department. "My officers did the best they could under unique circumstances. We eventually got our man."

"You were in the hospital, weren't you, while your officers took matters into their own hands? I heard it through the grapevine that officers Anderson and Wagner sort of colored just a tad outside the lines, without your direct supervision, to finally break the case. People lost their lives while those two were playing God, and skirting their responsibilities and the system."

"Look, I'm not commending them for the way they got there, but they got there, end of story, crime solved. Would I have handled it differently? Yes, but the maniac was not following any standard serial killer profiles. This was ground breaking and unheard of, especially along the Grand Strand."

"And they both should be respectful of you, Hank, since each received very nice promotions afterwards, especially Wagner. She hadn't been with your department very long, had she?"

"Pierce, her name is now Pierce. Woody had been in line for the constable position for too long. Pierce had the experience from her time in Ohio. She was the right person for the job. Hell, I don't have to defend them, or my choices to grant them promotions. You're walking a mighty thin line, Officer Burton."

"Sam," she reminded him with a smug grin. "And I thought I was a sheriff."

"I only call my friends by first name, and something tells me we won't be making too many inroads during this little transition...sheriff," snapped a highly frustrated Hank.

"Sorry, I didn't mean to step on your toes."

"In case you haven't noticed officer, I have mighty damn big feet. It would take more than the likes of someone like you to put a dent in them. Maybe I need to rethink this. I'm not so sure you're the best fit for this department or Horry County."

"Calm down Sheriff, we're on the same side aren't we?"

"I'm not so sure anymore. I'm in it for the department and this fine community, and I sense you're in for you. I'm a pretty good read on people. I think I will give this more consideration."

"Off the record so to speak, you may wish to consider just how far you're willing to cross the line, old man. Don't forget, I have a couple of aces up my sleeve. I can play the race card or female card anytime it serves my best interest. I'm an excellent poker player. You don't have a hand even close to match mine."

"Well, I certainly see why you were so available out there on the market. I didn't do my homework so damn good after all. Your threats are a piece of horse shit. You are not going to be sheriff. I can damn promise you that."

"You did your homework just fine, sheriff. I'm just better at playing the game than most. I wouldn't be so fast to make that call if I were you."

"If you were a man and white, I would have already knocked you on your butt," boasted Hank, now standing up and towering over her. "I might do it just for the hell of it anyway."

"Sad isn't it that times have changed, and you good old southern boys can't run roughshod over us poor little underprivileged Negroes, like you once could."

"Even sadder, people like you that use their color to manipulate the system and discredit those that stand on their principles, morals, reputation, and upbringing to promote themselves. You're a disgrace to your gender and color, and I will find a fair and ethical way to expose you for what you are. That, you can take to the bank. I'm surprised you played your hand so early in the game, when you could have so easily held firm and flown under the radar, until after I retired. That was mighty damn stupid for a seasoned poker player."

"Part of playing the game for me is rubbing my opponent's nose in it and watching them squirm like the worms they are and in this case, that would be you and your kind."

"My kind...I'm just a good old American law enforcement agent. If you would have taken the time to know me, you would have discovered that I'm color blind and gender neutral. I treat everyone the same. I ensure the cream of the crop is rewarded. I am proud of my service in this department and as a human being. You didn't do your homework, my dear, nearly as damn well as you think. That mistake is going to be your undoing."

"Give it your best shot. The press loves a good story. They just eat up this discrimination stuff. Leaks do happen."

"The press don't scare me, little lady. Play your cards, if you feel Froggy. I assure you, justice will prevail. I, for one, believe in our system," snapped Hank, red faced and now sweating profusely.

"Best thing you can do, Hank, old boy is forget about this little conversation and retire gracefully. You don't want to screw up your pension when you're this close, do you?"

"If bringing you down means doing what's right then deal me in," he warned her, feeling that familiar little twinge in his chest.

"I think we have your debriefing to attend, don't we? Try to put on a happy face for your troops. See you there," she said, turning and walking away.

"Screw you!" Hank managed to whisper as he slammed his fist on his desk, and then fell backwards into his old leather chair, scrambling for his nitroglycerin bottle in his desk drawer.

Conway Medical Center
9:35 AM

"I can't believe he's gone," sighed Trudy. "Just like that, just gone."

"After he didn't show up for the morning debriefing, I dropped by his office and discovered him slumped back in his chair, eyes closed like he was resting," explained Woody. "I yelled out to him from the doorway, but he didn't respond. As I got closer, I could tell he wasn't breathing."

Trudy placed her hand on Woody's shoulder, attempting to console him. She knew the two had a long history.

"I checked for a pulse but couldn't find one. He felt cold to the touch. He was clutching an unopened prescription of his heart pills in his right hand. He must have been having an attack, but it came on so suddenly he hadn't been able to pop one in his mouth."

"So close to retirement, and now this..."

"He deserved much better," barked Woody, still not wanting to accept Hank's death.

"I don't get it. I thought he had this heart thing under control."

"So he said, unless he wasn't telling us the whole story which is like the old cuss."

"What about next of kin?"

"He has a son in North Carolina, and a sister in Florida. I think that's about it for any close kin. The Mayor just left before you arrived."

Trudy heard clicking footsteps behind and turned to face the new sheriff. "Just came by to pass on my condolences. I know you were both close to Sheriff Singleton. Had he been ill lately?"

"Seemed to be doing just fine or at least as far as anyone of us knew," answered Woody. "Thanks for dropping by. It's a shame you didn't get a chance to know him like we did. You would have liked him. He was a straight shooter, and as honest as they come."

"I'm sure he and I would have gotten along just fine. He certainly embraced me and had bent over backwards to make me feel welcome," she put on an Oscar winning performance.

Trudy didn't buy it. She didn't believe for one minute that Samantha Burton had a sincere bone in her body. Like it or not, she was the new sheriff, for now. She would have to come to terms with that fact and deal with it the best she could. For now, she would mourn the death of a true lawman.

Thursday Night, 10:45 PM
Loris Countryside

Sheriff Hank Singleton had been laid to rest, with honors, at noon. The county still remained in shock over his sudden death, but the justice system must continue to function. The Mayor had sworn in his replacement at mid afternoon to expedite the transition, and begin the healing process, however; criminals don't take the day off to mourn a fallen police officer, not even Sheriff Hank Singleton.

She drove to the tomato farm, top down and enjoying the warm night air. Her quarry routinely visited a diner just over a mile from the old farm. He should be making his way back on foot. They all tended to travel by foot or by bicycle, she mused. She pulled down the access road to the farm's back forty. He would come this way to reach the compound. Here she would claim him for her own.

The syringe lay to her left. The forty-five rested between her legs, under her skirt, just in case more persuasive measures were required. She had only once before had to use the pistol. She had to unfortunately shoot the victim, leaving his corpse there to rot. She had staged it to look like a robbery.

She had watched the local television broadcasts and newspapers. It had been six months. His corpse had never been reported. She suspected his own had discovered the body and disposed of him. Illegal aliens were a dime a dozen. They were chosen for that very reason. Their families would not report their disappearances, couldn't report them without exposing themselves as being illegal, too. They were the perfect prey and in endless supply. Don't build that fence just yet, she thought.

Most were so predictable, but then aren't all men, regardless of skin color or nationality? Wave a little piece under their noses, and they would follow you anywhere. All of them are just dogs looking for the next bitch in heat. They can't help themselves. It's so primal.

She smiled. The fun part; lay the trap, reel them in, and then spring the snare. Wild eyed and in denial, the expression was always the same. Like a cat, she enjoyed playing with her little mice, prolonging the climax until an explosive ending. The poor little mice didn't fare so well in the game, but then again, the game wasn't intended for their enjoyment.

Carlos approached on schedule. Larger than most Hispanic men, he stood nearly five ten and possessed an athletic body. She licked her lips, contemplating what she would soon be doing with such a fine specimen. She watched him through her rearview mirror, the moon proving adequate illumination for her to make out his facial expressions. He had spotted her convertible.

She kicked into distressed blonde mode, crocodile tears and all, boo-hooing loudly. He stopped just a couple of yards shy of her back bumper and just stared toward the car. She kicked up the drama a tad, but he stood his ground. What was his problem?

He began easing backwards, small steps at first then quicker, more deliberate. He wasn't taking the bait. Something was wrong. Had he recognized her or the automobile or could the Hispanic community have implemented an alert system? After all, she had taken so many of them.

Game on, she could not allow him to escape. She stepped out of the driver's side, gun concealed on her blind side. She yelled to Carlos by name, begging for his help. He paused when hearing his name, stood motionless less than thirty paces away to hear her out. She beckoned him closer, but he shook his head, refusing her request.

Pissed, she realized it would be hopeless to drag this out any further. He would not play. The game had lost its appeal. She had grown short on patience.

The shot rang out, amplified in the open country side. Carlos fell dead, a single shot between his eyes delivered by an eagle eye marksman. She rushed over, ruffled through his pockets and removed what little cash he had, then quickly returned to her Mustang and made a hasty retreat.

Foreplay, all worked up and nothing to show for it. This didn't set well with her. She didn't like the thoughts of having to wait another night to claim her treat. Risky as it might be, she decided to take the long ride home. Just maybe, if she was lucky, she'd find a new mark. The two minute warning; time still remained on the clock.

CSI Team at the Crime Scene
9:20 AM Friday

"One shot to the head," stated Captain Kirk, forensics. "If I had to guess, looks like possibly a forty-five."

"And that kid over there found him taking a shortcut to join some friends fishing this morning," added Sly. "His pockets were turned inside out, no bills and just a few pieces of change scattered on the ground."

Trudy asked, "What about ID?"

"What do you think?" responded Sly. "He probably works on that farm back there," he pointed. "And my money says he's an illegal immigrant as is everyone else in that series of shacks. I've already called in a request for a warrant and back-up. We'll need all the help we can get if we intend to raid this farm."

"I haven't called in Dallas yet" advised Captain. "It's too early yet for a profile. It could be just plain homicide, one robbing the other."

"We did find some fresh tire tracks over there," Sly informed Trudy. "Tim is casting them and taking photos. We might get lucky."

Trudy sized up the crime scene. "Do we know when it happened?"

Sly answered, "Definitely last night by the condition of the body, plus we have one neighbor a half mile up the road that stated she heard a shot last night between 11 and 11:30. She shrugged it off, said she hears shooting from back in here quite often and has reported it before, and no one ever took any actions. We're checking the prior reports."

"If he's indeed an illegal, I don't expect we'll receive much cooperation from any of the workers, if we're lucky enough to interview or apprehend any of them," chimed in Captain.

"Cap is probably right. If they've gotten wind of this, and have seen our cars, then I expect most of them have high-tailed it already," confirmed Sly.

"How's Woody doing?" asked Tim, strolling over from the CSI van.

"He's still dealing with it pretty hard. I'm betting there are plenty of other folks still shell shocked over Hank's death," answered Trudy. "He's taking the weekend off and spending time with his kids. How's your wound, Captain?"

"Just call me scar face," responded Kirk Cardoon. "It should make me look more convincing the next time I go under cover."

"A real badass for sure," she chuckled.

Captain Kirk asked, "What's your read on the new sheriff?"

"I'm probably not the best one to ask. We don't share the same work ethics. I'll just leave it at that right now. Speaking of, I have a meeting scheduled with her this morning, so you guys proceed without me, but keep me posted."

"Will do," replied Sly. "Remember, she is the sheriff now, so be on your best behavior."

"Do I have a best behavior?"

"You're right. Cancel that last statement. What the hell was I thinking?"

"You boys try not to screw-off too much while I'm gone. Pretend I'm still here."

"Hey Tim, cancel the keg and pizza," yelled Captain.

"Tim, just put it on hold until I get back," shouted Trudy.

Driving to the police station she contemplated the next meeting with the pathetic excuse for a sheriff. With Hank Singleton clearly out of the picture, she just couldn't fathom where this woman would take the department. She totally regretted feeling this way about a woman, but it seemed justified.

Her dilemma, how could she expose the she-sheriff for what she really was, without ruining her own reputation? Her colleagues wouldn't take kindly to her discrediting one of their own, even if it was the appropriate thing to do. This had all the signs of a train wreck.

Maybe if she fed her enough rope, she would hang herself. Not likely, she thought. She didn't envision the one that wished to be called Sam making any stupid mistakes. She planned and calculated every move much too well to stumble over her own feet.

I'll play along with her and see where it takes me. There has to be a chink in her armor, if I can maintain my patience long enough to discover her flaws. After all, the she-sheriff didn't know who she was dealing with either, an equally dangerous adversary.

Sam sat in Hank's office, thinking extreme office makeover. She had the urgent need to customize her surroundings to better fit her personality and cast out those evil good old boy spirits that presently haunted the room and the dead man's leather chair.

With Hank permanently out of the picture, she only had to rally enough allies over her interim stint to ensure her election to this post. She foresaw only one obstacle in her path, the high and mighty CSI detective. There just wasn't room for more than one head strong career hungry female on the force. She had to either entice Pierce into her fold or ruin her career. Today she would make that assessment. She had no high expectations. What timing; Pierce now stood in the doorway.

"Enter," said the spider to the fly.

Trudy poured on a truck load of charm. "How might I help you sheriff?"

"Come in, have a seat and I repeat, please call me Sam. I'm sure your head is still swirling over the untimely death of Sheriff Singleton. You, as well as this department, must overcome your grief so that we can restore order. We must convince the tax payers we will practice diligence moving forward."

"We're professionals. Neither the general public, nor any of your constituents will notice a ripple in the pond, I assure you, ma'am."

"Tell me Detective Pierce, or may I call you Trudy?"

"Detective or Pierce is fine with me, just so that we maintain a cordial and professional demeanor. Perception and proper protocol should be maintained, don't you agree?"

"Don't you think that behind closed doors we can drop this crap? It is just you and me. I firmly believe we can shoot straight with one another. It's obvious to me that we'll never be best friends. You seem to have a bug up your butt towards me for some reason."

"You're the sheriff and I will comply with your wishes, providing it doesn't compromise either the integrity of this department, or my team or mess with my personal convictions."

"Well done, dear," she smiled, applauding. "I'm glad to see you let your hair down. Your integrity and convictions, it's time to knock you off that high horse of yours."

"Why am I really here, ma'am?" Just what do you really want?"

"To discuss your future, your role with this department, moving forward." The new sheriff remained cool and collective.

"My role, I thought that was perfectly clear. I am assigned to the CSI unit, no great mystery."

"If we can be frank, what are your aspirations, your goals, where do you wish to be, say in the next five years or so?"

Trudy smiled, so much for playing the game. "I scare you don't I? You see me as a major threat. Is that frank enough for you?"

"You, intimidate me? You give yourself far too much credit. I've studied your career thoroughly, from shall we say, your wild and youthful days, your journey through the academy, your turbulent time in Ohio, that little leave of absence of yours and some very interesting facts about your personal life prior to choosing this occupation. Best I can tell, you are damn lucky to be here right now. If I so choose to feed the right dirt to the news media, I could snuff you out, just like that." She snapped her fingers.

"What kind of silly game are you playing here sheriff?"

Sam retrieved a file folder from her desk drawer and slid it in front of Trudy. "Open it, and then we'll continue this discussion."

Trudy took a deep breath and opened the folder. She hadn't seen this one coming. It had rattled her cage terribly. She had no immediate come back.

"Speechless, I have indeed struck a nerve with you. I bet that new husband of yours doesn't know everything about your sordid past either, does he? You're so easy to read for such a sweet little blonde one, aren't you? And you are a natural one at that. Those pictures prove that fact clearly. You were quite the exhibitionist in your day, weren't you?"

"Where the hell did you get these, and what do you want?" Trudy almost choked on the words. She had not expected this meeting to go the she-sheriff's way, but she did indeed hold the upper hand right now.

"Let's just say we have a mutual acquaintance in Ohio, a person who had high aspirations for advancement, and now he works for me after I discovered his dirty little secret and covey of photographs. Just for the record, that's not my only copies. Actually you can keep those to remind you of our rather unique relationship."

Trudy flipped through the remainder of the folder's contents before she slammed it closed and eyed the sheriff as a cold blooded murderer probably assessed their next victim. She knew the son of a bitch well but how had she gotten her hands on these? He had said he destroyed them. She had seen him do it. It was all for show by the bastard.

"My, if looks could kill, we would have you judged, sentenced and fried about now for my murder. Don't fret my dear, I can certainly be persuaded to keep our little secrets under wraps if you play nice and do exactly what I ask you to do, when I ask you to do it. Essentially, from here on out, I own you, Pierce. You're my little girl toy for as long as I desire keeping you in my little playhouse, and how long I keep you depends on your loyalty. Your redneck sheriff underestimated me too. He didn't have the heart to take me on, may he rest in peace. I know how to play the game and how to climb to the top, stepping over and on whomever is necessary to achieve my goals. Now may I call you Trudy?"

Trudy didn't answer. She placed her hands on the desk instead. "You seem to hold all the cards right now, but don't get to comfy and cozy. I don't take blackmail lightly. My gut told me you were untrustworthy and it never lies."

"Tell you what, why don't you plan to drop by my hotel suite after work this afternoon and we'll continue our discussion about your future. Wear something sexy. You can go a long way in this department. Every queen has her little princess, but just don't forget the pecking order."

"Can I be dismissed now?"

"Say pretty please, and I'll consider it, Trudy."

A knock came on the door. Trudy stood up immediately and closed the few short strides to grab the door knob, opened it quickly to see Sly standing there.

"Is there something we can do for you Detective Stone?"

"Sorry to interrupt, I was looking for Detective Pierce."

"I believe we are finished here. I enjoyed our conversation, Detective Pierce. Keep up the good work and I do so look forward to a long relationship here in this fine department."

Trudy walked down the hallway, Sly jabbering in her ear and her not hearing a word. She couldn't believe how badly she had underestimated this bitch. She had dug up skeletons Trudy thought she had buried too deeply for anyone ever to have found. She could just read the headlines, Dark Side Revealed, CSI from the Inside Out. The stakes had been raised much too high and were not stacked in her favor. Her professional career as well as her personal life now hung by a thread.

For the first time, she regretted her decision to return to South Carolina. This was bad on so many levels she couldn't think straight. Murder certainly seemed like a viable option. She envisioned her hands around Burton's neck.

"So what do you think?"

She snapped out of it and stared expressionless at Sly, who was waiting anxiously for some sort of feedback. "I'm sorry; can you repeat what you just said?"

"I asked, what do you think about my little theory?"

"I meant before that."

"Which part?"

"All of it..."

"Where the hell have you been"? You mean to tell me you haven't heard a thing I've said?"

"Sorry, I have a lot on my mind."

"Anything I can do?"

She shook her head no. "So what is this theory of yours?"

"I was just saying I've been speculating whether the missing associate pastor, the allegedly kidnapped illegal immigrant, and this dead illegal migrant worker from this morning are related, and if the Klan could be our link to all three."

"Go on," she told him, trying to maintain focus while clutching firmly to the incriminating cache folder of photos.

"I'll wager that those tire tracks we discovered at the scene this morning will match a sports car of some sort. If it does, it could establish a link to the kidnapping. The anonymous caller reported seeing a sports car used."

"But we have no make, no model; nothing so we would really be grasping at straws, don't you think?"

"Okay, you got me there; however, we do have three Hispanics, one dead and two missing, compounded by Stewart Patrick's death, with him being chased by possible Hispanic gang members, drug related. We have the Klan making this big connection to Hispanic activity in the county. You can't tell me all of this is mere coincidence."

"All right, I'll concede to the fact that there is definitely a pattern of elevated Hispanic overtones here but we don't have anything that specifically ties them all together other than the proverbial race card. We can't hang our hats on that."

"What if this is plain and simple, the Klan's doing. Maybe they have hit squads out there with a dual purpose, eradicate as many illegal immigrants as possible while trying to incite a war between the whites and Hispanics to further elevate their agenda."

"Why would the Klan purposely wish to infuriate and antagonize Hispanic gangs? These same gangs would probably lash out at the Klan and I don't believe for an instant that today's KKK is ready for that war."

"Okay then, what about this? What better way to get the American citizen's attention and entice more recruits into the KKK?"

"I can't say I buy into this theory of yours hook, line, and sinker, but I give you permission to pursue the angle and see if you can connect any dots that actually support it, but that being said, I don't want any of this leaked to the press. Okay, that look, spill it, you have something else on your mind don't you, Sly?"

"You're not going to like this one any better."

"Pile it on. My day can't get any worse."

"Serial killer, a female version," he blurted.

"Whoa, let's not go there at all! First of all, the chances of us having a second serial killer here in Horry County has to be astronomical. Secondly, females just don't fit the serial killer stereotype, exception being the likes of Aileen Carol Wuornos, the famed Florida interstate killer. Sly, let's face it. You only have a female mentioned in the one possible kidnapping, so drop that line of deduction right now."

"Not exactly, we found foot prints, small, female and high heeled, but I'll stick with the Klan theory if you wish."

"Holy crap, now you're talking. On second thought, play both angles. Keep me posted and only me. That means keep the sheriff out of it until I decide to bring her in."

"You got it. You want to go grab a late lunch?"

"Thanks, but I need to call Brady and see how his doctor's appointment went."

Horry County Police Department
Sheriff Sam Burton's Office, 5:40 PM

"Well, hello Doctor Hawthorne. I correct myself, I meant to say Lincoln. I really didn't expect to hear from you so soon. I'm sorry, I would really love to join you for dinner and that tour but I have an engagement tonight. Could you give me a rain check? Why certainly, tomorrow night, it would be my pleasure. Why don't I just plan on meeting you there, say around seven? Marvelous, I look so forward to your company. Yes, me too."

Hanging up the phone, she settled back into Hank's oversized leather chair, a monstrosity. This had to go tomorrow. She felt dirty just sitting in the seat where her predecessor had died.

Those thoughts were quickly extinguished and replaced by the anticipation of the scheduled rendezvous with Detective Trudy Pierce. Tonight she would seal the deal that would guarantee the detective's continued loyalty and set the wheels in motion to achieve her final goal.

Tomorrow she would build the foundation for her political future, snaring the white doctor with what she would have to offer him. Once they have tasted black, they never go back, she laughed. Fooling these crackers was much easier than she could have ever anticipated. She smiled, thinking no one played the game better than she.

She had outsmarted them all. The spineless twerp in Ohio had been her best discovery. He had tried pulling that photo scam on her and she had so easily turned it on him. That had been years ago, when she, too, had been entering the academy. His little library of photographs had been taken and filed away to advance his agenda.

The poor bastard had chosen promising rookies, ones he figured he could blackmail once they had secured their place in law enforcement. His mistake, trying to scam a scam artist and she had confiscated his files, turning the tables on him. Granted, she had waited years to play her hand with Pierce, but she had successfully used many others at opportune times.

Keeping people in her hip pocket had become old hat. Her aspirations would not stop at being mere Sheriff of Horry County. This was just a stopping place until she launched her next campaign. Sheriff simply looked good on her ever growing resume. There was nothing like having a little fun with those she was blackmailing. They were never in a position to refuse her perversions. No one had ever bucked her and never would. Life was certainly good.

Denny's
Ocean Boulevard, 7:25 PM Friday

The white Mustang was conveniently parked out of sight, across the street from the construction site. The driver sat in Denny's in a booth that gave her full view of the workers scurrying around like little ants. She had already singled out her ant from the bunch.

Normally she would not have been back out so soon, especially after the messy, thwarted attempt last night, but she already knew this one's patterns and he should be easy enough to snare, providing he didn't drag any of his buddies along with him after work.

She had never tried a two-for before and she had to admit it did send a little tingle up her leg and into her nether regions just contemplating the possibility. No, better to play it safe and stick to the plan, she warned herself. Getting too greedy could be costly. She glanced at her watch. It should be any time now.

As if choreographed, she watched as her unsuspecting ant snatched up his simple belongings and departed on foot, while a few peddled away on bicycles. Her little ant didn't disappoint her. He departed solo and toward his modest apartment, a seven block walk.

In no particular hurry, she finished her hash browns and coffee, and then paid her tab in cash, and strolled to her car. She knew where he was headed. The final destination would provide better cover for what she had in mind. She paused; applied fresh lipstick, blush, and a splash of Clinique, before she fired up the Mustang. "Irresistible," she whispered, eyeing the beauty in the mirror.

She lingered three blocks back until she saw him turn down the narrow alley way. Satisfied he had gone inside; she eased her car down the alley and parked at a sharp angle, concealing her vehicle from view, a few short paces from his door.

She stimulated her nipples with her fingers to ensure they pressed fully erect against her thin blouse. Her mini-skirt barely clung below her panties. She popped the hood on the Mustang, and then walked over and rapped on his door.

She saw the curtain move slightly in the only window facing the alley. Once he made sure the police were not outside, he cautiously opened the door. He smiled and greeted her in Spanish. She smiled back and pointed to her car. He nodded and followed her; so predictable.

She asked him to sit in the driver's seat and try to start it. He obliged and turned the key in the ignition. The Mustang fired up on the very first try and he jabbered something, grinning and expressing his surprise and joy for helping a damsel in distress. She inserted the needle into his neck. It shouldn't be so easy; mission accomplished without a hitch this time, and in broad daylight.

Dragging him over to the passenger side, she sat back in the driver's seat. She adjusted the rearview mirror to assess her appearance. It was tough to improve on perfection. She hadn't even broken a sweat. She glanced back over at her catch and smiled. Let the games begin. She shifted Mustang into gear, and exited the alley undetected.

Holiday Inn Hotel Parking Lot
8:15 PM Beach Front

Trudy sat in her vehicle, gathering her thoughts. Why did life have to always throw her so many curve balls, she asked? She contemplated her options one more time to ensure she had chosen the right one. Plan A or Plan B, she was probably screwed either way. Oh well, she thought, the best way to take nasty medicine is just gulp it down and be done with it. Dreading it didn't improve the taste.

She slipped from the leather seat of her vehicle. The silky red dress almost rode up past her thighs as she exited. High heels echoed on the parking garage pavement, sounding like a Clydesdale horse pulling a beer wagon. The steady ocean breeze pressed the fabric snuggly against her breast, highlighting her impressive areola twins. Brady often commented on how they were God's gift to him.

Entering the lobby she greeted the desk clerk, and then headed to the elevator. She pressed the seventh floor button. The doors swooshed open almost immediately, offering her no escape route. Exiting the elevator, she made the slow walk toward room 722. The gallows awaited her. The matching scarf around her neck choked the life out of her like a well-tied noose.

Arriving at 722, she took one of the deepest breaths of her life, and then exhaled like a deflating balloon. She pulled and tucked everything in place. She paused, and then knocked on the door. She hoped no one would be at home, but no such luck, the lock clicked, and the knob turned and her worse nightmare smiled, motioning her to come inside.

In equally skimpy attire, she-sheriff bared a full mouth of fangs and said, "You look quite delicious my little lovely. I am so happy you decided to make the wise choice and join me here. It will do wonders for your career."

"You're the new law in town and I do as ordered, Sheriff Burton. My job is to comply with my boss's instructions."

"Come on honey...I've told you to call me Sam. This is after hours. What can I fix you to lighten the mood?"

"Vodka, straight...a double would work for starters."

"Straight," Sam giggled. "I don't think that will fly tonight."

"Look, I'm here as you requested Sheriff, I mean Sam. Can we cut to it? What do you really want?"

"My, my, aren't we just a bit snippy? Slow down and enjoy. I plan to. Hike up that skirt. Let me see what you have on underneath."

Trudy complied, flashing her best frilly little Victoria Secret's. Sam smiled, wet her middle finger in her mouth then slid her hand inside her own micro panties.

"If you deliver what I envision awaits me, we're going to have one hell of a long relationship, my little princess," purred a very aroused Samantha Burton.

"Before we proceed, I need to know what's in store for me. I don't play for free."

"Behind every successful woman is her equally effective woman. You can be that woman in my life. As I move up the ladder, you fill the vacated slots. It's win-win for both of us. My throne will eventually be yours once I become mayor and so forth."

"You forget I'm married. I have never been unfaithful to my husband."

"Now is woman on woman really considered being unfaithful? You can always say I never cheated on you with another man. You won't be telling a fib. Besides, you really must maintain the smoke and mirrors. Your staying married protects both of us."

"And if I get cold feet and decline?"

"Now you really don't want to travel down that road do you my dear? After all, you love what you do and I really wouldn't enjoy ruining your career."

"You don't give me much of a choice, do you, Sam?"

"There are always choices, sweetie. Choosing the correct one is the key. I promise you one thing, once you try black, you won't go back, or at least you won't enjoy that hubby as much as you once did. Let me just show you what black gold looks like," she said, allowing her nightwear to drop to the floor, standing naked, except for her high heels.

"You really don't waste any time, do you? I haven't had my drink yet. Whatever happened to good old fashioned foreplay?"

Sam walked over and stood inches from Trudy. Trudy flinched when she placed a hand on her left breast. "Let me show you how it feels to have a woman do things to you that only a woman can do." She knelt down in front of Trudy and in one fluid motion and slid her panties to her ankles. Trudy almost puked when Sam made brief contact with her nether region.

"Thank you Sheriff," whispered Trudy, as the hotel door burst open filling the room with blinding light.

Trudy stood with her back to the door. Sam was still crouched on her knees. She peeked around Trudy's torso to identify the source of the sounds and bright lights.

"Homemade porn, you got to just love it,' yelled Woody, holding the camera, zooming in on Sam as Trudy stepped aside, leaving the Sheriff fully exposed, full frontal, on her knees with her clothes out of reach. Her facial expressions were just priceless, mouth opening and closing like the lips of a carp.

Finally regaining her composure, she stood, defiant, arms crossed, legs spread eagle and asked, "Just what the hell are you two trying to pull here? I'll have both of your badges."

Woody, still rolling the camera said, "Interesting threat, Sheriff Samantha Burton, so tell me, where's your badge?"

Sam leisurely walked over, and picked up her negligee from the couch. She slipped it on, but before she could speak, Trudy asked Woody "Is that camera still rolling?"

"Oh yeah, we're rolling."

"Good, get this," she said, walking over to Sam and delivering a right hook, sending her sprawling backwards, bottoms up over the couch.

"Okay, that's a take," yelled Woody.

Sam, holding her chin, peeked over the back of the couch, and started pointing a finger at the two officers.

Trudy slipped on her panties, keeping her backside to Woodrow. "Hush," ordered Trudy. "We have a new sheriff in town and here's the only option you have on the table, so choose wisely, Sam."

Horry County Police Department
9:00 AM Monday

"I have called this press conference to announce my resignation as interim Sheriff," spoke Samantha Burton, with the Mayor standing beside her. "I owe Sheriff Hank Singleton my highest praise for giving me the opportunity to attempt to fill a great man's shoes. Regrettably, due to personal reasons, I must step down and ask you to respect my decision and privacy for doing so. I met with the Mayor over the weekend and made my recommendation to him for a person that I feel can serve this post. The Mayor agreed. I am honored to announce your new interim Sheriff, Constable Woodrow Anderson."

"Come on up here," Motioned the Mayor to Woody "and say a few words, Sheriff Anderson."

After the dust settled, Woody and Trudy watched as the one who had aspirations of being called Sheriff Sam Burton, hailed her cab and rode off into the sunset with no fanfare.

"Well, Sheriff Anderson, how does it feel?" asked Trudy.

"Well, I'd rather have Hank back, but I'm glad we're rid of the self proclaimed, black prodigy."

"That's a fact. You are sure you have edited that footage to mask my voice and remove any mention of my name."

"Done...no voice, no name, no head shots but some fine ass footage. Here you go," he said, handing her a manila envelope containing the only copy.

"Well, it was my best side," she grinned.

"Damn good idea, wearing that wire and signaling me when to enter with the camera. There's nothing like one upping a blackmailer, but you never did actually show me what she had on you."

"And that's the way it will stand. Sometimes we have a tendency to do stupid things in our youth. We don't always think of the ramifications. She assured me she gave me all the copies of my indiscretions. If she didn't, I'll hold onto her little Academy Award performance, just in case she ever has any second thoughts."

"And you say you shared your indiscretions with Brady?"

"I did. He has seen the photos and knows the whole story. It was just one of those bad decisions I made when I was young, stupid, and too naïve. I had a tough time prying them from his hands and keeping them out of picture frames on his desk. Let's just say he sees me in a whole new light and leave it at that. And he already has dibs on this little movie footage of ours. He wasn't so keen on you being the photographer. He had actually volunteered, but I told him you were my only partner in crime. He conceded."

"And all I got is a butt shot," laughed Sheriff Anderson.

"But you got to see the best butt in the department."

"Well I must admit the Sheriff sort of stole the show with her classic performance. What makes a person be so ruthless and power hungry?"

Trudy shrugged. "What's sadder, partner is, again, we've bent the rules, and broke the law ourselves. I had promised after allowing Road Rage to finish his trek across country that I would do better."

"You did. Nobody got murdered. I would say that qualifies as continual improvement, partner."

"All right, I think we've run this one in the ground enough. You need to rush off and do some sheriffy stuff, don't you?"

"Don't worry, my lips are sealed forever. I'm just glad we're rid of her."

"I better get that in writing, Sheriff, and I agree."

"Go do some detective work, how about it, and solve some of these unsolved crimes."

Trudy stood at attention and saluted her new superior officer, then exited his office to catch up with her team. She pondered her case load. She and the team weren't exactly clearing the backlog.

There were no new leads on the Stewart Patrick case or Jorge Cruz, the missing associate pastor. They weren't exactly dazzling anyone with the unidentified, murdered, Hispanic illegal migrant worker case. And still there loomed this alleged kidnapping of another Hispanic male. Was there really a connection to all of them, she asked as implied by Sly? Could the Klan be behind them? Maybe with Sam out of the picture she could think about them with a clear head now.

Horry County Police Department
One Week Later

"So how's Brady doing?" asked Woody.

"Coping, I suppose. We both are. He just started his medication so we don't yet know what impact it may have on his Parkinsonism. They did diagnosis him as having one of the worst kind, so we probably have fun times ahead. He's experiencing the mild tremors and some slight stiffness, muscle tone problems; but otherwise, you know Brady, he forges ahead like nothing is wrong."

"Don't hesitate to ask if you need my help, day or night."

"I know you've got my backside covered, Sheriff."

"Backside, now I must admit that does bring back visuals."

"I have no idea what you're talking about," smiled Trudy.

The phone rang. Trudy watched Woody's facial expressions and could tell more crap was about to hit the fan. Nodding, he hung up the phone and said, "Got another one for you."

"Shoot..."

"A hiking tourist and his son think they have stumbled onto a possible shallow grave off a dirt road out toward Loris. He said the stench was awful. Here...I've written down the location. How about taking your team over and check it out. It's probably just an animal carcass buried by spotlighters. Game Management told me a while back that they had reports of poaching going on over that way. The usual...people spotlighting deer at night, shots fired and so forth."

"We're on it chief. Maybe we can finally solve one and restore our diminishing reputation, and then you can promote us to dog catchers."

"Sorry, you're raising the bar way too high. Keep me posted. Be careful out there."

Trudy smiled, thinking how that sounded just like something Hank would have said. The team arrived at the secluded dirt road, about forty five minutes later. A State Highway Patrolman greeted them when they pulled down the road.

"Pierce, I see you brought your entire team. Business slow over at the beach," said Patrolman Giles.

"You know how it goes, I can just take so much sand between my toes and beautiful ocean scenery before I guilt myself into checking on you deprived road warriors. Actually, the chamber sent us here to audit your handling of tourist. Now, are you stopping them heading to the beach, or after they leave?"

"Always the smartass aren't you Detective. That's why I like you. Come with me and I'll introduce you to the hiker and his son who found the fresh grave site. They can take you to the actual location. It's about a mile and half in that direction." Giles pointed toward dense woods and swampland. "Hope you brought your snake chaps and gator repellent. You better watch out for the state bird too. Those mosquitoes can be damn nasty out there."

"Thanks for your assistance, Giles, but it already looks like my team members are conducting formal introductions over there. We'll take it from here. I'll keep you posted on what we find."

"I look forward to hearing what type of critter carcasses you uncover. It sure was sad what happened to old Hank. We all miss him, and good for Woody on his little promotion. What's the scoop on that female sheriff's resignation any way?"

"I think she just realized she may have bit off more than she could swallow. Take care."

She joined her team, hovering around the two hikers. Dennis Graham, thirty five, and his twelve year old son, Freddy, had discovered what they had perceived as being a fresh grave mound in an extremely secluded area on the edge of swamp territory. Trudy wasn't sure she bought into the animal carcass theory because why would anyone bother to bury animals, legal or illegal, in such a desolate area. Her gut told her something smelled fishy if indeed it was a grave.

"All right troops...let's pack up everything we could possibly need for our little investigation. It is a tough trek back into that swamp so we don't need any unscheduled return trips to the van," advised Trudy.

"After hauling all our crap out there, I'm going to be really pissed off if we end up only digging up deer or bear bones," commented Captain.

"If that's what we find, then we turn it over to Game Management," replied Trudy, giving Captain *the look*, indicating for him to stop his bitching and moaning in the company of civilians.

Cleaning up his remark, Captain said, "What I meant to say is I certainly hope it's not human remains." Dennis Graham's rolling eyes indicated he wasn't buying it.

The mile and half hike did offer up an abundance of wildlife, the likes that would have excited the now deceased, Marlin Perkins, of Wild Kingdom fame. The team jumped deer several times, their white tails flagging their hasty retreat, bounding effortlessly through the thickets as if they had springs on their hooves.

Stepping over a fallen tree, Dallas disturbed a coiled and slumbering copper head. Luckily the startled poisonous snake opted not to strike at the intruder and took more of a defensive stance. Dallas, not particularly the outdoorsy type, let out a bloodcurdling scream that prompted more than one of the detectives to go for their revolvers.

Skirting the edge of a murky stretch of standing water, too small to actually be called a pond, Tim Burroughs heard a splash and spotted a seven foot alligator skimming the surface. Too his relief, it swam in the opposite direction. Startled, Tim eyed the water hole with new respect.

"Always check for ticks," warned Dennis Graham, plucking one from his son's jeans. "They're really bad this time of year. They carry Rocky Mountain Spotted Fever and Lyme Disease. Trust me, you don't want either."

"Thanks for the heads up," replied Trudy.

"You ever see any bear out here?" asked Dallas.

"We go hiking every time we come here on vacation. A couple of times we've caught a glimpse of a black bear, but typically they are pretty shy and avoid human contact. Keep your eyes open for wild hogs though. They can be quite aggressive, especially if they have piglets," answered Dennis.

"What about gators?" asked Tim. "I just saw a monster one in that water?"

"Same as bear," explained Dennis. "Most are harmless. They avoid human contact. It is rare that a gator goes after anything larger than they are; however, they can be somewhat territorial, especially if they have eggs or young. If you just so happen to fall into one of those deep gator holes in the marsh, try to get to dry land as quickly as possible. You never know if the area is occupied by one of those rare ten-twelve footers and the splashing could be like ringing the dinner bell."

"How do I avoid gator holes?" asked Tim, looking about.

"Stay out of the water, if possible. I saw one of my hiking buddies walking in water ankle deep one minute, and then he dropped out of sight under the water his very next step. Gator holes can be deep and undetectable in these murky swamps."

"Did a gator get him?"

"Lord no, but it sure caused him to soil his shorts though," laughed Dennis. "It shouldn't be much further." He pointed to a large stand of mossy oaks, less than forty yards ahead.

"Yeah," spoke up Freddy for the first time. "I can smell it already."

Sly turned to Trudy. Both smelled the same stench. No mistaking it, it reeked of death. Hugh green blowflies buzzing their faces, indicated decaying flesh was certainly nearby.

"Right there, that's the spot" confirmed Dennis. "I mentally marked it by that twisted and crooked old oak directly ahead."

The mound sure looked like a grave, thought Trudy. It had been discreetly covered with pine needles and leaves. A one foot deep hole signaled that an animal had attempted to dig into one end. The smell of decomposition overwhelmed her senses. Her gut churned, warning her that this wasn't going to be good.

Cash and Carry Pawn Store
Little River Location

Brock had dismissed the manager of the store for the afternoon. He had flipped over the *Sorry We're Closed* sign on the front door and had retreated to the back storeroom where Scat and three cleanly shaved, skinheads waited for him.

The strangers, all heavily tattooed and burley, were members of a neo-Nazi chapter from Brock's home state, Louisiana. All three knew Brock by name, each responding to his request to come without any second thoughts. Brock had cashed in on some long overdue favors.

Scat eyed the three ominous figures and felt like a choir boy in their presence. He surmised these boys were no bullshit, no questions asked, get the job done types. He still had no idea what Brock had in mind and even wondered if he really wanted to know. For the first time, he was feeling he could be in over his head.

Brock slipped each a plain white envelop, obviously stuffed with cash. He then laid out his detailed plan. The designated leader of the trio verbally verified, piece of cake. The scheme confirmed Scat's worse fears. This was going to get ugly and he wasn't too happy with his designated role.

He kept his mouth shut though, figuring being part of the solution instead of the problem served his best interest with these ruthless scoundrels in town and on Brock's payroll. He thought, you really wouldn't want to cross them, and aspire to live to tell about it. Still, it didn't mean he had to like it.

Brock eyed Scat, looking for signs that he was still in this. Scat, sensing the scrutiny, spoke up, "Badasses, you mean business don't you, Boss?"

"You got dat right. You wit me on dis, Scat?"

"Damn straight, let's mix it up and bring the beach to its knees." Scat thought what the hell had he gotten himself into with this crazy Cajun.

"Long live di Klan."

CSI Team
The Swamplands of Loris

Trudy had dismissed Dennis Graham and his son after discovering the first bones, one obviously a human femur. It had become a crime scene. The team meticulously removed the dirt, continued to uncover more human remains, mostly just skeletal. She heard Tim Burroughs yelling. Turning she saw him waving frantically from the underbrush. She and Dallas covered the short distance to see what he wanted.

"I think I have another one," he replied, pointing to the raised surface.

Kneeling down, Trudy could tell that indeed this had to be another grave. "Mark it," she ordered. "Then you and Dallas fan out. See if these are the only two."

Captain and Sly continued to excavate the first grave, tagging and photographing the find. Over the next hour, nine more potential grave sites had been identified and marked. Trudy called it in to Woody and he was on his way.

By the time Sheriff Woodrow Anderson arrived, twenty six mounds had been flagged. The team huddled around the first grave, strategically discussing their next move.

"This is going to incite a media circus once we break it," warned Woody. "Is it too late for me to resign?"

"I say we halt digging in the first one and widen our perimeter sweep. We have about four hours of decent daylight remaining. Let's just see how messy this thing really is," stated Trudy.

The six of them combed the terrain and finally called it quits with less than thirty minutes of daylight left. Comparing notes and finalizing the tally, the number of possible mounds they had found now numbered sixty three over a three acre perimeter. Trudy suspected more might be uncovered in the swampy region bordering these sites.

"Damn," exclaimed Woody. "Just what the hell have we stumbled into out here? We don't have this many missing persons in the three surrounding states."

"Something tells me we're not going to find these people, if indeed all do conceal bodies, on any missing person's report," stated Sly.

"What are you getting at?" asked Trudy.

"One of my theories...the abducted Hispanic illegal, could that have been our first warning sign. And my second theory...could this be the work of a female serial killer, also connected to the alleged kidnapping?"

"Hold on, Sherlock, you're getting way ahead of yourself," warned Woody. "We've learned our lesson babbling about serial killers. We're not making that mistake again."

"Well these bodies certainly didn't bury themselves," Sly reminded them. "And you said; they're not likely to be on a missing person's report because there are too many of them. What better targets for a deranged serial killer than illegal Immigrants...no records, no names, no reports of disappearances," Sly built his case.

"Could be hate crime related," added Captain. "It might be the Klan or some other minority hate group."

"Can we keep this close to the vest until we exhume the bodies. I'll make the call to bring in the cadaver dogs."

"Woody, I doubt that we're going to be able to keep it hush, hush," answered Trudy. "We have witnesses to the first site, the hiker and his son. They saw the bones."

"But they only saw one grave," added Captain.

"All right, so here's the plan," explained Woody. "We release the discovery of the first grave to the news media, but we don't mention the others until we know more. I'll post a couple of deputies out here tonight. We'll bring in lights and more equipment tomorrow to keep this thing going around the clock. And let's dig up the freshest ones first because they should give us our best leads."

"We're going to require plenty of body bags and a temporary morgue," stated Trudy, "And more assistance."

"We're certainly going to be back on the map again and in the headlines, for all the wrong reasons," commented Tim.

"Woody, we better play it by the book this time. We can't afford to crap and fall back in this one. We allowed our emotions to override our common sense with ole Road Rage. It almost cost our careers."

"I know partner. Thanks for reminding me. Let's just get a handle on it first, before we go public."

Trudy nodded. She certainly didn't wish to relive those mistakes. What had happen to the Grand Strand? It had transformed into a murderer's paradise.

Pierce Beach Home
Just after Midnight

"You can't be serious?"

"Brady, I don't want to believe it either."

"Another serial killing spree here in Horry County...what are we, serial killer central now?"

"What really concerns me is the fact that some of those mounds appear to have been there for quite some time, possibly even years. I fear there are more."

"If you're correct, then you have quite the monster on your hands, a lot worse than Preston of road rage fame."

"Or monsters...I'm not so sure one person could have hauled those bodies out to such a secluded area without help, unless the perpetrator has super human abilities."

"You're talking a real monster then."

"I don't know what I'm saying anymore. Pour me another drink, and then make love to me until I beg you to stop."

Thirty minutes later Trudy curled in Brady's arms. "Well that didn't go as planned," he sighed after being unable to achieve any sort of an erection. "The doctor warned me that the Parkinson could play hell with my libido."

"Don't short change yourself, Circus Boy. You did a fine job during the warm-up ceremony." She kissed him, reminding him about his amazing foreplay action.

"The pleasure was certainly mine." He reciprocated with a long passionate kiss.

"So when is your next appointment?"

"Couple of weeks with more prodding and poking, I'm sure."

"Prodding and poking...," she repeated.

"Get you mind out of the gutter, officer."

She slid under the sheets and successfully woke the sleeping monster, and for the next hour they basked in a slow burn. She whispered the lyrics of the Conway Twitty tune, "I'm looking for a man with a slow hand..."

Restaurant Row
Myrtle Beach

Over the next two weeks, break-ins, robberies and vandalism reached levels never experienced on the Grand Strand. All law enforcement agents were overwhelmed with the onslaught, unable to catch a break and apprehend any perpetrators. In every case, the calling card indicated Hispanic gangs were behind the rash of violence.

Local gangs weren't taking the accusations lightly. Increased numbers of Valtos Locos and Sur-13s had been spotted on the Grand Strand, much more organized than ever before in the beach community. Brock's hired guns were working their magic, leaving graffiti and other mementos to raise the gang flag and support the Klan's insistence of complete gang extermination.

Ironically, this served as a distraction, masking the ongoing excavation of bodies from the ever increasing burial site. The CSI team had set up a temporary morgue in the wilderness and so far had been able to conceal the unfolding secret.

"Well, at least we have closure to one unsolved mystery," stated a hoarse and exhausted Sly. "I recognized him from his photograph, even in his present state. We have a positive ID. He's our missing associate pastor, Jorge Cruz."

"Probably mistaken for an illegal immigrant," added Trudy.

"That would be my guess," replied Sly.

"I can't believe this hasn't already leaked out," commented Dallas.

"It will hit the fan soon enough," replied Trudy. "We're just lucky this location is so remote and Woody has been spoon feeding them the one or two grave story, saying we're still searching the area. It has temporarily satisfied the news hounds."

"That rash of gang activity has kept the media preoccupied too," Tim reminded the team.

"Speaking of crap hitting the fan," added Captain, "When the gangs find out about this, we're going to be lucky if we don't have a full blown riot and war on our hands."

"But who are they going to go to war with?" asked Dallas. "We don't know who murdered these people."

"I don't think it will matter to them. Every white citizen could be fair game," warned Sly.

Woody arrived carrying a sealed envelope, marked for Kirk Cardoon (forensics). Captain opened it and eyed the team. "Well, the coroner has confirmed my suspicions. We have our motive behind this crime spree and it's going to blow your socks off."

"Fire away," ordered Trudy.

"The coroner's preliminary results support a theory which might just get us off the hook with the hate crime assumption. What you're looking at here is an organ mining operation."

Woody exclaimed, "A what?"

"Random autopsies performed thus far indicate that in every case, various organs have been surgically removed. What we have here is a body organ factory. Whoever abducted them had one thing in mind...harvesting marketable organs to sell. Report indicates that diseased or suspect organs were not removed which means the person or persons doing this, has a medical background."

"This is just too incredible," stated Woody.

"There's more, and I don't get this part," continued Captain. "All so far are males. None of the cadavers have been females."

"Are our organs not good enough?" snapped Trudy. "Anything else?"

"So far the established time frame spans from as recent as just a couple of weeks ago, as our associate pastor supports, to possibly five or six years. Somebody has been at this for a while," stated Captain.

"You mentioned surgically removed," recapped Trudy. "So this is not the work of the typical hacker-slasher then?"

"No, like I said, someone with medical experience and skills are involved. And they probably have one fat bank account by the looks of it, or possess very expensive habits or life styles requiring extreme cash flow. This can't possibly be the work of one individual. This is much too sophisticated."

"So the term serial killer doesn't really apply here," stated Woody.

"Not as defined by the text book definition," confirmed Dallas. "If what Captain Kirk states is factual, this is purely a lucrative business we have uncovered. Serial killers kill to satisfy their twisted needs and follow primal directives, cravings of one sort or another. This appears to be more driven by supply and demand."

"I'm too old for this crap," exclaimed Woody, realizing how he so sounded like Hank Singleton. "Any more surprises?"

Tim Burroughs spoke up, "The cadaver dogs indicate we have more out there in that swamp as suspected. Possibly they used the swamp as an early dumping ground or maybe this area became flooded. I saw activity of beavers in the area."

"So where do we go to find our suspects?' asked Woody.

"We should start with our medical professionals, active, retired, part time, and any showing signs of living well above their means so to speak," advised Captain. "Doctors, nurses, interns, medical students, emergency responders, those with military medical experience, and I wouldn't discount grocery store meat department personnel, or those with slaughter house experience."

"Something tells me we have a tough row to hoe here," exclaimed Trudy. "But, we have the best team to solve it. I have no doubt that we will persevere."

"How does the saying go? Failure is not an option," stated Captain.

Woody asked, "Do you think there are any other burial locations other than this one?"

"Based on the evidence I would say no," answered Trudy. "It had been used up until the time it was discovered by the hikers. I think our killer or killers were confident they were safe."

"Now that they obviously know that we know, do you think they will stop?" asked Woody.

"Maybe, but if this is their business, and they still have orders to fill, clients to keep happy, my bet would be they continue operations as normal and find a new place to dump the bodies," suggested Trudy. "Look at it from their point of view. Nothing has really changed other than our discovering this particular dumping ground. Their victims are not likely to report the crimes, so why should they stop?"

Captain stated, "Once we break this to the Hispanic community, it should put them on notice and they should have their guard up for suspicious activity, even if they're not willing to report it. This alone should hamper our harvester's ability to cash in on their prey. Plus, it could at least lead to some anonymous tips."

"I still think that female, driving a white sports car, could be a valuable key," added Sly. "She could be some sort of high dollar bait, possibly a hooker or exotic dancer. Our killers don't know we know about her, so all we have to do is catch her and possibly we have them."

"Women on the grand strand driving sports cars...now that really narrows down our search, doesn't it," spewed an exasperated Sheriff Woodrow Anderson, wishing he was still a Constable.

"We'll take any crumbs thrown our way," replied Trudy. "I'll drop by and break the news about Jorge Cruz to our Pentecostal Preacher, Raeford McCrery, if that's okay with you, Woody.

"Go ahead, but ask him to hold back making any announcements to his flock right now, until I can break it to the media. I dread calling this news conference but the longer we wait, the more likely it will be leaked."

Horry County Police Department
Two Days Later

The cat now out of the bag, 103 bodies had been exhumed so far. The media frenzy had begun and every major network swarmed the tourist town. The sudden publicity served was a double-edged sword. The hospitality industry flourished. Hotel occupancy had maxed out and restaurants were hiring extra staff to support the influx of news personalities and their staffs. The county prospered monetarily.

Sheriff Woodrow Anderson had been slammed for his department's inability to apprehend any suspects for what had been dubbed by locals as the Mexican Meat Market Murders. Constituents were equally frustrated by no breakthroughs in the soaring gang related crimes.

Brock Boudreaux up until now had stirred the pot vigorously, using his well orchestrated plan to triple the Klan's membership. He had cited the alleged gang related robberies as a call to all concerned white citizens to thwart the influx of illegal Mexicans trying to take over this country.

Brock was now taken by surprise with the reports of the unearthed Hispanic killing field. He feared the gangs and Hispanic community would hold them responsible and retaliate against the Klan. He had gotten more than he bargained for, and decided to temporarily halt his hired squad from staging any future crimes.

Trudy sat across the desk from Woody, exhausted and without any leads, fighting for what little reputation remained. The stress and strain could be seen on both their faces.

"We're still stuck here on square one," sighed Woody. "No suspects, no new leads and our jobs in jeopardy."

"Well, at least we've unearthed no more bodies."

"But our killers could still be out there harvesting more body parts and we would never know it. Has your team of mighty investigators made any headway?"

"Detective Cardoon is leaving no forensic stone unturned I assure you. He reported that whoever is behind this has left no incriminating evidence. He says the bodies have been squeaky clean; no fibers, hairs, tissue or blood that didn't belong to the cadavers. He thinks the surgeries occurred in a clean room environment."

"Just wonderful," said Woody, throwing up his hands.

"And Sly is working the Hispanic community, but that's a tough one to crack too. They remain mum in fear of being returned to their own country."

"Unbelievable," snapped Woody.

"Dallas has a few profile angles but nothing to really hang our hats on yet. Tim has been diligently data mining, looking for any similar cases but has found zilch so far."

"To be blunt, your answer would be *no* then," stated Woody, their friendship becoming more strained. "You have absolutely nothing. Some crime scene investigation team we have here."

"Look Woody, we're all doing the best we can. I don't like this any better than you do. This is a well oiled operation we're dealing with, and they went to great lengths to remain anonymous."

"Why here though? We're not exactly the illegal immigrant capital. There are a lot more areas of the country that would have been riper for the picking. There has to be a reason why they chose running their little factory here. Solve that one and I bet we solve the crime. Do we have anything on our female predator?"

Trudy shook her head no.

"We're pretty damned worthless aren't we?" "Worthlessness must be rewarded with promotions because you two have certainly moved up the food chain haven't you," spoke a familiar voice from the doorway.

"Oh crap," exclaimed Woody. "Tell me I just imagined that."

"Lance Rocker is back in town. And I'm here to rock your world and help you solve your little crime spree, but maybe I'm already too late. It looks like your world is a little shell-shocked already."

"How the hell did you get in here, you sorry ass bastard?"

"That would be *Deputy Sorry Ass Bastard* to you Sheriff," Rocker replied, holding up his deputy badge. "Remember, you deputized me to help you break the Road Rage case. I don't remember you de-deputizing me."

"Trust me. We stripped you of that honor. Why are you really here, Rocker?"

"And I've missed you too, Sugar Britches. Actually I'm here to follow your story. In case you haven't noticed, you're national news. I'll be doing my syndicated show live from here over the next few weeks. This will do wonders for the ratings for my investigative reporter show, Rocking Your World. Like I said, with me on board, we just might solve this puppy."

"I've dreamed about having another opportunity to kick your ass, and I guess Santa Clause has come to town."

"Hold on *Mister One Man Vigilante Force*. Hear me out. If you let me shadow your investigation, I promise I will return only positive PR for your department, and you could sure use a friend right now."

"He's got a point, Woody," Trudy reluctantly said. "We're sinking to new lows every day. With Deputy Rocker on board, we cannot fail."

"No damn way," snapped Woody.

"I assure you Sheriff, with Deputy Rocker as part of our team, we will not receive any negative PR on his watch," winked Trudy.

"Right..." winked Woody.

"Either you two have something in your eyes or I just got snookered again. Okay, you got yourself a deal. I get the exclusive, and you two come out smelling like a bouquet of roses."

"Welcome aboard, Deputy," grinned Trudy, "and if you pull any funny stuff I will personally neuter you, and I promise you, you will not enjoy it."

"You don't mince words do you, Detective?"

"And if you mess this up, I assure you I will finish the job. We're sitting on a powder keg with this case. There's absolutely little margin for error."

"So where do we start?"

"You can start by using your charm and your syndicated show to warn the Hispanic community. We'll provide you with a toll free number to be used for any anonymous tips. We are specifically interested in any reports of coercion by a Caucasian female driving a sports car," explained Trudy.

"Interesting," replied Rocker. "So is this female suspect waving a little snatch under their noses then swapping it for body organs?"

"You do have your unique way of phrasing a question don't you Rocker?" commented Woody. "But, yeah, that's what we think could be happening."

"Do you have any little Mexicans on the police force that could pull undercover duty? If not, with my dark tan and a little makeup I might be able to pass for one."

"Yeah, we're working on that angle," replied Woody. "We do have a couple of part timers that we're thinking of planting in the community and we have one Highway Patrolman that fits the bill, but you, forget it."

"Six-one, blonde hair and blue eyed...I don't think you could pull off that disguise very well," added Trudy.

"Don't underestimate me. I am quite the actor."

"Just how long do you really plan to remain in town?" asked Woody, clenching his fists by his side.

"For as long as this serial organ harvester boosts my ratings, or until I help break the case," replied Lance.

Woody put his finger in Rocker's face. "Let's try not to use that serial term if you don't mind?"

"So what do we want to call our killer or killers; something catchy for the viewing audience, I hope?"

"Look we don't want to over sensationalize this," advised Woody. "It's a very touchy subject because all of the victims have been Hispanic, and except for one, we have not been able to identify any of them. We think the abduction of the associate pastor was a case of mistaken identity and a slip up by the killers."

"So, what are we going to call them?" Rocker asked again, unfazed by Woody's concerns.

Trudy weighed in and said, "Let's just refer to them as individuals wanted for murder and conspiracy to harvest and sell body organs illegally."

"Too boring and it doesn't roll off your tongue. We've got to do better than that. How about this...the *Grand Strand Body Snatchers*?"

Woody rolled his eyes. "That would do just wonders for our tourist industry, now wouldn't it?"

"I got it, simple but to the point; I'll call them *The Body Parts Bandits*."

"Okay, I'll live with that one," replied Woody.

Rocking Your World
The Body Parts Bandits

Unlike Lance Rocker's *Alive at Five* news days, his syndicated program did not normally transmit live. The pre-recorded weekly program available on cable, an hour long segment, was a mixture of investigative reporting and Rocker's slanted opinions. He had received mixed reviews thus far. He had built the format based on the Road Rage events, but he could milk that story just so long, and the new had long worn off. His new format would consist of a mixture of pre-recorded segments and live reports.

Maintaining the viewers' attention, while ensuring a firm foothold in the ratings, had been more of a challenge than even the great Sir Lancelot could have imagined. This unfolding tragedy could be the break he had been waiting for to launch him back into the limelight if he played his cards right. Being privy to the case couldn't hurt either.

Rocker sat in his hotel room, flipping through his notes, preparing his opening statements for next week's show. His crew would be joining him tomorrow to begin filming preliminary footage that would include the burial site, interviews with Sheriff Woodrow Anderson and Detective Trudy Pierce. He would then focus on the Hispanic angle and pursue a potential Klan twist. Brock Boudreaux topped his list of people he intended to interview.

His cell phone rang. Glancing at the caller ID he saw his agent's name, Murray Hall, on the digital readout. "Well how's it hanging there slick?" asked Murray, a real sleaze ball, but a highly effective agent. By hook or by crook he could spin the deals, but he didn't come cheap.

"This could put us back on top, Murray. I've already established my inroads with the sheriff's department. They never learn."

"I read your e-mail and think playing up the illegal Mexicans against the KKK angle will be quite explosive for the first episode. What's the chance of us getting a gang member and Klansman on the same segment, face to face?"

"Brock Boudreaux, leader of the local chapter has agreed to meet with me tomorrow. I'll fish him. Let me check with a couple of my local informants and see if I can dig up a gang rep. I've got another incoming call I need to take. I'll check back with you tomorrow afternoon."

"I smell a big one here, Sport. Do me proud. Talk to you tomorrow."

"Hello Sweetheart; longtime, no hear," spoke the smooth tongued Rocker to the caller. "You been missing me? I thought so. Sorry things didn't work out for you. Sure, I'd love to see you. When? That sounds good. Yeah, I can meet you in Georgetown tomorrow night. I love that place, very secluded little spot. So you have something spicy for me? Turn down the sheets and try not to start without me. I'll be there by nine. You too, and I promise I will rock your world as always."

Rocker, strolling down memory lane, suddenly had a craving for chocolate, and called room service, ordering a double hot fudge surprise a la mode. Yep, things were looking up.

Horry County Police Department
Conference Room A

Trudy stood in front of the oversized white board, striking through the list of locations and individuals, as her team confirmed interrogations and discounted suspects. The list had gotten extremely shorter but no leads had resulted.

Rubbing her hands through her hair, she sighed, "So, we've got nothing."

"Either our perpetrators are damn good liars or we haven't interrogated them yet," commented Sly.

"Still nothing further from forensics?"

"We do, with reasonable certainty, now believe all the cadavers were Hispanic. We have no clothing or personal items so they were stripped down, clothes most likely disposed of where they performed the operations. There is evidence that the victims had been injected with what appears to be some new concoction of anesthetic. We're still trying to analyze and determine exactly what it might be."

"So they were definitely drugged," commented Woody.

Captain nodded then dropped a bombshell. "There were signs of sexual abuse on the most recent victims."

"Sexual abuse, please explain."

"We have forced anal penetration by a very large object," continued Captain. "Some of the men's nipples were missing. There were a couple of them with bite marks."

Woody had to sit down on that one. "Are you telling us someone bit off their nipples?"

"And the heads of several penis's were missing," stated Captain. "This new evidence could lead us to a dental or DNA match once we have a suspect."

Woody stood back up and said, "Wait a damn minute. I thought we had an organ factory going on here. Now you're sounding like we may have some sort of sadistic killers on the loose."

"Sorry, but it threw me a curveball too. I'm not sure what to make of our killer or killers now. I can tell you one thing though; the biter wore lipstick. She got sloppy on some of the victims. I would say she enjoyed playing with the prey before they harvested the organs."

"Is there anything else?" asked Trudy.

"Once the fun was over, they were very selective with which organs they removed from each victim, like they were going strictly by a shopping list. The same organs were not mined each time."

"Could they have known the victims?" asked Sly.

"Or, better still, they knew the victims' medical history," replied Captain.

"Shit, then we are talking doctors aren't we?" asked Woody.

"Or nurses," added Trudy.

"Or maybe a network of medical professionals," blurted Tim.

"Not likely," stated Dallas. "This behavior doesn't indicate a group sexual perversion. I suspect what we have here is one person performing the acts and another person or persons using the byproduct for lucrative reasons. Profile: Let's envision the female, our sports car driver, as the lure and seductress with sadomasochist tendencies. Once she has finished with her little playthings, a second party retrieves the organs, checking them off their order list and then they are sold to a pre-arranged buyer. The second individual is possibly just a voyeur, but I'll bet a round of drinks that the other person is actively involved in the show, one way or another, if for no other reason but to ensure the goods don't become damaged."

"Well that was quite a mouthful professor," exclaimed Woody. "Why didn't you just say S&M?"

"My contribution, and yes, S&M," she replied. "It's also my opinion that these are not racially motivated crimes. I concur with Sly's original theory. Hispanic illegals offer a convenient and endless supply for our harvesters. Crimes within the illegal community are seldom reported because deportation scares them more. I suspect the families of those abducted thought the disappearances were either gang or racial related and feared further retaliation, if they brought them to light."

"And there is absolutely no reason for us to believe that they would stop just because we found their dumping ground. Business is business, and I suspect the demand has not diminished, and heat will be on the suppliers," surmised Trudy.

"But what has changed in the game is we know what they are doing, and that gives us the upper hand. I do agree that the female is definitely the key," stated Woody.

"Hopefully Rocker will enlighten the viewing audience and warn them to be wary of any strangers luring them to their vehicles. This will be the adult version of cops telling kids to not get in the car with strangers, don't help them search for a missing dog or take their candy," stated Trudy.

"I just hope the Hispanic audience understands the message and heeds the warning," added Woody.

"You do realize we're damned if we do, damned if we don't on this one, because we'll be tipping our hand so to speak," warned Sly. "The Killers will figure we're on to them. They could change their tactics. I would if I were them."

"I'm beating a dead horse, but I'll repeat it any way. I think we all learned our lesson in the Road Rage case," Trudy reminded the team. "We withheld the warning from the public and other law enforcement agencies, and our killer continued his rampage on the unsuspecting community nationwide. I still feel guilty about that one because we could have probably prevented some of those deaths, if given a do-over and handling things differently."

"Don't beat yourself up over it, Pierce," consoled Woody. "We all agreed to keep it under wraps and rolled the dice...end of story."

"Tell all those victims and their families we were shooting craps with their lives. I don't think they would have exactly appreciated our gambling ways, given the outcome."

"Let it go Pierce, we can't rewrite the past. In the end, we got our man."

Trudy knew that better than anybody. Hers had been log jammed with mistakes and bad decisions, selfish and self serving. She thought about her mom, and how she could have handled her sickness differently. She had too often put her career above everything else. Trudy Wagner had always come first; how pathetic, what a legacy.

She had an opportunity moving forward to make things right with Brady, this case, and the community by learning from her past failures and making her world a better place. The key; don't backslide. She smiled, thinking all she needed now, chirping birds, a smiley, sunny face, blooming flowers, a few singing munchkins, skipping and frolicking, and she could portray Dorothy from a scene right out of the Wizard of OZ. Nah, no one would ever believe that one, she thought. Now, wicked witch, she could pull that one off.

"Pierce, you're with me, aren't you?" asked Woody.

"Yes sir, Mister Dillon, let's go catch us some cattle rustlers."

Dead silence, the entire team stared at her as if trying to decide which one of them should go for the straight jacket.

"Y'all lighten up, you hear," she said in her purest southern slang. "And bless your hearts, you little pea pickers. Come on guys, cut me a break here."

"Pay close attention team, your mind is a terrible thing to waste," stated Woody, giving Trudy the nod. "The southern belle has gone psycho on us."

White Convertible Mustang
Tanger Outlet Stores, Hwy 501

The voluptuous female sat in her car, top down, sunglasses in place, catching some rays, conversing on her cell phone. Picture perfect, she passed for any tourist with shopping bags from Calvin Klein, Ann Taylor and Jones New York, all piled in her back seat. She frowned, her free hand waved wildly as she expressed her displeasure to the caller.

"Look, I'm just doing a little shopping, girl stuff. Yes, I know how important it is to keep our clients happy. I always have the itch but I still think we should cool it for a while. You just have to call the shots, don't you, while I do your little dirty work?" She paused and held out the phone giving the caller the finger.

"You're right; you would be in my way and would certainly cramp my style. I so enjoy the thrill of the hunt." She wet her finger tips then slipped her hand underneath her white mini shirt. She closed her eyes and massaged her neither regions. An accomplished masturbator and exhibitionist, she exploded under the ripples of an endless tide of climaxes, while watching the many unsuspecting shoppers passing less than ten feet away.

Without missing a beat she continued her conversation. "Yes, I've scoped out our next resource. I'll take care of it tonight. Did you locate a new site?" She shook her head in disbelief. "Not yet, what the hell have you been doing all day? Do I have to do everything for you? Next I suppose you'll want me to perform the surgical procedures and handle the marketing too? Do I need to round up a shovel, or do you still have that covered?"

She rubbed her fingers together, examining the moisture she had stirred, then she applied a fresh coat of lipstick, her flavor for today, a loud purple.

"So what are your contacts telling you about their investigation? Oh, I see. It sounds like I better use the Jeep for a while and park the convertible. Absolutely not! I've told you a million times, I don't do women! I don't care if it would foul up their investigation. For the last time...no! You would really be bored with them too, and you know it. I know what you like and it isn't women, not as a staple anyway. I'm the exception."

She set the phone down on the seat and thrust both hands into the air, cursing under her breath, before resuming the conversation. "Have you got shit for brains? Damn, I can't believe I'm saying this. I'll do a few women, if that will make you feel better."

"Fret not dear, I will stick to the plan tonight. We'll make the next shipment. I love you too...chow."

Harbor Lights Inn, Georgetown
Thursday Night (just past 9 PM)

Lance Rocker sipped on his glass of wine and eyed the skimpily clad vixen sitting on the edge of the bed next to him. Such wonderfully seductive lips, he thought. He had not seen her in quite a few years, but he had to admit, she still had it and then some. She placed her hand on his knee, and immediately he became aroused. She noticed it too, and shifted her hand to confirm her suspicions.

"You haven't lost your touch I see. What's it been, four, maybe five years, Sam?"

"At least, and you certainly haven't lost your edge either, have you Sir Lancelot?"

"So, just what prompted you to contact me after the long absence?"

"Pleasure first, then we'll discuss business," she smiled, loosening his belt and unzipping his trousers.

"It's all about prioritization my dear, and you certainly have yours defined correctly," replied Rocker, slipping the strap off her shoulder to expose one perfect all natural breast.

Over the next hour the world rocked for both of them. Each worked hard to one up the other. Exhausted, sweaty and smelling of unbridled sex, the two collapsed; face up on the bed staring at the ceiling.

"Excellent meeting so far," commented Rocker.

"Mighty fine, and I haven't had a real man in ages."

"Sorry for them," smiled Rocker. "You haven't been in any satisfying relationships lately."

"Oh, I've been in some very fruitful relationships, but not with a man," she smiled, turning over and kissing him full on the mouth. "Present company excluded, and no insult intended, but I do prefer my kind if you catch what I'm saying."

"Well, we do have that in common I suppose. I have a fondness for women too."

"Let's shower and clean up then we can talk business," she told him sliding out of bed, grabbing his penis and leading the way to the bathroom. His immediate arousal indicated the shower would be filled with more escapades of good clean fun. Thirty minutes later they were refreshed, dressed and sipping from their second bottle of wine.

"I really am sorry your sheriff position didn't work out. I sense that it wasn't entirely your decision."

"Let's just say, I had a little help. I was reluctantly nudged into withdrawing my bid for the post."

"Someone had the goods on you, didn't they?"

Sam just smiled. "What can I say? I'm flawed and do have a weakness for the female anatomy. I must learn to practice restraint and not leap at every little twat waved in my face; especially when they report to me."

"Take it from one who knows, it just isn't that damned easy. We could probably swap war stories the remainder of the night, but that's not why I'm here is it? Spill it dear."

Sam reached in her purse and retrieved the manila envelope and slid it across the little table to Lance. He opened it and his eyes enlarged to the size of saucers. He licked his lips, flipped through the photos then asked, "Where the hell did you get these?"

"It doesn't really matter. They're yours now if you promise to use them and not expose where you got them. I want that little bitch's reputation totally destroyed, and I can't in any way be connected to her demise. I checked in here under a false name and paid cash, so I couldn't be traced to the area. This has to be your doing alone, understand?"

Rocker grinned. "So this is the little twat that did you in, Sheriff...fine choice. I've wanted in those britches for a while myself. And she has the goods on you too, doesn't she? The blackmailer is being blackmailed. Damn, this is so good. Tell me more and don't leave out any details if you want my help, including what she has on you."

"You drive a hard bargain."

"Hard is my middle name. Now spill it."

Pierce Beach Home
Almost Midnight

Trudy couldn't sleep. She slipped out of bed, intent on not disturbing Brady. He really needed the rest because his day had been filled with Parkinson bumps in the road. He had suffered from Dystonia much of the afternoon. This could best be described as painful muscle contractions in his feet and ankles. It had definitely affected his gait and posture.

He had appeared stooped over when she arrived home. He normally has excellent posture. He had almost tripped more than once; all signs straight out of the medical pamphlets she had read.

She had noticed his voice had been quite hoarse, too. Brady had complained that his tongue felt like it weighed five pounds. This too was symptomatic of the disease. It seemed to be progressing much quicker than they had anticipated.

She sensed his depressed state and her heart ached as she watched the man she loved unravel at the seams, knowing she could do nothing to stop it. She had poured herself a class of brandy, hoping it would ease her own stress.

Determined she would do it right this time, she assessed her caregiver role; something she should have taken more seriously with her mom's sickness, Alzheimer's. Both Parkinson and Alzheimer's were such cruel diseases. She could not believe she had to deal with both in one short lifetime. How selfish, she thought. She suffered from neither and should be thankful.

And then there loomed this body snatcher case. Who was the mystery woman and the potential network behind the profiteering scheme? Short of catching the culprits red-handed, too much relied on the Hispanic community and their cooperation in the case. She hesitated to hold her breath, because the stakes were even higher for any informants to step forward and jeopardize deportation.

She feared what they were up against had to be very organized and sophisticated. This was no fly by night operation, and up until now, they had gotten away with it much too easily and way too long.

Trudy had yet to shake the timely surfacing of those photographs from her past indiscretions. She had been tempted to call that bastard from her past, and tell him she knew he had supplied them to the one that had wished to be called Sam. She thought better of it. She had them now, and good old Sam was history. Let it go, she convinced herself.

Speaking of ghosts from the past, now, they had to once again deal with Lance Rocker. His arrival on the scene would definitely test Woody. He still resented Rocker for his affair with Janice; more like hated his guts. Well it couldn't really be called an affair. It had been more of a one night stand, but only because Preston, the Road Rage serial killer, had taken her before the relationship had an opportunity to develop. Rocker had been smitten by her for sure, and Rocker wasn't the type to fall in love easily.

She looked at her empty glass and decided no amount of adult beverage would induce sleep tonight. Her brain, in overdrive, could not be subdued by an overdose of alcohol. She would just have to deal with her little deepening pile of dung the best she could, one crisis at a time. Why did she always have to play the role of protagonist? For once, why couldn't she just be the antagonist in this little novel of hers, wreaking hell on other people's lives?

She stopped by the bathroom to relieve her bladder then eased back into the bed beside her broken hubby. Morning would arrive soon enough and with it she would take on the day's challenges and deal with them. Unlike Brady, she did have choices and some control over her life. He had been robbed of that luxury way too young. Life was so unfair.

1:03 AM Friday Morning
Forestbrook

She cruised to a stop in her red Jeep Commander, just a half block shy of her destination. She preferred the Mustang for these jobs. She knew better than to bring uninvited attention, if the authorities were on alert for suspicious activity involving a sports car driven by a beautiful white female. Yes, she was indeed beautiful, she thought.

Knowing that the jig was now up, it only excited her more and raised the stakes in playing the game. Her panties were wet, anticipating her next rendezvous with the unsuspecting target. She always became extremely aroused imagining what lay ahead.

She had once been able to control and regulate her perverted desires but now, because of the business and its demands, suppressing them was no longer an issue. She abducted two, sometimes three marks a week and could pick and choose her toys at will. Tonight she felt particularly spunky.

So focused on her objective, she never noticed the approaching group of males from behind. The five Valtos Locos gang members had spotted the jeep and the sole passenger and had smelled a target of their own.

Two passed on the sidewalk along the passenger side then stopped, turned, and chanted vulgar obscenities to distract her from the three that now hurriedly charged the jeep from the driver's side. Through the open window one clutched a hand full of blonde hair, instantly penning her against the door while a second snatched the door open, and the third placed his hand over her mouth.

The other two scampered to join in on the melee. Within seconds they drove off with their bounty, the Jeep Commander and their little blonde bonus firmly subdued in the backseat.

Already she was being stripped of her clothing and the first of the five was sexually assaulting her. The tables had quickly turned. The dominator was being brutally dominated, and she didn't like it, but had no say in the matter.

One of the men, waiting his turn shuffled through the white woman's purse while the three in the backseat were having their way with their new play thing. He found a small case. Opening it he discovered a vial and a couple of syringes. The vial had no markings.

Speaking in Spanish, he asked the white woman what it was, but realizing she didn't understand, he shouted, "What is this shit, bitch?"

In the middle of the gang rape she couldn't muster a response. One of her rapists slapped her hard across her face and yelled "Did you not hear the question, whore?"

While they preferred speaking in their native tongue, all could speak perfect English. She stared wild eyed but still did not respond.

"All right then bitch, you get to try this shit first," he said plunging the syringe into the vial.

She didn't have the strength to fight. She figured being sedated would ease her pain. Her little concoction could not be found in any medical practices. It could not be detected through any routine toxicology test or during autopsies. If it did show up, it could not be identified without extensive research. It had been developed to work quicker than any known anesthetics, and had been purposely developed to not be easily detectable.

She watched as the needle penetrated her bare buttocks and managed a little smile, knowing she had been saved. Seeing how quickly the clear chemical reacted, the deliverer of the drug shook his head and tossed the drugs from the jeep, wanting no part of this stuff. They turned off the main road but their captive was now at peace.

Parking on the edge of a secluded soybean field, the five gang members took turns raping and sodomizing the white princess. They urinated and defecated on her afterwards because they could. Unconscious, Nurse Cassandra Guy was spared the pain and indignity inflicted on her lifeless body. The vial indeed had contained her personal miracle drug. There would be no Hispanic donor delivered on this night.

Horry County Police Department
10 AM Friday

"A Mister Brock Boudreaux is here to see you, Sheriff," stated the receptionist over the intercom.

"I don't remember this appointment," replied Woody.

"He doesn't have one. I told him that, sir."

Woody paused, rolled his eyes and thought what had he done to deserve this. The Wonderful Grand Wizard of Oz wants to talk. He longed for his constable job back and thought, screw this sheriff position. There would be no run for re-election. He just hoped the public remembered that and would show some compassion and mercy. So far they had demonstrated neither.

Ex-Sheriff Samantha Burton had certainly gotten the last laugh hadn't she? Woody sensed she had a method to her madness by recommending him for this position. He sure missed Hank Singleton. "Send him in," he finally informed the receptionist.

"Sheriff Woodrow Anderson," greeted Brock, offering his hand.

Woody reluctantly accepted and shook the Klansman's hand, performing is Civil Duty. He could almost feel the corruption oozing from Brock's palm. He subconsciously wiped his hand on the side of his trouser leg, discreetly of course.

"What can I do for you today? And, without an appointment, you have about one minute of my busy schedule."

"Dim killings what you be looking into, dey got not one chôse to do wit da KKK. Me tink sometin stink real bad bout it though. Don't got me wrong. Dim whut you dug up don't mean nuttin to me. I just wonder where you at on it."

"First off, we haven't accused the Klan of any wrong doing or involvement in these murders, but we haven't ruled out any suspects yet either. Second, I'm not at liberty to share with you any specific information pertaining to the case. Third, you've lived here long enough to be able to talk so people can understand you instead babbling that Cajun gibberish."

"You got no repek you coo-yôn peeshwank. You ain't nuttin to me and I squash you like a little bebette and not tink bout it. "

"I didn't say I didn't understand you. I said you need to learn to speak English. I know exactly what you just said. Who the hell do you think you are coming in here and calling me a stupid runt, and threatening to step on me like a damn bug? Get the hell out of my office before I lock your ass up and toss away the key. Not exactly your best move threatening a law enforcement officer you sheet wearing sonofabitch! I just moved you up on my personal most wanted list!"

Brock put two fingers to his eyes then pointed the same two fingers toward Woody then said, "I dun put da gree gree on you, beb!"

"I'm not afraid of your stupid ass swamp curses. One last time, you best make like horse shit and hit the trail before I put my shoe up your Cajun ass. By the way, this conversation never happened. We had a cordial little visit didn't we my good triple K friend?"

I'm not cut out for this sheriff crap. I'm just too direct and to the point. I don't think I have to worry about being elected when my interim turn expires.

Brock stormed out of the office, cursing like a banshee. This had not gone as he had hoped. Why should he have expected any better? He and the new sheriff had never seen eye to eye in the past. Obviously he hadn't gotten over the Pavilion incident. Looking on the bright side, someone was eliminating the Mexican population so he should be thankful. He just wondered who deserved his appreciation. If it wasn't the Klan's doing, then who was doing the dirty deed?

Marion County
Saturday 2:15 PM

A passerby had reported finding a body dumped off the roadside in a drainage ditch near Brittons Neck off Route 908, approximately 20 miles from Conway. Police officers, arriving on the scene, had cordoned off the area after identifying the body as a nude female, Caucasian, blonde hair, severely beaten and battered.

Preliminary results from the investigating officers and the coroner indicated the female had been brutally and repeatability raped. Her face was so badly battered and swollen, she almost didn't look human. She smelled of urine and feces, not her own by all indication.

No identification had been found. The victim wore no clothing, indicating the body had probably been brutalized somewhere else then dumped in this location. The killer or killers had made no attempt to hide the body. Tracks at the scene supported that they had pulled to the side of the road and shoved her from the vehicle. One officer commented the tire tread looked like they had been made by a four wheel drive vehicle.

Based on the condition of the deceased, the coroner stated she had been murdered within the previous six to eight hours. He commented that he could see tissue under her fingernails. She had fought her attackers and most likely inflicted some severe scratches.

There were no missing person's reports filed in any of the surrounding counties. Officers surmised either she wasn't a local or friends or relatives didn't know she was missing yet. One of the veteran officers on the scene stated he had never seen a more gruesome or malicious attack in the county. The small community would surely be shaken by this murder.

Myrtle Beach
Saturday 5 PM

He paced the floor nervously, not coping well with her disappearance. It just wasn't like her to behave like this. He remembered the last conversation with her. She had shown some concern about abducting another so soon after the police's involvement in the case. Maybe this was her way of protesting.

No, he thought. She wouldn't respond like this. It simply wasn't her way. Something had gone badly wrong. Could her target, alerted by all the publicity, have fought her and injured her. No if she had been injured, he would have heard from her by now.

Maybe the police had caught her in the act and she was being held and interrogated. Even if she didn't talk, the trail would eventually lead to his doorsteps for sure. That jeep was registered to him. No, the police would have already been here by now, he rationalized.

He certainly couldn't report her missing just yet. That would bring them snooping in his direction. No, best thing to do was to wait. He would ride it out and see what happened. Right now he had bigger problems, pissed off clients asking about their order. He had to solve this and solve it quickly.

He had already accepted their money and deposited it in an offshore account. These people didn't play around if crossed. He could end up a missing person if he didn't come through for them. Close calls in the past had taught him that failure to meet a promised delivery was not an option in the black market. He desperately needed a plan B.

The phone rang. "Hello. Why yes the offer still stands. I would love to meet you. Why don't you come by first then we can... Oh given the circumstances I fully understand why you wish to keep this our little secret. No, I'm sure we can settle in here afterwards. Perfect, I'll see you within the hour then. You have the address, right? Wonderful."

After hanging up the phone he sighed loudly, "Things could just be looking up after all. I now have a potential plan B. This is indeed my lucky day."

Murrells Inlet, The Hot Fish Club
5 PM Saturday

Trudy sat on the deck just outside, The Gazebo, the Hot Fish Club's outdoor bar. Lost in a third Margarita and staring at the marshland, she waited patiently for Brady, who had been sponsoring a golf event at the Tradition Golf Resort. He had phoned her to say it would be closer to seven before he would finish up. She had first met Brady here. She remembered how goofy he had looked wearing that golf knickers outfit. That's when she had dubbed him Circus Boy because his attire had reminded her of a clown.

Their life had certainly been a three ring circus, for sure. Both he and she were accomplished jugglers, keeping two careers going while still trying to find time for each other. Too many times she had walked a fine line just like a tightrope walker, not always maintaining her balance when it came to career and their home life.

With the more recent events, she felt like she had been shot from the circus cannon and missed the safety net, battered and bruised from her fall. She still tried to pick up the pieces of her life.

Suddenly sensing someone standing behind her, she turned, expecting to see Brady, but instead made eye contact with one whom she first pegged a biker, and then she recognized him. Scat Crowder hovered over her, sipping on a long neck Bud.

"Hey honey, need some company?"

He apparently didn't recognize her out of uniform. She almost blurted out her identity, but then decided to play along, and see if she could pick him for information on Klan activity, specifically anything concerning Brock Boudreaux.

"Hi yourself," she replied, pouring on the southern charm and an accent to boot.

"Are you from around here?"

"Just visiting from Charlotte...you a local?"

"Born and raised," he smiled, "And damned proud of it. Are you here alone?"

"Bastard stood me up. Screw him. I'm here to have a good time. I can do it without the likes of him. He thought his gang was more important than me. Are you a skinhead too? Your shaved head reminds me of his. Boy some of the stuff he's told me he's done to the blacks and other minorities, man, I just get all hot and bothered just thinking about it. It's such a turn on, you know what I mean? I hate those monkey bastards." She had quickly gotten into character and poured it on, baiting the hook and dropping the line.

Trying to jump in while she paused for a breath, he said, "Sort of a skinhead, but not exactly, and I know what you mean about those Niggers and worthless Mexicans. How would you like doing a few shots? My name is Scat."

"Sounds like a mighty fine idea to me, bring them on, Scat. Call me Sadie. You can tell me more about your gang. I just love this white supremacy crap. I ought to shave my head too. Wouldn't that just be a hoot?"

Several shots later, old Scat had kicked into brag and confess mode. She set the hook and had begun reeling him in.

Staying in character she said, "I didn't even know the Ku Klux Klan was still doing stuff like that. They used to be the real badasses." She slurred her speech and couldn't help it. It wasn't an act, that's for sure.

"We still are. We're not anyone you would want to mess with, that's for damn sure. IKA is what we really go by now days."

"IKA, KKK, whatever...come on, I haven't heard anything about the KKK stirring up crap here at the beach. Are y'all new in town?"

"Well, we stay behind the damn scene now, but we do more stuff than you could shake a stick at."

"Liar...like what? Tell me something you've done recently; something that I would recognize, so I'd know you weren't jerking my chain." She rubbed her hand across her breast just to keep him off balance. Scat took notice and licked his lips, hoping this was his lucky night.

"You read anything in the paper about all the break-ins, the ones they say were being done by some of those Hispanic gangs?"

"I don't know. I might have seen something about them. Hell, do I look like I read the damn newspaper? So what? A bunch of Mexicans break in some stores or restaurants or something; what's that got to do with you and the Klan? If you're trying to impress me honey, you're losing your audience."

Scat rolled his eyes. He leaned over to her and whispered, "It wasn't any Mexican gangs doing it."

"I don't get it. What the hell are you saying?"

Scat winked. He pointed toward himself.

"Holy crap," she exclaimed. "You didn't do those, did you?"

He smiled, then whispered, "We certainly did. We pulled those robberies and staged them to look like those stupid ass Mexican gangs did them."

"What did y'all get out of it besides the loot?"

"It was fine propaganda against illegals and gangs. It didn't hurt our recruiting either. Yeah, the money and goods came in handy too. See this ring. It came from one of the safes; real diamonds and gold."

"That's so hot! Did you mastermind it, Honey?"

"I can't take all the credit, but I was right there in the middle of it, Sadie. Our chapter leader, he recruited some real badasses in here to pull it off. We paid them big bucks too, let me tell you."

"Man, that's a lot better than that bastard that stood me up ever told me."

"What you say we get the hell out of here and see if I can put out that little fire you got blazing in your britches?"

"Am I interrupting something?"

Scat turned to see Brady standing there decked in mustard yellow knickers, matching argyle socks and flat hat, black shirt. "Who the hell are you, fancy pants?"

"He's the guy I was telling you about; the one that stood me up."

"He doesn't look like a skin head. Hell is head ain't even shaved."

"My bad," she replied. "I just communicated with him on one of those chat lines. The picture he posted doesn't look anything like him. I tell you what, give me your address and number, and I'll catch up with you, after I finish giving him what for."

Scat nodded and wrote the information down on a napkin. Brady just stood their dumbfounded and played along.

"Call me. I don't live that far from here. What a damn loser," he mumbled as he walked away.

"This ought to be good," said Brady as he sat down.

"Better than you could ever imagine," she answered, giving him a kiss. "That boy is dumb as dirt."

"And apparently he brought out the slutty side in you..."

"All in a days work...that's why they call it undercover."

The Clinic

"That was quite an impressive tour," commented Samantha Burton. "I admire what you are doing here."

"I have lived a most fortunate life, my dear. I feel it is my obligation to give back to the community and to those less fortunate souls," replied Doctor Lincoln T. Hawthorne.

"And you say you operate this along with your sister and voluntary interns?"

"That is correct. My sister, Cassandra Guy, is a RGN. Excuse me for the acronym; she's a Registered General Nurse. Cassandra and I wear numerous hats," he explained, showing Sam a picture of his sister displayed on his desk.

Sam moistened her lips with her tongue and said, "I regret I won't have the opportunity to meet your sister. She is quite gorgeous. I can tell you are very proud of her." *I may have to look her up some time.*

"Yes, she's the jewel in our family for sure. May I pour you a drink?"

"That would be simply wonderful, but just one. I have to hit the road shortly. I have to be back in Charleston tonight."

"I am so sorry the position of sheriff did not work out for you. It is certainly their loss. What brought you here? Did you have unfinished business with the powers that be?"

"No, they don't know I've returned to their precious county. I must admit I pulled a little cloak and dagger and covertly slipped in under the radar."

"I'm sorry, I don't follow."

"Excuse my babbling. I had personal business and didn't wish to be spotted and hounded by the local media; I used a false name and stayed down in Georgetown to avoid them. No one really knows I'm here, and I'd like to keep it that way, if you don't mind. Is that much too naughty of me?"

"Not at all, my dear," he smiled, handing her the glass of Scotch. "I think it is simply intriguing. You're a regular little secret agent, aren't you?"

Sam laughed, "I really like you, Lincoln. Sorry I won't be seeing more of you." She took a long drink then continued. "I must invite you and your sister to the low country. I have a quaint little place near Edisto, a couple of extra bedrooms, and fabulous view of both the ocean and the marsh."

"Speaking on behalf of Cassandra, we most certainly will take you up on your gracious invitation."

Sam began blinking, attempting to focus. She shook her head, warding off a sudden bout of drowsiness. She yawned several times, then in a slurred voice said, "Pardon me, it has been a long day. I assure you I am not bored by your company. Normally one drink doesn't have this sort of effect on me."

"No offense taken. Please rest here as long as you like my dear," Lincoln replied, removing the glass from her hand before she dropped it. "Now, I have orders to fill and my little covert queen, you are here just in the nick of time to assist me with my grocery list."

Lincoln scooped her up in his arms, and prepared for surgery. He would dispose of her car and any traceable belongings once he completed the task at hand. First, he may just indulge and partake of her exquisite chocolate pastry. Waste not, want not, they say. Shame she wouldn't be awake to enjoy it too.

SurfSide Beach
11 AM

Scat sat in his modest two room apartment, sipping on a cold one, still fantasizing about that Sadie he had met last night. He hoped she would call him. He really wanted in her britches. Hell, he wanted in anyone's britches.

He hadn't had a good piece of ass in almost a month, if you didn't count that knob job he had gotten from that crack-head neighbor of his about a week ago. She was ugly as sin but she needed drugs and he needed relief from the blue balls. He closed his eyes so he didn't have to look at her while she performed the dirty deed. Good thing, he didn't have to kiss her afterwards. He gave her a little meth and sent her on her merry way.

He hated this dump. Brock had promised him better digs but so far had not delivered. That old Bayou bastard had done a lot of promising and he was getting damned tired of him not following up. Sure, he kept him in spending money but he had expected a hell of a lot more when he hooked up with this Klan crap.

The damn gun slingers Brock had brought in to pull all those robberies had been paid a pretty penny to lay blame on the Mexicans. Scat begrudged them because he had only been tossed some of the scraps. Sure, he had this expensive ring but look around, he thought. I live just above poverty level. He was exaggerating, but he just needed to vent. Problem, no one was there to hear him.

He couldn't figure why Brock hadn't given him more responsibility, a higher profile position. He had to do all the dirty little jobs and he was no dummy. He figured Brock would allow him to take the fall if anything went badly wrong. He was no damn stupid flunky. Hell, he could have been one of those college freaks if he had wanted to be. Hindsight, he probably should have made something more out of himself. Oh well, one has to play the cards dealt them.

Man, this massacre ground they had uncovered was heavy duty crap. Those were a lot of damn dead Mexicans they had found out there on the edge of that swamp. It sure sounded like something the Klan or some white supremacy group would pull, but Brock and his flunkies denied any involvement. Word on the street, a couple of the badass Mexican gangs were looking to take it out on somebody. He just hoped like hell it wasn't the Klan or him.

Scat had heard that the Valtos Locos and the Sur-13s were boasting revenge. The notorious MS-13 gang, who up until now had never shown their ugly faces at the beach, were also said to be taking notice. He couldn't figure why they were getting so worked up. They didn't really care about their own people. Those staged robberies had them also hunting for the perpetrators, gangs blaming other gangs, and not suspecting Klan involvement.

"Yep," Scat spoke out loud, rearing back in his worn-out leather Lazy Boy recliner. "Old Brock wanted the white people to get pissed at the thieving Mexican gangs, but he sure has bitten off more than he had bargained for with the gangs now getting all riled up. Of course he didn't count on this other mess though. If he would make me his right hand man I could help, but I'm not going to be his little flunky fall guy any more. Hell no, he can saw that limb off behind his almighty ass." He took another pull from his beer.

A knock came at his door. He adjusted the Lazy Boy from the reclining position and slid out. Barefooted, he wobbled his way to the door. The six-pack he had consumed for breakfast was working on his balance. He swung the door open and low and behold there stood, his little Sadie.

"I've been sitting here just thinking about you, honey. You must have read my mind!"

"Dwayne Allen Crowder, how about I read you your rights instead," said Detective Trudy Wagner Pierce, flashing her badge and a search warrant with Captain and Sly flanking her, standing like bookends in the doorway.

"Monkey shit..." exclaimed Scat. "You're a friggin cop."

"Didn't ever dream of that, did you, Mister Klansman, when you were spilling your guts last night. I can be quite the charmer when I want to be."

"This is damn entrapment and illegal as hell."

"Whoa cowboy, I was there waiting on my husband when you strolled over, spewing all this braggart crap. I'm just a mighty good listener with memory for detail. Thanks for sharing."

"Bite me, bitch. I'll be out before you can finish your damn paperwork."

"You really do need to pick better friends," said Captain.

"Come on Scat, your taxi is in the drive," added Sly.

Scat dropped a series of f-bombs. He didn't exit gracefully but knew better than to resist arrest.

The Clinic

Doctor Lincoln T. Hawthorne, business as usual, greeted his morning appointments. Three had been Hispanic, one black and another poor white trash. None had been very promising prospects to fill upcoming orders. His sister had not shown up for work. He had pulled double duty at the desk. Only one intern had reported so his meager staff had him very shorthanded.

His instincts told him that something terrible had happened or Cassandra would be here. She never missed work. He agonized over reporting her missing to the authorities. He certainly didn't need to bring any attention to him or the clinic, especially after the discovery of his burial grounds.

Last night's guest had satisfied his clients' immediate demands. She had been in phenomenal physical shape, offering up an amazing yield of organs. Shipments had gone out on schedule but he hadn't had time to dispose of the dear ex-sheriff's remains. Lucky for him no one would be looking for her in Horry County so time would be on his side.

The problem at hand, he had to have his brother locate another remote area for disposing of the leftovers. Brother Eugene, a mortician, transported the cadavers and conducted unceremonious burials of the donors. Eugene obviously had assisted in digging the graves and disposing of the bodies, but he never asked any questions. Big brother had been paid well for his services and preferred not knowing the details of their business arrangements.

An even more critical issue, Cassandra...with her missing, the operation came to a standstill. Lincoln identified her victims through their medical records from visits to the clinic. He knew which ones were healthy, were illegal and would not be reported. She collected them and brought them to him.

Lincoln couldn't count on a steady supply of Samantha Burtons.

Faced with aggressive goals, he required at least three donors for next week's demands. He had two men, identified from the clinic already, but didn't know how he would manage to harvest the goods. A third still depended on the upcoming week's clients. Up until last night he had chosen only illegal Hispanic males, easy targets, never reported as missing. Samantha Burton had been a dangerous stretch.

Where was Cassandra? He discounted her being arrested now. Had her last abduction gone wrong? Had her mark been aware of the killings, and maybe had turned the tables on her? His sister could be dead or worse. Possibly she was being held captive somewhere by vengeful Hispanics? He decided he would keep his mouth shut for the time being. Maybe she would show up, unharmed and apologetic. Maybe she was just trying to teach him a lesson.

The task at hand, he had one dead police official on his premises and still had two pre-selected donors requiring harvesting. One of his potential donors sat in his waiting room right now, twenty three and in perfect health except for a broken right hand. He appeared to have come here alone. Could he risk taking him now? He had never done this at the clinic. Did he really have another choice?

He dismissed the young intern for the day then motioned for the young man to come inside. The waiting room was empty for now so he flipped over the *Closed* sign, pulled the blinds and decided he must not allow this opportunity to pass.

Examining the man's broken hand, Lincoln advised him in Spanish that he would need to give him a shot to deaden his hand before he continued his examination. The man nodded, oblivious to the fact that this shot would deaden more than just his pain. Minutes later he sat limp in the chair.

Soon after, Lincoln had wheeled him to the back and had him on a surgical table. Typically Cassandra assisted him but he would perform this organ mining operation solo, and then he would have a second body to dispose of. Brother Eugene would have his work cut out for him. The game had changed dramatically. Contemplating what could have possibly happened to Cassandra consumed Lincoln like a cancer.

Interrogation Room
Horry County Police Department

Scat sat at the table alone and sweating bullets. He glanced over at the mirror, wondering how many stood on the other side watching him squirm like a red wiggler on a hook. He had really messed up, confiding in that little hot number, Sadie. He wished he could remember everything he had told her, but too many consumed shots last night had blocked most of those memories.

One thing for certain, crossing the Klan was inexcusable. It had to be the next worse thing to betraying the mob. The scent of fresh poon-tang had definitely clouded his thinking and had given him a bad case of diarrhea of the mouth. He just didn't know how much he had blabbed, trying to impress the undercover cop.

Scat's imagination took control of his emotions. Had she been wearing a wire? If she had, why did she wait until the next day to bring him in? Maybe he didn't actually spill his guts to her. Just maybe he had enough sense to make up some crap to impress her. Who was he really trying to kid?

The door swung open and in walked the high and mighty undercover cop with one of the cops that had greeted him at his apartment door. She wore plain clothes and still didn't look like a cop to him. She was a damn find figure of a woman, Amazonian like in stature. One thing for sure, he could certainly remember what had attracted him to her. She had the right bait to lure him in. He licked his lips and clutched his crotch then took a long deep breath but remained dry mouthed and speechless.

"Dwayne Allen Crowder, you have got a lot of explaining to do, now don't you? I can call you Dwayne, can't I?"

"I don't care what you call me, and I don't say shit without my lawyer present," he boasted, trying to regain his composure.

"It didn't seem to trouble you talking to me last night without your lawyer present."

"I always tell you bitches what you want to hear," he spoke up, his voice breaking up slightly. "You know the game, just like strippers in titty bars, they're all just working there long enough to pay for their college expenses or buy a new house. I'll tell you anything I think you want to hear to get me a taste."

"Well, you need to learn to be a better liar I suppose," she explained, opening her hand to expose his diamond ring in her palm. "Seems this ring of yours did come from one of those robberies just like you mentioned last night."

"Hell, I didn't know it was stolen, I bought it in a pawn shop."

"Which shop?" asked the black cop, standing next to her. "We'll wish to validate your story."

I don't remember. I do my shopping at about all of them around here. You can pick up good merchandise at most."

"Never mind, we'll ask around and help you with that one," replied the black cop. "I'm detective Sylvester Stone, in case you've forgotten."

"By the way, you have quite a little enterprise going at your place don't you?"

Scat just shrugged his shoulders. He had no response. He had already talked too much. Brock was going to be one pissed bastard when he got wind of this.

Let's see here," she said, pulling a note pad from her shirt pocket. "Meth, Ecstasy, Cocaine, Viagra laced Cocaine, Marijuana, Speed, just to mention a few of the goodies we found in our search of your apartment."

"I want my lawyer. I get a phone call, right? I want to make it now."

"Are you really sure you want **Brock Boudreaux** to know what a disappointment you have been? He's not going to like it when he finds out how you've been spilling your guts to the police about the Klan activities and fingering him."

Bingo, she had hit a nerve she thought. Scat was definitely squirming now. It might be time to let him sweat for a while, then he may just be ripe for the picking and ready to make a deal.

"We'll see if we can arrange that call for you," she told him. "Sit tight, we'll be back in a jiffy."

Woody watched from the mirror. Obviously his high school buddy was in over his head and he could tell Scat was unnerved and about to break. Clearing up that series of robberies could buy him and the department some valuable time. Good publicity for a change wouldn't hurt, either. This department was due for a break.

Trudy and Sly walked into the viewing room where Woody and her entire team peered at a now pacing Scat Crowder. Yes, Dwayne Allen Crowder looked pretty shaken for sure.

"So what do you think?"

"I think you have our boy on the ropes," commented Woody. "Hopefully he'll offer up Brock to save his butt."

"Seems too easy to me," replied Trudy. "I don't picture this Brock Boudreaux going down without a fight and right now all we have on him is Scat Crowder's testimony, if he offers it. Even that ring could be just all circumstantial. Being in possession of stolen goods doesn't mean he stole it. We can certainly pressure him with the drug charges but if he doesn't cough up Brock we're at a dead-end on the robberies."

"And even if he does snitch on Brock, it's not going to be a piece of cake bringing him down on those charges," added Sly. "It's just Scat's word against Brock's."

"Have I missed something, teammates?" asked Rocker, standing in the doorway just behind Trudy, eyeing her in a new light, after now possessing the photographs.

Woody asked, "What are you doing in here, Rocker?"

"This deputy badge works just like the key to the city," he smiled, holding the badge up for all eyes to see.

"Different case and you're not part of it," growled Woody.

"But my entire team has been assembled, it must be a biggie."

Trudy stepped between Woody and Lance. "Look, it's not related to the Hispanic murders so how about just waiting outside?"

"Where's the love?" asked Rocker, still visualizing her without her clothes.

Woody took a step around Trudy in Rocker's direction and he got the point. "I'll be outside if you need me."

Making sure that their attention had returned to the bald, tattooed gent on the other side of that mirror, Rocker kept the door cracked open just enough so he could hear their conversation. He had a nose for a good story and this reeked of it. Seeing the hallway clear, he clicked the record button on his mini recorder and held it in place so he would not miss a thing of what they said.

Woody and the CSI team reviewed their options before sending Trudy and Sly back in to pressure Scat. Rocker smiled and clicked the off button then quickly scampered down the hallway before they emerged from the viewing room. Once in his car he pressed the play button and smiled while he listened to his lead in for this week's segment.

The Clinic

"My dear brother, just what have you gotten yourself into this time that requires me to bail your butt out?" asked Eugene Hawthorne.

"We have a problem," explained Lincoln. "Cassandra is missing. I sent her for a pickup, but she never returned."

"What do you mean our dear sister is MIA? That's not like her. Have you reported her missing?"

"Don't be absurd. How could I possibly do that, Eugene? We can't have the authorities snooping around here, now can we?"

"I suppose you know best, little brother. Do you think she has been harmed?"

"I certainly hope not," answered Lincoln, sitting down and dropping his head in his hands.

"That's not why I'm here is it?"

"Without Cassandra, our little factory screeches to a thunderous halt."

"Look me in the eyes, Lincoln, what have you done?"

"We had orders to fill and you know how our clients get when we miss a deadline," he mumbled into his hands.

"I said look at me, brother. Just what have you done?"

Looking up at Eugene, a heavier and older version of himself, he said "I have two empty cases for you to dispose of, brother. One's here and the other is back at the house."

"Here at the clinic, are you crazy? I thought you never conducted business here at the clinic, Lincoln. You don't shit where you eat remember."

"Policy has changed until Cassandra returns."

"And if she doesn't, what then little brother?"

"We have a business to run so we'll do what we have to do to make those shipments, right?"

"There's something else isn't there?"

"The one at the house is a black female and her vehicle is parked in the garage."

"What the hell have you done, Lincoln?"

He recapped the events for Eugene, leaving out few details. The stakes had been raised and two cardinal rules had been broken. Never conduct business at the clinic and never use donors with identities.

"A sheriff none the less," commented Eugene, shaking his head in disgust. "Desperate men take desperate measures."

"Ex-sheriff and we had commitments. I weighed the risks."

"So now I have to clean up after you and dispose of the empty cases, as you like to call them, and a vehicle to boot. Guess it is time for me to earn my money. I'll take this empty case with me. I'll pull around back. Prepare it for transporting."

"We still require one more donor to make this week's order."

"That's yours and Cassandra's department,"

"Eugene, I am really worried about our sister."

"I know you are. So am I. I fear something terrible has happened.'

"What if she is..." but Eugene cut him short, placing his fingers to his lips, indicating for him to hush.

"Let's pray for her safe return, Lincoln."

Eugene collected both empty cases and did something that broke cardinal rule number three. He decided to bury both inside the caskets of two upcoming funerals. He had now been forced to mix this with his internal business.

He had quickly devised a plan for disposing of the ex-sheriff's car. He would have one of his men drop it off in a Hispanic neighborhood with the keys in the ignition. The rest would take care of itself. If and when it was detected, what better than the Hispanics being blamed and suspected for her disappearance? Now, how perfect was that he thought?

The Mayors House Restaurant
Litchfield

"What's the special occasion, Circus Boy?"

"They were running these $14.95 specials that include drink, appetizer, entree and dessert so you're special for joining me."

She watched Brady as he held the menu, hands shaking much worse. He noticed she had noticed and propped the menu on the table. She could tell his condition was advancing at an incredible rate just like the doctor had told them it would and, worse still, no cure.

Brady had agreed to be a human guinea pig and had begun taking a series of highly experimental medications that introduced their own set of risks and side effects. He had signed waivers to ensure the medical authorities could not be sued by him or any family members.

"So how was life in cop world today?"

"We tried to crack that Scat, the skinhead, but so far he hasn't cooperated with us. Woody is still holding him on the drug charges, but he's likely to make bail on those soon."

"And I thought you and he were a hot item," smiled Brady, reaching across the table to hold her hand.

"Well unlike you, he recognizes I have a brain. You just love me for my love monkey."

"And what's the matter with me being a monkey lover," he said loudly enough to raise the attention of a nearby table of four.

Trudy, realizing they had over heard his comments, looked over at the eavesdroppers. She turned three shades of red and shushed Brady. One guy gave them the thumbs ups. Brady saluted them. Trudy gave Brady *the look* to tone down the situation.

She attempted to get the conversation back on track. "We'll play good cop, bad cop on him tomorrow," she told him.

"Let me guess, you're the good cop?"

"Well bad is too easy for me. I need to practice on my good. How was your day?"

"Let's see. I almost fell twice, did fall once. I drooled in my coffee and I slurred on the phone to a man trying to sell me a timeshare. He thought I was flirting with him and hung up. I now have a new approach for telemarketers."

"I love you."

"No, you just love me for my drooling tongue."

"Every wet inch of it," she replied, squeezing his hand. "So how are all those drugs working?"

"I'm constipated and piss purple," he said in a very serious tone.

"Purple is my favorite color and the first time I saw you in that Ringling Brothers knickers outfit I instantly knew you were full of crap."

"I love you too. Where are your cuffs?"

"I guess we're going home now."

"You're so perceptive, my little love monkey."

"Let's go, Circus Boy."

Swamp Fox Hotel

"Murray, is your phone connection bad? You heard me, I want to do this as background information to feed the main story," explained Rocker to his agent.

"Rocker, baby, you told these officers that you would allow them to screen the material for the show. They're not going to buy into this. I do like it, but they won't."

"I told them I wouldn't run any material about that Hispanic graveyard without their approval. This has nothing to do with their ongoing investigation. They politely informed me exactly that and ran me out of their little discussion. I'm the master of the twist. You should know that by now, Murray."

"So let me get this straight, you're going to piss off the police department, the Klan, the Hispanic gangs, all for the sake of ratings. I love it. Let's do it."

"I want a film crew here with me tomorrow. I have a few surprises of my own. Have someone do research on this new Klan movement, the IKA. Get your hands on some file footage about it and those gangs I mentioned."

"You got it."

"Deputy Lance Rocker is about to break this thing wide open and do what I do best, *ROCK THEIR WORLD!*"

Interrogation Room
Horry County Police Department

Trudy, interrogating Scat said, "Tell me about that tattoo there on your right forearm."

"Where's my lawyer? I don't say shit without him being present."

"The court has appointed you one and he or she should be here shortly. I'm just making small talk until they arrive."

"Fine, it's the IKA Crest. Now will you shut the hell up?"

"It's different from any I've ever seen...strange markings. I'm not conning you. I'm really curious."

Scat rubbed his head then took a deep breath. "Some date back over a hundred years," explained Scat, attempting to relax. He needed to get out of here.

"And what's that?" she asked, touching his arm with her finger.

She still intrigued him, even for a cop. He still dreamed of getting in those tight britches. He might do just that if given half a chance. "It's the cross wheel."

"Interesting, it almost looks like the regular cross."

"It is a representation of the Christian cross. It's our cross within the circle. See the red inside the circle. That's blood from the white people and the white field is, what else, but the white race," he smiled, and zoomed in on her full and luscious lips. "How long have you been a cop?"

"Around eight years, give or take," she replied, still attempting to lure him in with the personal chat. "And what about those?" she pointed to other emblems on the tattoo.

"Cut the crap. I get it. You don't really give a shit about my tattoos. I know when I'm being played, missy."

"You're not that damn smart or you would have caught on to it the other night."

He stood up, his shackled hands resting on the table, veins pulsating in his neck and on the side of his shaved skull and whispered, "You don't have shit, or you would have already done something, Detective."

Woody, observing the antics from the other room, moved quickly. He stepped inside the interrogation room to intervene.

"Well, well, well if it isn't my old buddy Woody or I guess I should call you Mister Sheriff, sir."

"Sit back down, Dwayne," ordered Woody. Scat did, but not before spitting on the floor.

"Pretty damn interesting, don't you think, Sheriff?"

Woody didn't respond. He took a deep breath then stepped over to the desk and grabbed Scat's shackled hands, giving him a firm jerk toward the opposite side of the table.

"Big man, that's always what your little runt ass has wanted to be. She don't know what your old buddy knows about you does she?"

Woody gave the chain another swift yank almost, causing Scat to do a nose skid across the table's surface. Staring Scat down, he warned him to can it.

Trudy removed Woody's hand from the shackles and said "Sheriff, why don't you let me handle this?"

"Yeah, Woody boy, me and the PO-LICE WOMAN need a little privacy, so we can chat about mine and your old times. We did have some good old times back then, didn't we?"

"Detective Pierce, please excuse me and my old high school classmate, and turn off the recorders, and clear everyone from the room."

"But..."

"Detective, that was an order."

"Yes sir," responded Trudy, hoping he knew what he was doing and fearing he was taking this bad cop routine over the edge.

After standing in silence for a couple of minutes giving Trudy an opportunity to comply with his orders, he finally spoke. "Dwayne or is it Mister Badass Scat now? Cut your crap! You're way in over your head on this one, old buddy. Don't even think about digging up old bones about our pass, or

I'll bury you so deep that body sniffing dogs will never find you. And I'm in a position to do just that."

Scat, taken by Woody's abruptness, thought carefully about his next response. "I saved your little whiny ass from those teenagers when we were in the fifth grade...remember, buddy? You owe me for that and I'm collecting the favor."

Gritting his teeth and clenching his jaw, he responded, "That was a long time ago and no, I haven't forgotten."

"You know what they would have done to you if I hadn't come to your rescue, don't you?"

Woody took another deep breath but didn't respond. He had become swept up in a replay of that dreaded event. He was ten years old again and waiting in the park for the arrival of Dwayne. They were supposed to practice baseball. He killed time by bouncing the ball off the restroom wall and catching it in his glove. He never saw the three older boys emerging from the bathroom where they had been sharing a joint.

"Hey squirt, what the hell are you doing here at our ball field?"

Woody, always small for his age, had looked more like a second grader instead of a fifth grader, and these three were easily twice his size. He had decided to ignore them and walk away. He had made it about ten paces before one of them grabbed him by the shoulder and spun him around.

"Pipsqueak, we were talking to you," a second one shouted at him.

Woody remembered smelling the reefer on them. They were clearly stoned. The three had a reputation for bullying underclassmen. They never picked on kids their own size. Woody could be a little scrapper when he had to, but he was outmanned, and in no position to take on these three alone. To make things worse, he possessed a bit of a stutter back then, and it only made things worse when he attempted to speak, especially when in a stressful situation.

"What do we have here, Porky Pig?" asked the third boy.

"Maybe we need to slam the ham," another shouted, pushing Woody to the ground.

He quickly stood up and began brushing himself off, when two of them grabbed him by each elbow and hustled him, feet dangling off the ground, inside the restroom. No one witnessed his untimely abduction.

"So what do we do with little turds like this?" asked one of the boys, apparently the leader.

"I've got an idea," said another one. "Let's have a little fun. Get in that stall."

Woody tried to say no but the stutter wouldn't come out so he shook his head no instead. Two restrained him by the arms while the third yanked his jogging shorts and underwear down to his ankles.

"Look," taunted one. "He has a pecker the size of my pinky finger!"

Woody's face reddened with that comment. He had always been ashamed of his size and this wasn't helping his confidence any. The two held him firmly. There was no escape.

The boy standing in front of him unzipped his pants and pulled out his penis. "This is what a full grown dick looks like. Yours is just shy of making you a little squatter. Do you squat when you go to the bathroom?"

Woody said nothing. He realized he was in a world of trouble. The potheads meant business. He closed his eyes, tears ran down his cheeks. He braced for the worse. The boy behind him screamed, falling into him and knocking him free from the two holding him captive.

"Turn him loose you stinking bastards," shouted Dwayne, yelling like a wild banshee, and wailing away at the three boys with his baseball bat.

The one boy had dropped to the floor, holding his back, and scrambling for cover under a sink. The other two had their arms up trying to ward off the wild blows being inflicted by their bat wielding attacker. Woody jerked up his pants, and then scrambled towards the exit, but not before kicking the boy under the sink squarely in his exposed balls.

After a few more strategically placed blows, Dwayne followed, yelling to the three if they said anything about this or tried it again, he would tell everyone in school that they were a bunch of pothead queers.

"So buddy, are you going to cut me some slack here, or what?" asked Scat, snapping Woody out of the nightmare.

"I'll go check on your lawyer," responded Woody, still stunned by those memories. "And no, I haven't forgotten what you did." That had been one of the worst days of his life. He vowed after that day that he would be a force to be reckoned with and had gone out for all sports. He had excelled at every one of them. Life lesson, his size never mattered again.

Trudy stood by the coffee pot. Woody came over and poured a cup. He looked like he had just been interrogated instead of Scat.

"Are you okay?"

"Yeah," Woody replied, taking a sip. "We won't be getting anything further out of him. I expect him to make bail today."

"We still have the stolen ring and drug charges."

Woody nodded and returned to his office. His thoughts shifted to that day in the park, a time he thought he had buried long ago. He did owe Dwayne Crowder. If he hadn't shown up when he had, Woody cringed at where he may have ended up; bitter, suicidal, homicidal, certainly not in law enforcement.

He decided to step away from this particular case, pull the plug and just let it fade into oblivion. No evidence really linked Dwayne to the robberies. Possession of the ring was simple possession of stolen merchandise. The drugs, while a case could be made on intent to distribute, his old schoolmate could probably get off with fines, maybe a little time served and probation. He would refocus the team on the Hispanic murders and shelve this one. His debt would be paid in full.

The Hawthorne Compound
Pawley's Island

Lincoln reviewed his database of illegal clients from his clinical practice in an attempt to identify the final donor he would require for this week's commitment. Once identified, he still had the challenge of acquiring and delivering the merchandise. Cassandra remained missing so he would be forced to make this happen without her services.

Brother Eugene had made it perfectly clear that he couldn't be counted on to deliver the goods. He emphasized where he fit into the process and stood firm on his responsibilities in their little operation and it didn't include retrieving the live donors. He could not convince Eugene to deviate from his role. This now rested fully on his shoulders alone, so he would have to devise an alternate plan of action.

Lincoln contemplated whether he should risk a second abduction at the clinic. What other choices did he have? How could he really be assured that his chosen donor wouldn't tell a family member about the appointment? One thing for sure, they wouldn't confide in the authorities if the donor didn't return from the appointment. Surely they would never suspect him of any wrong doing.

Settled, he would have to do it at the clinic. He certainly couldn't approach the donor on the outside and accomplish what Cassandra had made so artful. What had happened to his dear sister? She had surely compromised their situation with her disappearance.

Lincoln thought, I could just walk away after filling this order. I have the wealth to do so. Eugene and I could retire and vanish to some secluded island where we could live happily ever after. No, it wouldn't be that simple he admitted. These people don't let you walk away just like that. They certainly offer no retirement plans nor allow you to work a two week notice.

Lincoln had not really thought of getting out before he had gotten in. He should have given it some thought but he hadn't. He had convinced Cassandra and Eugene to join him in the self proclaimed family business. It had been lucrative for all of them, but now Cassandra was missing, and Eugene was balking at stepping up to the plate to substitute for little sister. It all fell back on his shoulders, and he felt the weight of the burden.

Lincoln still had an endless supply of potential donors at the clinic but harvesting them posed a serious problem long term. He couldn't just post a job opening; Body snatcher needed for family owned and operated business, no questions asked, previous experience a plus but not necessary, good pay and benefits if you don't get caught.

The doorbell rang. He closed his computer file then accessed the security system and viewed the main entrance. He didn't recognize the visitor. He reluctantly descended the stairway to the first floor to inquire the identity of the stranger waiting patiently at his front door.

Using the intercom, he asked, "Please state your name and reason for being at my door."

"I'm Raeford McCrery, preacher at the Pentecostal Church on the north end of the Grand Strand. Are you Doctor Hawthorne?"

"Yes I'm Doctor Lincoln Hawthorne. I don't believe I have ever made your acquaintance, sir. What can I do for you? I already have charities that I donate to and really do not appreciate solicitors."

"Oh no, it is nothing like that, I assure you. I think Jorge Cruz was a patient of yours. I discovered an unpaid bill while packing up his things and I would like to settle his account. A young man, an intern I do believe, at your clinic, told me I could possibly reach you here at this address."

Lincoln opened the door and motioned the elderly pastor inside. He could not recall this Cruz fellow. He had never laid eyes on the pastor before.

"I do apologize for disturbing you at your home, but when I get something on my mind, I can't rest until I do something about it."

"So you say you were packing mister Cruz's things and found this bill," he recounted, viewing the $75.00 fee past due on his clinic's letterhead.

"I'm sorry, allow me to explain. Jorge was an associate pastor at my church. I am saddened to say he was murdered a while back."

"Murdered..." Lincoln repeated, acting surprised by the information. He still didn't remember Jorge.

"Yes sir...I'm sure you've either read about it or seen it on the news; all those bodies the police discovered buried along that swamp. Well, Jorge was the only one the police have been able to identify so far. What a waste, he was such a promising young clergyman. He really connected with the teenagers of the church."

"Heavens, please have a seat, Pastor McCrery. My condolences to you and his family for the young man's death. Can I offer you some tea or coffee?"

"Thank you for your hospitality but I'm fine. Jorge didn't really have any close family. I suppose we at the church were his real family. My congregation remembers him for that full smile and tender heart."

"So tell me, what do the police think happened to your Pastor Cruz?"

"Incredible circumstances to say the least, I'm saddened to say. The authorities said all those young men were being stripped of their internal organs, some sort of black-market dealing in the selling of body parts. Can you believe we could have something like that going on around here?"

"Truly unbelievable," remarked Lincoln, looking shocked. "So does our cracker jack police force have any substantial leads?"

"The detectives that have been talking to me think the murderer or murderers have a medical background. He said everything was so surgical and precise, like they knew exactly what they were doing, which organs were good, and which ones were bad."

"Interesting theory, surely they must have suspects. Something like this couldn't be so easily concealed here in Horry County."

"Well, they're beating the bushes for anyone who may have known Jorge or those others that have fallen prey to such diabolical evil doers. I can not fathom how human beings could have done something so horrific to their fellow human beings."

"We live in troubled times pastor. The mighty dollar can corrupt those we might never otherwise have thought were corruptible."

"But someone in the medical profession, that is so deceitful and sinful, don't you agree?"

At that moment the clergyman and the doctor made unmistakable eye contact. Raeford McCrery realized he had just solved the crime, and was now in grave danger. Lincoln saw it in the elderly pastor's eyes. The connection had been made.

"Pastor, we do seem to have a bit of a problem. It is most unfortunate for both of us."

"I pray for your soul doctor," responded the preacher, appearing remarkably cool and unshaken by the discovery.

"We all need prayers. Have you said one for yourself?"

"I pray this ends now, Doctor Hawthorne. Too many people have lost their lives, and for what, to have their precious body parts sold on some black-market to the highest bidders?"

"I'm insulted by that remark. Not hardly, my dear man; what we have is a well structured business with set prices and obtainable goals, I assure you. We do not run an auction house. Our clients expect only the highest quality. We deliver just that. What we do saves so many more lives."

"My son, you speak of this with absolutely no remorse, unbelievable. Just a business opportunity for you, but in America we call it murder."

"I could discuss the morality of this with you for hours but sadly it would still end the same, you with your religious and moral convictions, and me still doing what I do best. You must understand there's nothing personal about this pastor. I am truly sorry you had to stumble into this while just trying to do a good deed for your friend, Jorge Cruz. I do indeed commend you for that."

"I suppose because I'm a man of the cloth and a man long in the tooth, that you expect me to bow my head and accept your judgment as final, just roll over and allow you to extinguish my life just as you would a common house fly."

"I assure you my dear fellow; I do not look upon you as a mere insect. If I were in your position I would probably fight with my last breath, pastor, but that's just me. But, why make this difficult for both of us?"

Raeford McCrery stood to his feet and grabbed the nearest thing he could get his hands on, a candle stick lamp on the accent table. He ripped off the shade and yanked the cord from the receptacle. He began swinging it wildly in front of him, while slowly backing up toward the door.

"Well done pastor," spoke up Lincoln, applauding his effort. "So you really think you're going to pummel me with that? You are quite resourceful but I fear you suffer from a severe case of denial. Feel free to seek a second opinion. I'm sorry, pastor, this can be such a messy business."

"Stay back, doctor. I'm more formidable than I look, but then again that is only my opinion. Feel free to test my tenacity if you feel so Froggy."

"I really don't have the time or patience for this." Looking beyond the pastor, he shouted, "Eugene, please grab the dear pastor and let's end this!"

Raeford McCrery twirled around, swinging the lamp base with reckless abandon. No Eugene stood behind him. He so easily had taken the bait. Lincoln moved swiftly, plunging the syringe that he had previously retrieved from his desk drawer into the pastor's back. Raeford gained his footing and turned to face his attacker. He managed one glancing blow along the doctor's left cheek before he collapsed to the floor.

Lincoln touched his cheek, felt the gash, then saw the blood on his finger tips. Anger rose in him like lava in an erupting volcano. He planted a solid size ten and half shoe to the pastor's chin. Blood oozed onto the Persian rug from his mouth. "Fire and brimstone, so unbecoming...well best I perform a little autopsy, pastor. Maybe you have a few useful organs. Waste not, want not. I suppose I better phone Brother Eugene. He's not going to be very happy with this dreadful predicament you have brought upon us. If I can somehow complete the remaining items on our list, with your assistance of course, it could defuse some of my brother's anger. Thank you for being so kind as to pay Jorge's debt."

Rocking Your World Telecast Preparation

"Okay, sheriff, so I assume you and your team of crime fighters approve the content of tonight's show for the Mexican murders?"

"Footage of the crime scene is fine, Rocker. I see nothing wrong with the filmed interviews with Preacher McCrery or any of the investigating officers. I'm a little antsy about some of the interviews you conducted with the locals, but I suppose the public must show their mixed opinions about the case and our handling of the investigation. But let me make this perfectly clear. You can't show bias toward the department. What about you, Pierce?"

"Looks fine to me, Woody...I mean Sheriff. It can't be sugarcoated or the viewing audience won't buy it."

"Okay then," answered Rocker, glancing over to his producer. "You heard them, it's a go. We go live on prime time at nine tonight."

Surprised Trudy said, "Live, I thought you pre-recorded your shows?"

The producer spoke up, "Most of our shows are pre-recorded, but it's not uncommon for us to mix it with live commentary, or on location shoots if the story calls for it. Lance will be reporting live from the burial site then we'll cut to the various file footage we have filmed throughout the telecast if that's acceptable to you of course."

"Just keep your people on this side of the yellow tape and no closer."

"Sure thing, Sheriff, I see no problem with that."

"All right, then we have a go. We stick to the script just like you have approved, Sheriff, and I promise you have Deputy Rocker's word, as far as this case is concerned, no surprises."

After Lance Rocker and his producer departed from the premises Trudy confided in Woody. "So I hear that lowlife, Scat, has been released on bail?"

"That's correct; several hours ago just like I predicted."

"You should have allowed me to put a tail on him."

"Stay out of it and that's an order. You have plenty to keep you busy, so restrict your team efforts to investigating and solving those murders. I can assign others to the robbery detail."

"My, aren't we just a ray of sunshine today, Sheriff?"

"Goes with the territory, I'm afraid. I now understand how Hank developed heart problems, rest his soul."

Trudy departed to join her CSI unit but was still bothered by the robbery case and its connection with the Klan and the Hispanic implications. It all just seemed much too coincidental to her. She shrugged. Woody was right. She had plenty on her plate right now, this case and Brady's deteriorating condition.

SOS she thought. I still seem to have problems with my prioritization. I just subconsciously placed Brady second on the list. I suppose that's an improvement from third, but Mom is no longer in second, so what does that really say for me and my pathetic existence. I've always allowed my work to rule my life. I promised to do better after Mom died; broken promises again.

Walking into the room she smiled and greeted her team. "So catch me up to speed. Have we solved our little crime spree yet?"

Captain spoke first, "Nothing more from forensics; impeccably clean room practices were definitely used when doing the dirty deed, and even afterwards. Every cadaver so far has been squeaky clean except for those bitten and the lipstick. In all my years I have never seen anything like it."

"No new peculiar Hispanic murders or disappearances meeting our profile have shown up on the radar screen, I sadly report," stated Detective Tim Burroughs. "But I did see something you and the Sheriff may be interested in checking out."

"I'm all ears."

"A rental car, belonging to one Samantha Burton has been discovered off the beaten path down in Georgetown County. It had been stripped down and it appears that our ex-sheriff has been reported missing by her housekeeper."

"Damn," commented Trudy, hoping she wouldn't be considered a suspect in her disappearance. "Keep me in the loop on that one, Tim. I'll tell the Sheriff." What's the irony in this, she thought? Had Sam tried to blackmail the wrong person? She mourned for the loss of any human life, but selfishly thought it couldn't happen to a more deserving person, if indeed something terrible had happened to her. It would tidy up her little situation, providing there were no more copies of those photos stashed away on her premises. That would surely link her as a prime suspect in the woman's disappearance.

Any good investigator would quickly tie in Sam's resignation, those photos, her vehicle and her now missing as more than just coincidence. This could get ugly, very quickly she thought. Brady may have just gotten bumped back to third. This was more than a mere distraction. She could be in for the fight of her life if her worse case scenario panned out.

Yep, she thought. This could be a show stopper and career ender even, if she was ever proven guilty, which she certainly wasn't. Worse still, Woody was involved in her little counter blackmail scheme, if it came to light.

When had she become so corrupt and unethical? She sighed, thinking this just proved that crime doesn't pay on any level, especially for those responsible for upholding the law. Right is right; wrong is still wrong. She had definitely crossed the line too many times lately. Perfection is just a myth. Honesty is a flaw. Facing the music is not just for musicians. *Oh well, nothing to do now but hold my breath and cross my fingers, and hope like hell that Sam was alive and well somewhere.*

The Hawthorn Compound

"L.T., do you have this subconscious desire to bring us crashing down?" asked Brother Eugene.

Lincoln cringed because Eugene never called him L.T. except when he was highly irritated with him. Obviously highly irritated didn't do justice to his present mood.

"You murdered a damn Sheriff and now a minister, both of whom have received media coverage of late," shouted Eugene Hawthorne. "Let's set off the fire works, wave some flags and yell for them to come on over and cuff us. Cassandra vanishes and then you just lose it. This is becoming much too sloppy, Brother."

"Good news, I was able to salvage enough items from the case to complete this week's requests. I bought us some valuable time, Big Brother."

"And now you speak in your coded riddles, what's the point?"

"His car is in the garage and the empty case is still in the donor room."

"Did you not consider that someone from his church may know that he had been headed over here?"

"Eugene, he solved the puzzle while here to pay that young associate pastor's past due bill. I didn't invite him here with the intent of doing this. I had no choice. I could not allow him to leave and report his suspicions to the authorities."

"There are always choices but you're correct, allowing him to leave wasn't an option. I apologize for my rage. I'll make the necessary arrangements to dispose of the evidence and your empty case. Please promise me you will not collect any more celebrities."

"I promise, and I've been thinking."

"So that's what distracted you," Eugene chuckled.

"Maybe the time is appropriate for us to disband our operation and relocate."

"Wisdom, finally, I'm ready for retirement."

"We have ten days before our next order is due so that should be adequate time for us to make the necessary preparations don't you think?"

"Indeed I do. Only one problem, haven't funds already been deposited for that purchase?"

"Yes but if we make any attempt to return it, we would most certainly tip our hand, don't you think?"

"We're not going to be their most favorite people regardless when we close up shop, so I really don't think it will matter. I have a few connections so I'll have them prepare us a new identity."

"I'll liquidate what I can, and what you say we burn down the compound and stage three empty cases here to throw them off our trail?"

"You have been giving this considerable thought haven't you? Do we have three empty cases that match?"

"Not yet," he smiled. "If you will humor me just one more time..."

"I don't seem to have a choice, do I?"

"There are always choices," countered Lincoln, taking a dig at Eugene.

"Touché," replied Eugene.

Rocking Your World Telecast

Lance Rocker reviewed his material for tonight's show while pacing in front of the crime scene's yellow tape. Mosquitoes and gnats swarmed and buzzed his face. Luckily the repellent warded off any direct contact with his precious tanned skin.

"Live in ten minutes," yelled one of the crewmen.

Still shaken and troubled by news of the discovery of Samantha Burton's automobile in Georgetown County, Lance wondered if she had indeed covered her tracks well enough so that the dotted line wouldn't lead back to him. The larger mystery, where was Sam?

Interesting he thought, Sam giving me those explicit photographs of Pierce, and then vanishing into thin air. Could the lovely detective have had something to do with her disappearance? Had she been trying to retrieve the additional copies of the photos? Maybe she had gotten wind that Sam had not been on the up and up with her and decided to settle the score? Rocker just couldn't peg the detective as a murderer, but one can never know about these matters.

He could have gotten more juiced up over this if he, too, wasn't sort of caught in the web. He still had those photos so how best to use them to his advantage without incriminating himself? If Sam was actually dead and the she-devil detective had anything to do with it, then he could be endangering himself by confronting her. But would she try anything if she knew he had the photos? It didn't protect Sam did it, he thought. He could have been the last one to see her alive if indeed she wasn't.

He wondered how come all the woman he screwed lately seemed to end up dead or missing. This didn't sound very promising for his possible defense did it? He would weigh his options very carefully.

"Five minutes Lance," yelled the producer this time. "Makeup, see to him please."

Rocker ran through the scenario in his head, wondering if any of the recent events could actually be connected. He didn't have a clincher so he would just throw out theory. His viewing audience would eat this up. The ratings would most certainly sky rocket off the charts. Lance Rocker would be back on top.

"Okay, 5, 4, 3, 2, 1...you're live, Lance."

"Good evening and welcome to Rocking Your World. I'm your host, Lance Rocker. We're live from the burial site of what has been reported to be the graves for at least 103 Hispanic men. Authorities estimate these murders spanned a period of a half dozen years in what they have dubbed a well organized and highly proficient organ and body parts retrieval business. Tonight you will hear comments from the CSI unit, local and professional opinions and view actual excavation footage from the scene behind me. I warn you some will be graphic and is suitable for mature audiences only. I would suggest parental discretion."

Pierce Beach home

Trudy pulled into the drive, still stressed over Sam Burton's disappearance. The back floodlights were on which meant Brady was on the deck enjoying the sights and sounds of the ebbing ocean and beach scenery. She hoped he had cocktails iced and ready for consumption. She needed a drink very badly.

Entering the house, she quickly freshened up then disrobed to a tee shirt and undies before eventually reaching the back deck. "Lucy, I'm home," she announced in her best female voice, mimicking *Desi Arnaz* as *Ricky Ricardo*.

"I'm out here," he yelled from the deck in a thick tongued response, no mimicking on his part.

He handed her a chilled glass of wine, greeting her at the door. "Sweetie this will do, to break the ice, but you better break out the hard stuff, your Jack," she said, kissing him, then collapsing in his arms.

"Tough day huh, you never drink Bourbon.

"It's the perfect time to start. How are you doing?"

"Peeing orange tonight, and if I could figure a way to swirl the purple with it, I would try out for the Clemson mascot. What happened to get you so worked up? You couldn't have already seen Rocker's show."

"What, no I haven't," she said, confused by his statement.

"Not to worry, I recorded it for you, so what's eating you?"

"You do remember Samantha Burton. Well they found her automobile stripped down and deserted in a remote part of Georgetown County."

"Her car?" asked an astonished Brady. "I haven't seen it on the news."

"It hasn't made the wire yet and actually it really wasn't her car, which makes this even stranger. Woody has been in touch with the Georgetown authorities and, exercising professional courtesy, they have shared aspects of the case with him. The car was a rental. Why would she rent a car to drive from Charleston to Georgetown, when she obviously owns several vehicles?"

"It does sound strange, but given her perverted dark side, maybe she was up to something she didn't want anyone to know about."

"Yeah, that did cross my mind too. It gets worse. She's missing. Her housekeeper reported it. They found the car's rental paperwork in her name in the console and a receipt from a Georgetown motel, paid in cash."

"So maybe she went on a blind date and it got out of hand?"

"Makes sense, given her fetishes and preferences. Where's my Jack and make mine straight, none of that cola crap. Sorry, that sounded sort of demanding. Pretty please, could I try your bourbon?"

"Coming up, Princess," he smiled, standing very stiffly and awkwardly, walking toward the bar.

"I'm concerned, Circus Boy, what if she's dead? I could be a prime suspect, if they find more photos and connect it to me. And Woody, he assisted me in blackmailing her. Motive, motive, motive..."

"So did you whack her or did you have her whacked, *Tony Soprano*?"

"I'm not kidding here Brady. This isn't funny."

"I know you're not, and I almost hate to be the one to really send you over the edge, but we better go inside and watch Rocker's show. You're not going to like it I can promise you."

"We previewed the footage and script for the Hispanic murders and saw nothing offensive for the department or detrimental to our investigation. We gave him the thumbs up to proceed. He gave us his word."

"And he kept it about that case," he assured her.

She flopped onto the loveseat beside him and said "What the hell has that bastard done now?"

"Finish that shot first and then allow me to pour you another before I play it for you. Please promise me you won't throw something at the 52 inch."

Before Brady could start the recording the phone rang. Trudy recognized the special ring tone on her cell phone. "Hello Woody. No, I was just about to watch it. Brady recorded it for me. So what did he do? Fine, I'll watch it and call you back."

She looked at Brady and motioned for him to start it. She thought how Woody was sounding and acting more like Hank with every passing day. She downed her Jack, sending a shiver through her. She wondered how in the hell did anyone drink this stuff.

Horry County Police Department
6:25 AM

Trudy walked into Sheriff Woodrow Anderson's office and eyed Woody sitting behind his desk, CCU coffee mug in one hand and what looked like a Ziploc sandwich bag with ice held on the back of his neck. She recalled how she dreaded facing Hank Singleton in this very same office under similar circumstances.

"Good morning Woody or maybe not..."

"You look like dog crap yourself," he remarked after placing the Ziploc on his desk.

"So what do we do with our innovative Deputy Rocker?"

"Well I've slept very little and have given it a lot of thought. I've got to hand it to him. He stayed true to his word on our prime case. He didn't alter any of the footage or his script. I guess we didn't do a very good job calculating his allotted time or we would have realized he had that extra ten minutes or so remaining."

"So," prompted Trudy.

"So, we do nothing," finished Woody.

"Hold on Woody. He interviewed Scat when he exited the jail after making bail, and he allowed him to spew about the department, accusing us of trying to hang those robberies on him and the Klan instead of Hispanic gangs. Then he follows that up with how a rivalry could be brewing between the KKK and Hispanic gang on the Grand Strand, and you're going to do nothing?"

"And it's not KKK, its IKA, Imperial Klans of America. What can I do? Pressure him for his informant, lock him up, and beat the crap out of him. He didn't do anything unlawful or breach our agreement. I agree, he is still a lowlife, but that's not illegal."

"You do realize that Scat mentioned by name at least three Hispanic gangs that he has pegged for perpetrating those robberies, and how we had allegedly accused the IKA and him specifically of committing the crimes instead, in an attempt to stir the pot. He may have just single handedly instigated a war between those very gangs and this new version of the Klan."

"So we'll monitor the situation. Think about it. It could keep Brock and his boys in check for a while with his alleged conspiracy plan out in the open. He'll most certainly tone down their activity to displace any suspicion."

"But what if we have an increase in gang activity?"

"So who do you think they will be taking it out on? Not the community; they'll go after Brock, Scat and their hatemongers. It's win-win for us."

"I don't know about this Woody, it's too cynical, even for you," said Trudy, rubbing her weary bloodshot eyes.

"Let me try painting this shed a different way. We couldn't get a confession out of Scat, then what does he do? He blabs his mouth all over national television, bringing light to the case. How do you think the Klan is going to take him airing their dirty laundry?"

"So we wait and we watch, allow it to run its course, is that it?"

"And we hope they slip up. Who knows, they could request police protection if the gangs crank up the pressure on them. I bet my old school buddy would surely cough it up to save his sorry ass, and then we could cut him a deal if he offered up Brock and his accomplices."

"Then, case closed, we would have them where we want them, Sheriff."

"Exactly," he grinned, removing the ice bag once again from his neck.

"Is there anything new on Sam?"

"Georgetown police are following the lead to that motel and asking who remembers her and if they saw her with anyone. But we have another one that might perk your interest."

"I'll bite, what do you have?"

"You remember your Pentecostal Preacher, Raeford McCrery. It seems he's been reported missing."

"First his associate pastor, Jorge Cruz, and now him... this is no coincidence is it?"

"And he's not Hispanic so what does that mean?"

"Are you thinking what I'm thinking, Woody?"

"He may have identified then confronted our killers."

"Or he stumbled into the hornet's nest by accident. We're on it. This could just be the break we needed. And Woody, please keep me posted on any news about Sam."

"You know it. Try not to fret about that one right now. There's no trail leading back to us."

"Yet..."

"You didn't kill her, did you?"

"Woody, I can't believe..."

"Just kidding, go catch those low life murderers," he said, taking a sip of nasty cold coffee.

The Hawthorne Clinic

"They found her car, Eugene. It was stripped down like you said it would be, found down in Georgetown County. When you get this message, give me a call," said Lincoln, leaving a voice message on his brother's cell phone.

All files pertaining to the abducted donors had always been destroyed by Cassandra after she delivered the merchandise for harvesting. This included ensuring no entries existed on the sign-in log. Lincoln had failed to do the same for the donor he had retrieved and harvested on the clinic premises, an oversight on his part.

Too many days had expired since Cassandra vanished. Both Lincoln and Eugene feared the worst. Little sister had to be among the deceased. Hindsight told him he should report her and the jeep missing, but the jeep was registered to him.

What if he called it in as stolen and what if Cassandra's lifeless body was discovered in the jeep, he wondered. No, he had to keep mum. There wasn't anything he could do for her now. The office phone rang and after four rings he finally willed himself to answer it.

"What were you thinking L.T.?" screamed Eugene. "Don't leave incriminating messages on answering machines or cell phone voice mail. That's evidence, you big moron."

"Sorry, I wasn't thinking."

"You've been doing a lot of that lately. Yeah I saw it. It's all over the television about the police finding her rental automobile," said Eugene, calming his voice. "So what, they didn't find her and never will I assure you."

"What about the minister's car?"

"I torched it before dumping it into the swamp. It sank like a rock. Nobody will be finding it for a very long time."

"And the minister..."

"Stop your worrying. It's been taken care of too. How's it going here?"

"Hard copy records are gone and I'll be taking my laptop with me. There are no other electronic records," he replied

"We should have our new identities by the end of the week; passports, drivers licenses, birth certificates, new credit cards and such," stated Eugene. "I've been thinking, let's ransack this place before we torch the compound then it will make it look like whoever burned the house was here first."

"Good thinking..."

"This is turning into a real mess, L.T."

"Eugene, I wish you wouldn't worry so much. We've been doing this for years and we haven't come close to being caught."

"Wake up, Brother. Cassandra is missing. She alone supplied us with donors. She's our sister and she could be dead for al we know."

"I pray she is not."

"Speaking of praying, a pastor and his associate pastor are part of this now. This will not go away. Top that off with you murdering a sheriff."

"Must I remind you, she was no longer the sheriff?"

"Splitting hairs, my point is you colored outside the lines, L.T. We weren't supposed to harvest those with traceable identities."

"Circumstances beyond my control, I assure you."

"It really doesn't matter now. This over, and the sooner we can disappear, the better."

"Without Cassandra..."

"She's not coming back to us L.T. Face the facts."

"We can't just allow her to vanish."

"You mean like those we've..."

"I mean, we can't leave her out there, period."

"What are we supposed to do, L.T., go to the police and report her missing?"

"We should have a funeral for her."

"We can do that before we leave."

"That sounds fine, Eugene. I'll prepare our last shipment."

"You do that, Brother. I'll see you later."

Cash and Pay Pawn Shop
Socastee

Brock had flipped the sign to Closed, and then he walked to the back room where Scat stood and twitched nervously. He had already given Scat a severe tongue lashing. Brock had threatened him to within an inch of his miserable life for what he had spoken about on the news segment.

Brock had informed Scat that the Grand Wizard had called him and stated he expected extreme measures to be taken in alleviating the problem. Scat still didn't know what he had meant by extreme measures.

Brock stood there a second time, red faced, veins pulsating in his neck and speechless. Scat hated it when he said nothing.

"I know I really screwed up," Scat spoke up. "Tell you what. I'll just quit and get the hell out of Dodge. That should make the Grand Wizard happy. I'll just drop off the face of the earth. I don't want to face those drug charges anyway so it works perfectly for me. I have no intention of going to prison."

Brock remained silent but had gripped a pistol concealed just below the cash register. He had received his explicit instructions earlier and had hidden the weapon complete with a silencer before Scat had arrived. Murder was no stranger to Brock. He had proven his loyalty many times, but not in recent years.

"Tell them you disposed of me if it will help you save your reputation, Brock. I'll pack my things up and get the hell out of here today. I'll disappear."

Brock fondled the pistol's grip and eased his finger over the trigger while maintaining direct eye contact with the babbling Scat. A van had been conveniently parked in the alleyway behind the pawn shop. Its back floor was lined with plastic. An assortment of tools were stored in the passenger seat (shovel, ax, saw), everything he needed for dismantling then disposing of the blabber mouth.

A loud crash from the front of the shop drew both men's attention. "Damn it," whispered Brock, suspecting robbery because this particular site had been broken into numerous times.

Instinctively retrieving the pistol from its hiding place, Brock turned to face the intruders, making splinters of the entrance door in the shop's showroom. Scat caught sight of the silencer equipped gun and suddenly realized it had been intended for him. Brock had called him here to ice him.

Three men exploded though the entryway to the backroom, all clutching Uzis. Scat took advantage of the developing situation and dove behind storage shelves that offered him safe passage and cover toward the rear exit. If he remained low to the floor like a slithering snake he might just make it.

The MS-13 gang members opened up simultaneously spraying bullets in a sweeping motion. Brock Boudreaux had been practically cut in half by the barrage, but not before he got off a couple of clean shots nailing the middle shooter in the chest and dropping him dead.

Scat sprung up and shouldered his way through the back door, pressing the release mechanism and stumbling into the alleyway, almost crashing into the back doors of the white van. His face smeared against the back windows, he spotted the plastic and instantly knew that it had been positioned to keep blood from his body from contaminating the inside of the van.

Righting himself, he darted around the left side of the van, glancing over his shoulder for any sign of the shooters, but saw no one. He heard shots being rattled off inside. The gang members were leaving their calling card.

Just before he reached the corner of the building, two more Hispanics stepped into view, blocking his escape. Both sported Uzis. Scat stood there unarmed and defenseless, all hope lost. Turning to seek refuge behind the white meat wagon intended for him, he saw the other two gunmen emerging from the pawn shop's back door.

There was nowhere to hide and nowhere left to run. He did the only thing he could do. He dropped to his knees, tears running down his cheeks and pleaded for mercy, a deal, something. The four gunman opened fire, in no mood to negotiate a compromise. Sirens blared in the background but Scat never heard them.

Pentecostal Church
North Myrtle Beach

Trudy, accompanied by Detectives Sylvester Stone and Tim Burroughs, stood on the front lawn of the church's parsonage. Elaine McCrery, the pastor's wife, sat in a rocking chair on the front porch, being consoled by several of the church's members. She wore a long sleeved blouse buttoned up to her neck, a pleated khaki dress reaching just below her knees, her hair tucked into a little bun and she wore very little, if any, make-up.

Mrs. McCrery, some ten years younger than her sixty five year old husband, looked much older. Wide at the hips, flat bellied and with an eye catching pair of breast; she could have been a stunning lady dressed in a sweater and jeans, but she held firm to her faith and dressed modestly.

Trudy sat down in another rocking chair beside her and asked for the others to please be excused, because she had a few questions to ask her. She smiled at Trudy, an angelic smile, nothing put on about it. "Have you found my Raeford?" she asked.

"No ma'am," answered Trudy. "Are you up for a few questions?"

"Why yes. If it will help you in finding Raeford, please ask your questions," she responded in a tone that defined her moral fiber.

"When was the last time you saw your husband?"

She took a deep breath then replied, "He had been packing up Jorge's personal belongings. We so miss that young man. He was destined to be a wonderful pastor. He spoke and preached from the heart."

"Yes ma'am. I can imagine your grief. So what happened next?"

"Raeford found an unpaid medical bill among Jorge's things. I didn't even know our young pastor was having any medical problems. He always seemed healthy enough. That Raeford, he believed in doing the right thing. He told me that he owed it to Jorge to clear any debt."

"Do you remember the origin of this bill?"

"No dear. He didn't mention where. I do remember the amount was seventy five dollars because he asked me for the money. Raeford never carried more than ten or fifteen dollars in his wallet."

"So that was the last time you saw him."

"Yes, it was just after seven o'clock, yesterday. I phoned the police station last night at quarter past ten, but they told me he wasn't a missing person after only three hours unless I suspected foul play or he had serious medical problems. I insisted he was indeed missing, but the nice young lady told me she would file the report and for me to call back today, if he didn't come home. He was still missing at that time too."

"Police procedure, I assure you it was nothing personal. We react to missing children or juveniles immediately or someone handicapped or medically impaired. Unfortunately adults can come and go as they please and we don't have the resources to run down every single one unless you suspect foul play."

"Do you suspect foul play?"

"Not to upset you ma'am, but it does seem peculiar that two pastors from the same church have vanished. Your young associate pastor met such a tragic ending."

"Detective, do you think those same people wanted my Raeford for his internal organs? His aren't in prime shape I'm sure, but I love every fiber in that old body of his. We are supposed to celebrate our twenty-first wedding anniversary next week. We were both widowed you know. My first husband died of cancer and his wife died in an automobile accident. A drunk driver crashed into her car while she sat at a stop sign."

"I'm sorry to hear that. Do you remember anything else? My officers have the description and license plate of your car."

"No, I don't believe so," she replied, a tear rolling down her cheek. "Please find him and bring him back to me."

"We'll do our very best," Trudy assured her, suspecting he was probably already dead and the chances of them ever finding his body slim at best.

She walked over to Sly and Tim. "Did you two dig up anything?"

"Neighbor saw him leave and turn south around 1900 yesterday," responded Sly.

"The Caddie did have *On Star* so I've called to see if they can pinpoint its location. I'm waiting for them to call me back," added Tim.

"He had to have fallen prey to the same bastards, I'm sure of it," growled Trudy. "Jorge's unpaid medical bill led him right to their doorstep. He either decided to do a little private investigating of his own, or he just put two and two together during his visit. Regardless, that $75 debt most likely cost him his life."

Tim's cell phone rang. "Yes, oh, well thanks for your quick response. No luck. The system is not responding. They suspect it has either been destroyed or deactivated manually."

"You're right," pointed out Sly. "The good reverend is dead. I doubt we'll ever find his remains or not anytime soon."

"But now we know we're dealing with a legit medical facility of some sort," smiled Trudy. "So what type of facility would deal with mostly illegal aliens?"

"Clinics or emergency rooms, private practices," replied Sly.

"Let's rule out emergency rooms only because they're linked to hospitals and make available too many witnesses, too much activity and it would be more difficult to manipulate the records," stated Trudy.

"Private practices?" asked Tim.

"Same deal. There would be too many ordinary folks, people with insurance where everybody knows your name and, unless the entire practice was corrupt, record cover-up would be difficult," Trudy surmised.

"Then that leaves clinics," stated Sly.

"Clinics, wouldn't that be where most illegal aliens would go for repeat visits?" she asked. "But we did a preliminary of all the medical facilities, doctors, and so forth already."

"Only on paper or electronically," answered Tim. "We didn't actually go door to door. We screened them based on reputation, track records, dependability of their staff and so forth. Nothing really jumped out at us."

"Tim, give me a number. Just how big is the elephant we're about to try eating?" she asked. "Restrict it to just Horry County for now."

"This is retirement central, and with all the seniors here, there's no shortage of medical facilities."

"Break the numbers down for me when you have them...practical, dental, orthopedic, chiropractic, etc."

"Anything else?" asked Tim Burroughs.

"Location, location, location...tell me which ones offer seclusion, are off the beaten path or may be located south of here. Our female in the convertible sports car, let's keep her in mind, too."

Sly walked over to his cruiser to respond to an incoming call on the radio. He returned with a long expression on his face. "Robbery over in Socastee, pawn shop and the Sheriff asks us to investigate."

"What, no police officers in the area?" asked Trudy.

"There was some sort of a shootout with automatic weapons. We have two, possibly three persons down. It's owned by Brock Boudreaux. Officers are on the scene."

"Double crap," exclaimed Trudy.

"It sounds like this could be messy."

"If this Brock Boudreaux is involved, I can only imagine. He's probably instigated some sort of racial uprising."

"If we're lucky we'll have the opportunity to bust him."

"Sly, people like Brock always tend to skirt the law. It's like a gift. Let's roll and see what we have at that pawn shop."

"Maybe this will be our lucky day. We're due for a break, that's for sure."

"Beach life is never dull here along the Grand Strand."

Cash and Pay Pawn Shop
Socastee

Trudy had sent Tim back to the station to work on the clinics list. She and Sly arrived at the pawn shop to quite a mêlée. Over fifty people had crowded the streets and storefront adjacent to Brock's business. Lance Rocker was already on the scene and was the only news media inside the yellow taped barricade. She would have to remember to ask Woody to confiscate that deputy badge and de-deputize him. She should have done that after the Road Rage case.

"Well, well, Detective Pierce, dragging your ass in here as always, I see," smarted off Rocker.

"Stifle it," she snapped, pointing her finger in his face.

She approached the on-scene officer," So what do we have here, Officer Potter?" She asked, seeing his name on his shirt.

"Two dead inside, and another in the alley in the back," he recapped. "One witness said he saw three, maybe four Latino looking men exit the premises brandishing what he described as Tommy Guns, Uzis, I would say by the description of the gunfire."

"Do we know who the victims are?" asked Trudy.

"Well, one is definitely a Hispanic and by the colors, I would say a gang member. My partner over there says he thinks he may be a MS-19, but we've not heard of any presence of that gang in this area, so that has not been confirmed."

"And the other two..,"

"Wallet from the one inside indicates his name is Brock Boudreaux. Manager of the Dollar General next door says he owns the pawn shop. It's about as bad as it gets. He's cut to pieces. It doesn't look like a simple run of the mill robbery attempt to me. I think it was some sort of a hit."

"What about the one in the ally?"

"ID says he's Dwayne A. Crowder," he responded, noticing the expression on her face. "You know these men."

She nodded, yes.

"We found a forty-five by Boudreaux," said the officer. "Get this; it was equipped with a silencer. I don't know who was trying to assassinate whom."

Rocker spoke up, "I guess you're going to try to blame me for this because of that segment I ran last night."

"Let's do the math," stated Trudy, "You interview Scat. He spills his guts about the rash of robberies, and how the police are determined to blame him and the Klan for them. Then you point out to your viewing audience this little theory about the IKL possibly staging those robberies in order to pin them on Hispanic Gangs. Oh yeah, you share more file footage of Brock at that Pavilion rally and insinuate him to be the leader of possibly orchestrating the scheme. Wow...now we have this. Am I leaving anything out?"

Rocker stood speechless, enjoying the closeness and visualizing the photos Sam had given him. He had his own little Rocker fantasy in motion.

"Look around you. This was as good as putting a target on both men's backs. Thanks to you they're both deader than hell and we have one dead gang member on the premises to boot. What would you call it, Mister Rocket Scientist?"

Lance didn't respond but instead pressed against Trudy. She noticed his obvious maneuver and pulled away and motioned for the two officers to escort Lance Rocker to his car and to make sure he exited the area. If he didn't cooperate, they were to handcuff him and arrest him. "And don't fall for the deputy badge again," she warned them.

"Not so boring around here is it," commented Sly.

"Call Captain and get his butt down here. You two go over this scene with a fine tooth comb. I'll be back at the station. I need to have a friendly chat with our Sheriff."

"What about Lance Rocker?"

"He's on my short list."

Horry County Police Department
Sheriff Woodrow Anderson's Office

"Call for you on line three, Sheriff," advised the officer at the front desk.

"Sheriff Anderson, what can I do for you?"

"Up to your ass in bodies again I see," said the voice on the other end of the line. "Seems to be your trademark," the voice now chuckled.

Like a voice from beyond the grave taunting him, Woody cringed at the caller's sarcasm. Immediately recognizing the caller he responded, "Tim Ford, are you still enjoying your accommodations at Lieber?" Lieber Correctional Institute in Ridgeville, S.C. was where the state housed the worst of the worst, including those waiting on death row.

"Three squares a day and some of the most interesting roomies," he replied, smoothly as always.

"So, why do you honor me with a phone call? Do you have more confessions you would like us to record?"

"Enjoy Deputy, I mean Sheriff. My lawyer is working an appeal to get me out of here," Tim Ford advised Woody. "That little unlawful collaboration orchestrated by you, Deputy Wagner, and that District Attorney will be my ticket to freedom."

"You played that card during the trial and look where it got you, roommate of Big Bubba."

"We have a new angle and more evidence I assure you. It will prove just how unethical your department is, especially you and that Wagner."

"Pierce, you forget, she's happily married now."

"So tell me. Who are you framing for those Hispanic murders? I'm in here so I suppose I'm in the clear. Why don't you just leave them alone? They're doing what big government and law enforcement are afraid to do. Rid this country of the illegal cockroaches."

"Isn't your time about up?"

"I saw Lance Rocker's show. He certainly exposed your department for what it is, a bunch of incompetent stooges incapable of convicting a jaywalker."

"You're behind bars aren't you?"

"Not for long and when I get out..."

"This has been fun but I have a life to enjoy and you have...oh, I'm sorry twenty years of three squares and bubba-land. Whose little bitch are you this week?" Woody heard the guard tell Ford his time was indeed up.

"Not to worry Sheriff, you'll be seeing me soon enough and kiss Wagner's ass for me. Oops, sorry, that would be your job wouldn't it? Enjoy your life while you can, Mister Widow Man." The line went dead.

Ford had stung him good with that last reference to his deceased wife, Janice. Woody had done a good job putting that Road Rage mess behind him, or so he had thought. Ford had almost gotten off clean for the Bradshaw murder and if not for Pierce's tenacity and determination, he probably would have gotten away with it.

Yeah, they tiptoed down the line on obtaining that confession and conviction, but look how many times open and shut cases had been thrown out on a technicality. Justice had been served in the Tim Ford case and let his sorry butt rot in prison.

A knock at the door jarred Woody back into the real world. He looked up to see Trudy standing in the doorway. She had a pissed off expression.

"Okay, what's got your panties in a wad?"

"And I might ask you the same thing...Sheriff. You were certainly into that phone call. You didn't even hear me call to you."

"Oh, just one of those dreaded media calls that come with the territory." He fibbed, figuring she had enough on her plate without having to deal with Ford. "What about you?"

"What else?" she responded. "Lance Rocker..."

"What did he do this time?"

"Well he had already flashed his deputy badge at the local police at the pawn shop shooting and gained entry. He knows the whole story."

"And that is..."

"Brock Boudreaux and Scat Crowder were murdered and one unidentified MS-19 gang member was found dead on the premises from apparent return fire from Boudreaux. His pistol was equipped with a silencer."

"Silencer," replied Woody, now standing up and placing both hands on his desk, reminiscent of Hank Singleton's mannerisms.

"I think he planned to kill Scat but four, possibly five gang members disrupted his plan and the visitors killed both of them instead, all because of Rocker's implications on his show."

"Well, we certainly knew this would be a possibility, didn't we?"

"Woody, if Rocker reports this incident in his next telecast, you do realize we could have an all out war in Horry County, especially if the IKL retaliate."

"Couldn't happen to a nicer bunch of people," replied Woody, flopping backwards into his leather chair.

"Innocent people could be caught in the crossfire. My conscience has haunted me ever since our poor decisions on the Road Rage case. We should have involved the Feds instead of shouldering it ourselves. We went against Hank's orders just so we could be the ones to capture Road Rage and solve the crimes. Innocent people were killed because of our selfish judgment."

"Don't think you're alone in reliving that one. We talked about it then, and we certainly can't undo it now."

"This is our chance at redemption."

"Any ideas?"

"Rocker," she replied.

"I thought he was our problem."

"And our salvation," she replied. "How about having some officers pick him up and bring him in ASAP? Leave the rest to me."

Woody nodded and made the call. He took a deep breath and asked, "What about our Hispanic body snatcher case?"

"I have Tim running another check on clinics in Horry County after interviewing Preacher McCrery's widow. It seems McCrery had found an unpaid bill in Jorge Cruz's things and apparently decided to go pay it. We think he found our killers and, if he did, he is most likely dead too. We're close. I can feel it."

"Keep me in the loop, and I do mean in the loop; not how we undermined Hank, if you get my drift."

"Come on Woody. I'd never do that to you. What about Sam? Is there any news from Georgetown police on their motel investigation?"

"I haven't heard anything lately but I'll give them a buzz. Why don't you call it a day?"

"I will after I check with Tim. Afterwards, I do need to get home and find out what color Brady is peeing today."

Woody smiled, thinking at least she had someone to go home to, remembering what Ford had smarted off about Janice. Sure, she had been unfaithful and had slept with, of all people, Lance Rocker, but she hadn't deserved to die. He couldn't undo what had happened. His career had always come first. It had cost him dearly. He still had his litter of rugrats. He would try his best to put them ahead of his career, but right now his career was winning that battle.

Hawthorne Compound

Lincoln had tidied things up at the clinic, having destroyed all the hard copies. No incriminating electronic records existed there. His personal laptop did hold the truth. Still, no word about Cassandra and that kept him on edge.

Brother Eugene had gone to pick up their new identities. They had decided not to close any bank accounts nor withdraw any suspicious large sums. When the time came, the authorities must be convinced that all three died in the fire. That is if Cassandra wasn't found elsewhere before or after they departed the country.

His task at hand, locate three individuals that matched their profiles. Three bodies had to be planted and discovered in the compound fire. The fire would have to be intense to prevent any dental matches or possibly of DNA confirmation. He and Eugene still had a lot to accomplish if they planned to leave within the next nine days.

Missing the deadline would not be detrimental but it had been established as their goal. Neither Lincoln nor Eugene had any reason to believe they were under investigation. No lawmen had come sniffing around. Their little enterprise had been operating flawlessly, until dear sis had gone MIA.

The phone rang and the caller identified himself as Marion County law enforcement. Lincoln tried to remain calm. "Yes, this is Lincoln Hawthorne, how may I assist you, officer?"

"Mister Hawthorne, we have a Jeep Commander registered in your name," stated the officer, reciting the license plate number and description of the vehicle.

"Yes, it does belong to me," he confirmed, trying not to hyperventilate, preparing for news about his sister.

"Two Hispanic males are being held on various charges. They were driving your vehicle. Had you allowed them to borrow your vehicle?"

Lincoln hesitated. He didn't know how to answer. Did this mean they hadn't found Cassandra? The officer had not mentioned a woman, only two men. He weighed his options and chose his words carefully but before he could answer, the officer stated, "I could find nothing about the vehicle being reported stolen."

"My sister, she had borrowed it," he blurted out. "Is my sister all right?"

"Sister, when is the last time you saw your sister?"

"I haven't talked to her in several days but that's not unusual. Cassandra does her own thing, comes and goes."

"And what is your sister's name?" asked the officer.

"Cassandra Guy..."

The officer took a description of Cassandra Guy from Lincoln then asked, "And where does your sister reside?"

"Here," he replied, almost regretting saying it but what else could he have said. "She lives here at this address with me."

"And you haven't heard from her in several days?"

"She was going to visit and stay with a friend in Florence for a couple of days," he thought fast and made up the tale.

"Can you give me the name of this friend?"

Realizing he had screwed up he responded, "No sir, I can't."

"Pardon me sir; you can't tell me this friend's name?"

Lincoln was perspiring profusely and was glad the officer couldn't see him on the verge of a panic attack. He finally answered, "She was going to meet a man and all I know was that she said he was married. She never told me his name and I never asked. It wasn't any of my business. I didn't want to get involved in such deceitfulness. Officer, where is my sister?"

"I don't know sir. The two males were arrested after they ran a stop sign then attempted to outrun the officers. We found drugs in their possession and unregistered firearms."

"Where is my sister," he yelled.

"I'm not sure sir but we did find blood stains in the back seat. The two gentlemen we now have in custody belong to the Valtos Locos."

"The what?"

"They are Hispanic gang members and are most likely in this country illegally. Could you provide us with a photo of your sister?"

"Absolutely, I can e-mail you one immediately if it will help you find her." Lincoln jotted down the e-mail address. "Do you think these men have harmed Cassandra?"

"I don't know sir. Once I have the photo we will begin that line of questioning. I'm sorry we had to break it to you like this sir."

"Thank you, officer..."

"Detective Peron Davis," he answered, giving him a number where he could be reached.

"Please, Detective Davis, find my sister."

After ending the call, Lincoln phoned Eugene and explained what had happened. They both agreed that this altered their plans. They couldn't do anything with Cassandra now confirmed missing by Marion County police.

Lincoln had always feared one of these abductions could go awry but it never seemed to concern Cassandra. She lived it, breathed it, embraced it and afterwards she so enjoyed toying with the captors, her version of cat and mouse. She did nothing malicious. Hers were acts of sexual foreplay at best, but how she did take pleasure in her little games.

Now she was gone. Lincoln wondered if gang members held her captive somewhere, making her their little sex toy, their play thing. He and his sister were close, so very close; much closer than even Eugene had ever known. He surely missed her.

What if they never found her? What if they did find her alive? But what if they found her dead? What best worked for their situation? Surely there would be publicity either way. Her disappearance would make the news. Hispanics, they were the cancer of this country, he thought. There was no cure for them.

Lincoln poured himself a Cognac and flipped on the television. The lead story, a shootout between a notorious

Hispanic gang and the Ku Klux Klan, there was just no end to it, he thought. Perfect, the attention would focus on gang violence in his sister's disappearance or murder.

Cassandra, just another senseless victim, in the wrong place, at the wrong time, and he and Eugene would mourn like a normal family. The public would view them as victims too. Island life awaited them eventually.

Complicating matters, another deadline approached and this one would require at least two donors. Two, a magical number, he chuckled. They required two also. This could work after all, he smiled. "To Cassandra," he toasted.

Pierce Beach Home

Trudy sat in her police cruiser in her driveway and stared at the house. She watched Brady's silhouette pass the kitchen window. Could they really cure him with all these experimental drugs, she wondered? Maybe she should be spending more time with her husband instead of acting like Super Police Woman.

Life had been so simple back in Ohio. Hers had been work, work, and more work; no mom, no husband, no real life, other than being a detective. She had replayed this scenario in her head way too many times and where had it gotten her? Certainly not back in Ohio, she thought.

Ohio, right she thought. That's where her infamous photographs had been taken. And why, because a stupid relationship had gone bad. Yep, she could pick a loser. She regretted she had just thought that. Brady was no loser. She would be the loser if she ever lost him.

Screw Ohio. I've never been happier.

Speaking of losers, Woody had called her on her way home and they hadn't located Lance Rocker. His producer wasn't sure where he had gone. His cell phone was either off, or Rocker wasn't answering it because the voice message picked up every time. She figured he was just trying to avoid them; the bastard.

Her thoughts ran the gambit. Brock and Scat both dead, she hadn't really expected that, at least not so soon after Rocker's airing of that segment. Sure, she had expected trouble but not to this magnitude. And Sam, just what the hell had happened to her? These distractions made it difficult to focus on the Hispanic organ harvesting case.

Preacher McCrery vanishing had definitely thrown the case a curve ball. No doubt, his disappearance had to be tied to the murderers. And the only known potential suspect, the mystery woman, who was she? Just how big was this operation, and who were the players?

Not to forget about Lance Rocker, she reminded herself. He was an ever present thorn in their sides. They had to bring him under control if that was really possible. She took a deep breath and eased out of the cruiser. She could still see Brady moving about in the house.

Making her way down the pathway that lead to the back she thought, when was the last time I talked to my sister? She had promised herself that after their mom's death she would keep in touch. They had worked hard to repair their fragile relationship. Lately they were sort of backsliding.

Sis hadn't called her in a while. What a hypocrite. She hadn't called her sister either. Atlanta was less than a six hour drive but it may as well be on another planet. Neither of them seemed to feel it important enough to make the drive or even meet one another half way.

Why worry about this now, she wondered. She surely couldn't fix it on her own and wasn't really sure it was worth the effort. Sure it was. She loved Allison. They had bonded since their mother's death. Once the case was over, they would again. She would make sure.

Right now she must focus on Brady. He needed her more. She should go inside and see how her hubby was weathering his storm. Why did she procrastinate so?

Gazing out over the ocean while climbing the deck's steps, Brady completely startled her sitting on the porch swing, an adult beverage in hand. "Glad you decided to join me. I thought your ice would melt before you did. I saw you sitting in your car...another tough day or just dreading the return to the convalescent home."

She sat down next to him in the swing and pulled him close to her. She hugged him like there would be no tomorrow then kissed him passionately. She smiled. "Just checking your drool level and it seems about right to me, Circus Boy."

"And your day...I saw the news about the pawn shop shooting."

"Well so much for pressuring a confession out of Scat and incriminating Brock Boudreaux."

"What about that Samantha what's her name abduction or whatever you're calling it?"

"Woody said there are no new developments."

"We're knocking items off the list. What's left?"

She filled Brady in on the preacher's disappearance and her theories concerning him. He agreed it sounded like an obvious assumption that the preacher had crossed paths with the murderer.

"Tim ran the inquiry and we have thirty clinic type facilities in the county. Those include chiropractic, dental, and a splattering of specialty practices. We'll divvy these out among the team and begin prodding and poking our noses into them. We'll see what we sniff out."

"Oh yeah, I forgot to tell you. Allison called just before you got home and was asking how you were doing. She said she had had you on her mind lately. She mentioned something about us planning on coming down for a weekend in Atlanta real soon."

Trudy smiled then downed her drink in one quick gulp. "Excuse me while I call her back. I love you, Brady."

"Same here, you call that sister."

Georgetown Police Station

"Don't I get a phone call or something?" asked Lance Rocker.

"Mister Rocker, you're not under arrest," responded Detective Rabun.

"Maybe I should call my lawyer anyway."

"Look Mister Rocker, we're just asking your cooperation in this investigation. If you would feel more comfortable having your lawyer present, please make your phone call."

"You would like that, wouldn't you? Then it would look like I had something to hide. I would be guilty until proven innocent!"

"Mister Rocker, you're here only because we have two witnesses that recognized you being at that motel. One placed you in Samantha Burton's room. You could have been the last one to see her, and we need any information you can provide us. That's all."

"You think I murdered her, don't you?"

"That's your story. I never said she was dead. She's missing."

"Don't try to twist my words," snapped an out of character and distressed Lance Rocker. "And for the record, I had absolutely nothing to do with Janice Anderson's murder either!" He regretted saying that immediately.

"We understand, Mister Rocker, and have no reason to question you about that. You're certainly fixated on murder aren't you? Can you simply share with us your business for meeting Samantha Burton at that motel?"

"Well I certainly never admitted meeting her there now did I?" What a stupid thing to say, Lance, he thought, seeing the detective raise an eyebrow. I'm floundering here.

"Okay, I did meet with her. She contacted me and asked me if I could drop by."

"Can you share with us the purpose for that meeting?"

Take your time, Lance. How you answer the detective's question is critical he told himself. Keep those photos out of it. "Well, how can I say this? We had a past."

"A past...what sort of past?"

"A sexual past," explained Lance. "We hadn't seen one another in years, but we had this little fling some time back."

"So she called you to reminisce about old times?"

"That's correct. She was in the area and heard I was too, so she called me."

"Can you explain why she used a fictitious name and paid for the room in cash?" Rocker took a deep breath, "Okay, I was there to screw her. Are you satisfied? We both have careers to protect and thought it was best we keep this low profile."

"Well that didn't work out so well did it?" said a very sarcastic Detective Rabun. "You probably should have worn some sort of disguises."

"So you have a sense of humor..."

"Do you know where she might have been heading after your little rendezvous?"

"Back to Charleston, best I know."

"She said nothing about any side trips or seeing other long lost acquaintances?"

"I'm sure she had a list and was crossing them off as she went. No, she didn't mention any other appointments."

"And you haven't heard from her since."

"We both got what we wanted, completely satisfied. We went our separate ways afterwards, officer. I certainly hope you find her safe and sound."

"We wish for the same outcome, Mister Rocker. You are free to go. We have your number if we need to ask you any further questions."

"I am always glad to help in solving a murder."

"There you go again. We never said this was a murder investigation, Mister Rocker. I find it quite interesting how you have called it murder numerous times."

Lance gave the detective a cordial nod then made a hasty retreat. He kicked himself in the ass all the way to his car. He had allowed the detective to unravel him, and had obviously elevated his status as a suspect, or at least a viable person of interest.

Just what had happened to Sam? His thoughts again returned to Detective Pierce. He vowed he'd not hesitate throwing her under the bus and exposing those photos, if he became their prime suspect.

He needed a drink but decided to exit Georgetown County before quenching his thirst. He didn't need to give them a reason for bringing him back in to that station. Could Pierce and the Sheriff have killed Sam? After all, Sam had told him they had the goods on her.

Marion Police Department

Lincoln and Eugene Hawthorne sat patiently in the Chief of Police's office, waiting the chief's return. He had stepped out to talk with another policeman in the hallway. Lincoln had wondered if the discussion concerned them. The Chief had given them a strange look after taking a phone call, just before the other officer entered.

Neither he nor Eugene had uttered a word to one another since arriving. The Chief had asked them to meet with him and discuss evidence concerning the jeep and their sister. So far they had learned nothing new from the previous phone call. They had found the jeep. They hadn't found her. The two Hispanic gang members remained in custody. Neither had mentioned their sister.

The Chief returned, sat back at his desk and eyed both of them mysteriously before speaking. "Gentleman, it saddens me to report to you that we have a *Jane Doe* at the morgue that fits the general description of your sister. Could one or both of you accompany my officers there and see if you could possibly ID her."

"I'll do it," spoke up Lincoln.

"I must warn you that the coroner says that this *Jane Doe* has been brutally assaulted and may not be recognizable by facial identification, but if your sister has any other distinguishable marks, tattoos or scars, it could help in making the identification."

"She has a piercing and tattoo," remarked Lincoln.

Eugene spoke, "She has? When? Where? I didn't know she had either!"

"We were close, Eugene. She has confided in me numerous times." He had actually accompanied Cassandra when she had both done, and had even helped her pick out the tattoo. There were a lot of things brother Eugene didn't know about their relationship and never would.

Escorted by the officer, they arrived at the morgue less than fifteen minutes later. Lincoln advised Eugene to stay in the waiting room. He would accompany the coroner to view the body. He hoped it wasn't his sister.

The police chief had been correct. He did not recognize the woman on the table when the coroner uncovered her face. She had died a horrible death for sure. Her attacker or attackers had disfigured this person, making it difficult to determine her gender by facial features alone.

Taking a deep breath, Lincoln asked the coroner to pull the sheet down further. He did, exposing the woman's nude body to the waist. Her breasts were black, blue and bloodied, covered in what appeared to be excessive bite marks around the breasts themselves. This had been a savage rape if rape was really the correct term.

Shaking his head in dismay, he requested the coroner to please uncover the rest of the body. The coroner complied and removed the sheet from the cadaver. Lincoln gasped at the carnage inflicted by the attackers on her lower extremities. In all his years of medical practice he had never seen anyone punished as badly as the person before him.

Rigor mortis had contorted her body badly. Her hips were swung and twisted in a rightward direction from her torso, legs spread open. He walked to the other side of the table to gain a better view. The coroner eyed him like he had him pegged for some sort of pervert. The inflicted savagery almost made him puke, and he didn't puke easily.

He found what he had been looking for and said, "It's her. It's our Cassandra. This is definitely our precious little sister. What could possibly make a human to do this to another human?" He had flashbacks of the donors and what had been inflicted on them before harvesting the bounty.

"If you don't mind me asking how you recognized her as your sister, I'll have to mention it in my report."

He pointed to the Ladybug tattoo well below her bikini line and just above her privates. The unique piercing through her clitoris left no doubt. Lincoln didn't share that bit of information with the coroner nor would he with Brother Eugene.

"Thank you Doctor Hawthorne. I will make the necessary arrangements for releasing her body once the police complete their investigation."

"Their investigation?" he asked.

"Yes, blood samples, salvia, semen, DNA, those bite marks...I'm sure you're familiar with the drill, being a man of medicine. This is obviously a murder investigation. Those men they have in custody, surely they were responsible for this, don't you think?"

"Sorry, I'm not thinking too well right now. I must now do the next worst thing and inform my brother that we no longer have a sister."

Lincoln actually distracted by thoughts of retribution, contemplated how he and Brother Eugene would make these Hispanic bastards pay for what they had done to Cassandra. He said a silent prayer for their quick release. An eye for an eye, the jury was in and the verdict...death, slow and as agonizing as possible. He would render the punishment. He would personally, but discretely, ensure they made bail if offered. They would never make it to trial.

The next day the lead story on television and the local newspapers had been the murder of a prominent Horry County citizen. The Hawthorne family was no longer in the shadows. Their escape plan had been drastically altered and delayed indefinitely.

Horry County Police Station
Sheriff Woodrow Anderson's Office

Trudy sat across the desk from Woody. She eyed him while he read her report and digested her proposed game plan. He certainly didn't fill that chair like the mountain of a man, Hank Singleton, had but her old partner hadn't made a half bad sheriff so far. The news media had not been fair in their portrayal of him. Then again, they had not always been kind to Hank either.

"Looks good to me," he finally stated. "Do you need any additional resources?"

"Thanks, but my team should be able to handle the clinic inquiries, and we're still working the Brock-Scat case, although I believe that one is a wrap, other than apprehending the other members."

"I wouldn't hold your breath on that. We probably have a slim to no chance of bringing in anyone else. The eye witnesses have not been that much help. They fear retaliation. I can't say I blame them."

Trudy nodded.

"Focus your attention on this one. Neither Brock nor Scat has actually contributed that much to our fine community. Other than the IKL, I don't expect to hear many screams for justice. Considering the circumstances and sudden demise of these two, the Klan may keep a low profile to avoid any further retaliation."

"Understood, you're probably right on that one."

"I talked with Georgetown this morning. They picked up Lance Rocker for questioning on the Samantha Burton case."

"What's his connection?"

"Seems he was seen at her motel, specifically her room before she up and vanished," spoke a gloating Woody

Anderson, leaning back in his chair, hands resting on the back of head.

"Do we know why he was meeting her there?"

"Sam old Rocker...and that's why I really hate that son of a bitch."

"Are you telling me that he and Sam were...?"

"Pounding one another..." Woody finished. "Rocker admitted that was why he was there. He claimed they were old friends...the bastard."

"No, there's more to this," she exclaimed, rubbing her chin and closing her eyes.

"Sure there is," admitted Woody. "Women tend to end up dead when Deputy Rocker is around."

"Surely you don't think he killed her and stashed her body some place? What would be his motive?"

"Maybe their little sexual interlude got out of control. It could have been an accident, and he had to get rid of the evidence. Wouldn't that just be fitting?"

"Is that what Georgetown is saying?"

"Nah, that's just wishful thinking on my part, Rocker behind bars for good."

"Sam and Rocker, and why now?"

"Spill it."

"What if this has something to do with us and what we did to her? Think about it. Who best to share that sort of information with than Rocker?"

"But you have the photos..."

"Do your really believe she gave us the only copies and destroyed the others like she promised?"

"We have those on her so checkmate, right?"

"No. Sam is not the type to just let it go that easily. What good are our photos if she is dead? Plus she had a fondness for women, not men. She confessed that to me. She had to be using Rocker. Trust me, I'm right on this."

"So let's say, hypothetically, she gave Rocker a copy of those photos because she wanted to get even. How would he use them? And she would have to know we would figure out where he got them."

"We both know Rocker. He would use them to his advantage; to boost his ratings or more Lance Rocker style, use them to blackmail us, too. She would never have turned any copies over to him, unless she had made him promise to go public with them. She was beyond blackmailing us now."

"It still doesn't explain what happened to her."

"If she isn't dead, then maybe she faked her disappearance, staged it to throw us off her trail, if and when Rocker used the photos."

"If he even has a copy of the photos," said Woody, tiring of all this crap. "Yours is mere theory, my dear detective, and it's out of our jurisdiction. We don't have a real dog in that hunt, not one that we would be willing to share with Georgetown; unless you want them to add both of us to the suspect list. Do the math, we had motive."

"So what do we do?"

"We do nothing. You work on our case and you let them work on theirs. We had nothing to do with her vanishing."

Trudy didn't respond, still thinking about the Sam and Rocker connection.

"Where were you on the date in question?"

"You don't think I killed her do you?"

Woody hesitated, "That's what I would like to believe, unless you give me cause to think otherwise. It would make life easier if we knew she was dead for sure."

"First Rocker, now me?" she remarked in a highly agitated tone. "Are you losing it, Sheriff? Are you so desperate to solve a crime, any crime?"

"Gotcha!" he said leaning forward and grinning like a possum.

Trudy gave him the one finger salute and stormed from his office. This Rocker thing is far from over, she thought. She could feel it, intuition, and it never failed her. Like Woody had told her, focus on their case. Murderers were still roaming free out there somewhere and possibly still dealing in the body part's black market.

She had this sudden urge to talk to Lance Rocker, but first things first. Meet with her CSI team and divvy up the clinics.

See just who they could flush from the bushes. Somebody in one of these clinics was guilty as sin, intuition again.

Swamp Fox Hotel

Lance sat in his hotel room, sipping on a second Bloody Mary while admiring the photos of a young Trudy Wagner Pierce. They left absolutely nothing to his imagination. The jury was in. She was a natural blonde. Her ex-lover had certainly caught her in every possible angle. By the looks of the photos, she had thoroughly enjoyed every frame too. She had an admirable dark side.

Even after his stressful night, under the intense interrogation of Georgetown's finest, he caught himself becoming aroused by the scenes portrayed by the much younger looking Amazon. He figured she had been eighteen, possibly nineteen, years old when these had been taken. One never thinks of the consequences when doing foolish things.

He stared at those deep alluring blue eyes and wondered if they could possibly be the eyes of a cold bloodied killer. Had she whacked Sam? Maybe she had them under surveillance at the motel. If so, maybe he was next. He shook his head. "Get a grip Lance," he mumbled.

Lance tried to get his act together. He hadn't returned any calls from messages left by his producer or his agent, and they had left plenty. He had another show coming up in a few days. He had to hold the audiences' attention, but how would he top that last one? Detective Pierce had been dead on. Two Klansman were dead because of that incriminating segment he had included. Boy, how it had skyrocketed his rating though. What good would that do him if old blue eyes knocked him off next.

The knock at the door almost caused him to soil his under pants. He sat on the sofa, dressed only in his silk drawers. His erection had retreated like a turtle in its shell after being startled. He slipped on a cotton robe, provided by the hotel, and opened the door leaving the security chain in place just in case.

One vivid blue eye stared at him through the narrow crack in the doorway. He instinctively shifted his weight and removed himself from the line of any potential fire just in case she might be concealing a gun and preparing to fire it. He heard no shot, only her familiar voice.

"Is this your rendition of a Peeping Tom?" she asked him. "It's supposed to be conducted from this side of the door in case you've forgotten."

"What do you want? Why are you here?"

He could see the right side of her mouth turn up in a smile. "Were you expecting the boogey man?"

"I'm not in the mood, Detective. I asked what the hell you want." He held his position and scanned her torso for any sign of a weapon.

"Open the damn door, Rocker. We need to talk."

"You got some sort of warrant?"

"Why in the hell would I need one?" she asked, now more convinced than ever that he had something to hide.

"Hold on a minute, I'm not decent," he replied, closing the door and thinking how stupid a comment that had been.

He heard her mutter, "When has that ever stopped you?"

Trudy waited impatiently at the door. What was he hiding, she wondered. Could he and Sam actually be in this together? She would keep this close to the vest and would not mention she knew Georgetown had picked him up for questioning. What was taking him so long?

Lance scooped up the photos and hastily stashed them inside a desk drawer. If the detective was indeed Sam's killer, she didn't need to lay eyes on those photographs. They may be his only protection from her. He took one last deep breath, ran his hands though his locks, and then opened the door.

"About time...what were you doing, trying to hide a body in here?"

Lance, taken by her comment, had no immediate come back; very uncharacteristic for him, indeed. Trudy had picked up on it too. "Okay, just why are you here?"

"To see what you have planned for your next show. I didn't know if we needed to order more body bags."

"I'm sorry those people were killed but…"

"But what?" she cut him off. "It was good for ratings, wasn't it?"

"I didn't break any promises with your department, and you know it," he babbled, again uncharacteristically.

"You always know how to color outside the lines don't you? Staying on the fringes of the law is an art form for you, isn't it? You enjoy it. Admit it."

"You're one crazy bitch. What's your real reason for being in my hotel room, Detective?"

Trudy eyed him and discreetly perused the hotel room, master of the detail, unsure what she was hoping to find.

Rocker allowed his robe to fall open and expose his silk boxers. "Are you here to have your world rocked?"

"It's uncanny. That's exactly why I am here. In your dreams, Dick-Head, and you can close your robe. Your little Mickey Mouse isn't what's it's cracked up to be." She noticed he was sporting Disney World boxers.

He grinned, then closed and tied his robe. While he did so, she conducted another visual scan of the room and noticed the corner of something protruding from a desk drawer. It resembled photo paper.

"All right, so we've completed the formalities. Why are you really here? Do you have any new information on the serial killings?"

"We asked you not to refer to them as that, didn't we?"

"Call it what you want, but you have a hell of lot of dead Mexicans. In my book when you get past two or three dead ones it is serial, whether you and Sheriff Short Stuff want to admit it or not!"

"We're following some leads."

"That means you don't have doodley squat, doesn't it?"

"Doodley squat, you learn that term in journalism school, same place you got the Mouseketeer shorts?"

"You're really obsessed with my boxers and the package they contain aren't you?"

"Do you have a script for your next show yet?"

"I assure you that my producer will send you a copy for approval before we run our next segment."

"Make it a complete one this time, and no damn surprises."

"Sure thing, Detective," he answered, looking her up and down, remembering those photos and becoming aroused again.

Trudy picked up on it. She felt like the bastard was undressing her with his gaze and she noticed his increasing erection, bulging from the terrycloth robe. He had a copy of those photos. She just knew it. "What does your schedule look like today?"

"Keeping tabs on me, detective?" Rocker, now more suspicious than ever, wondered if she planned some sort of ambush.

"In case we need to contact you..."

"You have my cell phone number."

"And we were unable to reach you last night on your cell so that's why I'm asking for a snapshot of you itinerary. Did you have it turned off, or were you just screening your calls?"

"I saw no messages from you. As a matter of fact, I don't remember seeing any incoming calls from you or Shorty."

"We talked to your producer and he told us he had been unable to reach you."

"I had personal business. Is that against the law too?"

"Good day, Rocker. We'll be keeping in touch and don't think about pulling any of your bullshit."

"And you have a wonderful one too, Sweet Cheeks."

After he closed the door, he replayed that little visit in his head. Something is not right here, he thought. She acted strangely. She knows something. I should have gotten dressed and followed her. No, that might be just what she wanted.

Walking down the hallway, she turned and took one last look at his room. He knows something, she thought. He's up to his ass in this Sam thing and I'm going to get to the bottom of it one way or the other. He has to leave that room sometime.

Grand Strand Clinic Search

Detective Sylvester Stone, Sly to his cohorts, and teamed with Detective Tim Burroughs, had already visited three of the ten clinics on their list. Neither had picked up on anything suspicious during the questioning process. All appeared to be on the up and up, as best they could tell.

Sly had been impressed with Tim. He had certainly come a long way. Trudy had been dead on. The killing of that deputy by Tank had awakened a side of him just begging to get out. He had become an integral part of their team. He really liked Tim, but he was almost too nice of a guy to be a cop. That worried him a little because he would have to depend on him to have his back when the time came.

Doctor Dallas Solomon, the team's resident psychologist, had paired with Detective Kirk Cardoon, known as Captain Kirk to his pals, forensics, and so far they were not faring much better. They were at their fifth stop. One had been closed, and another had such a full waiting room that the doctors had not had time to meet with them, but after eyeing those waiting for treatment, none looked Hispanic.

Sly, still troubled by the pastor's sudden disappearance, tried to imagine just what type of ruthless individuals they must be up against. If they killed him to cover their tracks then they were probably capable of most anything. He advised Tim to stay alert each time before they entered a clinic. While he certainly didn't promote a shootout among civilians, they had to be prepared for the worst case scenario. If that meant guns in hand and blazing, then so be it. Dead cops served no purpose.

Sly, a good read on people and their mannerisms, had been concerned lately about their leader. Detective Pierce had seemed distracted, almost detached at times. Aware of her husband's illness, he could chalk some up to her being worried about him but there was more. He couldn't quite put his finger on it. Something else was definitely going on with her. He just couldn't peg whether it was business or personal or possibly both.

The stress of this case had probably taken a toll on her. It had impacted all of them. The media and citizens wanted these killers caught. Yesterday was already too late in their eyes. He had not been part of the department during the Road Rage incident but could sense that the public, after being shaken by that one, would not be so forgiving a second time.

Sly pulled up in front of the next clinic on their list and noticed the empty parking lot on the side, not a good sign. The clinic owned and operated by a Doctor Lincoln T. Hawthorne had a sign posted on the front entrance indicating office closed. Tim circled this one on his printout and made a note to follow up later. They headed to their next destination.

"What you say we swing back by the Pentecostal church after we finish and go through Jorge Cruz's things. Maybe we'll get lucky and find another receipt or something," said Tim.

"Brilliant idea, detective," responded Sly. "We probably should have done that in the first place."

"I find it hard to envision a doctor doing this, especially here. It is even more difficult to fathom a second case like this one In Horry County. I know you weren't part of Preston's serial killings, but what is the statistical chance of us having another murder case like this here? It must be astronomical."

"I agree, Tim. One in a lifetime is extreme but a second is tough to absorb. Interesting enough, this case was ongoing even before your Road Rage killings had even begun."

"Both were happening at the same time but we never knew it. That's just unbelievable."

"While we were chasing down a maniac, we had another predator seeking out illegal aliens. You can't make this stuff up, can you? It would make a great novel, intertwining the two crime sprees, don't you think, Sly?"

"No one would believe it. This would be tough to swallow as fiction. The critcs would not be kind."

"Yeah, I guess you're right. This is so far out there for sure."

"Let's grab a bite to eat, partner, before we head to that Pentecostal church. How does River City Cafe sound?"

"Perfect," smiled Tim.

The Hawthorne Compound

"Cassandra's funeral is scheduled for Thursday," advised Lincoln. "Then we can focus on our original plans."

"Two more days before we bury our little sister," sighed Eugene. "I still can't believe she's gone."

"She knew, as did we, the risks involved. I just wish we could get our hands on those bastards that killed her."

"As long as they're in custody, there's fat chance we can do that, Little Brother. And it won't bring Cassandra back to us."

"I want those two dead, a slow and torturous death."

"You do indeed have an ugly dark side, L.T."

"Darker that you could ever imagine, brother, but I suppose one has to have thick skin to do what we do."

Eugene thought about what he had just said. He, himself, was no cold blooded killer. He had never killed anyone and never intended to do so. Getting rid of the bodies and all the incriminating evidence had been his specialty, his niche in their little prosperous enterprise. Even doing that still bothered him.

He had not found it so easy to embrace their evil doings. Neither Cassandra nor Lincoln flinched. They did what had to be done when the time came to do it. Snuffing out an innocent life for mere profit seemed as common to them as sneezing. How had they become so ruthless and without conscience? Maybe he had been adopted, he thought. That could at least explain why he was so different from them.

He could hardly wait for retirement on some luscious tropical island. He didn't share his brother's obsession with killing the two Hispanic men that had most likely murdered their sister. He thought why not let the judicial system earn its keep rather than them burdening themselves.

The funeral would be simple. Cassandra Guy's body would be cremated so there would be no reason to receive friends or view the body, going against southern tradition. Soon it would be over, and he could begin the new chapter in his life.

He just hoped Lincoln could transition back to being a real doctor. Hell he would settle for him not practicing medicine at all, but could he really walk away from this?

Had the killings already devoured him like an incurable cancer?

"So, are we really going through with torching this place and the clinic?" asked Eugene.

"Absolutely, I just need to locate our doppelgangers. You don't have a couple of cadavers that would fit the bill do you, brother?"

"Not presently..."

"Too bad those two murderers of our sister aren't a match, too short," he laughed.

Eugene thought, even Lincoln's laugh sounded a little over the top and just a tad too deranged for his taste. He had this bad feeling that his brother might just mess this thing up before they made their clean getaway.

"L.T, have you decided a destination for our rebirth?

"How does a trip down under sound? We could probably vanish in Australia don't you think? The outback sounds quite intriguing doesn't it?"

"Don't start thinking you're *Crocodile Dundee*, Lincoln Thomas Hawthorne."

"I was thinking more *Kangaroo Jack*," he laughed again, almost sounding like a mad scientist. "You could be my trusty sidekick, *Platypus Pete*."

"I don't think so. I'll just stick with the one on my new passport, Ken Zimmer. And you're my brother, Wayne Zimmer. "

"Two simpletons just trying to make a meager living," added Lincoln. "Maybe we could run one of those tour excursions and take people into the wild and wooly outback wilderness."

"Being that we know absolutely nothing about the Australian outback and neither of us really like that outdoorsy camping experience, I think we best settle on something else."

"Where's you sense of adventure?"

"I'm leaving that here. I just want a quiet fly under the radar existence wherever we end up."

"Dull, so dull," stated Lincoln. "How can you go back to living such a boring life after what we've accomplished here?"

"Don't even think that we're going to set-up shop again, brother. This is a fresh start with no more of this crap. I mean it."

Lincoln just smiled at him and shrugged it off. This whole thing stunk to high heaven. He would have to keep a watchful eye on big brother, at least until they departed. He was even thinking that he might just distant himself from Lincoln afterwards, just in case. He thought if indeed Lincoln was headed down a destructive path, why should he get caught in the aftermath?

Swamp Fox Hotel

Detective Trudy Wager-Pierce waited patiently in the hotel parking lot, hoping Rocker would leave. After almost an hour she had been disappointed. She had to access his room and snatch those photos, if indeed he actually had copies. Instinct told her he did. If Rocker was a murderer, she couldn't afford being sucked into the muck along with him.

She had returned a call to Woody but had given him a false location. He didn't need to be drawn deeper into her personal problems so she remained mum on her suspicions and plans, at least until she could confirm them.

She contacted each of her two teams investigating the clinics but so far they hadn't turned up anything. Tim Burroughs had mentioned searching through Jorge Cruz's belongings so she told him she would take care of that task. She decided she would go by and pick them up after she finished with Rocker. Sloppy detective work, she thought. We should have done this after his body had been identified. Some CSI leader she had turned out to be.

She had allowed the Samantha Burton debacle and Brady's situation to cloud her judgment. She had never had a problem multitasking before returning to her southern surroundings. In Ohio she had been a disciplined machine. Here there were simply too many distractions. She smiled, remembering she hadn't really had a personal life before.

She made a quick call to Brady but ended up leaving a voice message. He was sponsoring a golf event at Myrtle Beach National King's North course. She suspected he had turned off the ringer so as to not disturb the golfers. She left him a message telling him he did not have to return her call. She would see him tonight.

She had nothing better to do so she decided to call her sister in Atlanta. Again, she had to leave a short message telling her sister she would call her this coming weekend.

Trudy returned her thoughts to Lance Rocker and Samantha Burton. What if she did find those photos in his suite? What then? She certainly couldn't use them to further the case, and if she did find them, what exactly did it mean? Were they in a scam together? Was she dead, and did he kill her?

How could she prove any of it without exposing compromising photos of herself? She had been so damn naive to have allowed him to photograph her in all those poses. That was before she had chosen a career in law enforcement or at least before she had gotten that far along at the academy.

Maybe it would work out better if she didn't find them there? Should she wait? If Rocker did have them, he would play his card eventually, or would he? Given his perverted past, that collection of women's underwear they had discovered in his closet during the Janice Anderson murder, he could be keeping them to jerk off by. That pissed her off even more.

Trudy had to find out, one way or the other, or she would never be able to move on and put this behind her. What had she been thinking posing for those racy pictures for that low life boyfriend, Eric? She should have taken pictures of his little pencil dick, and then he wouldn't dared have done this to her.

Add this to my to-do-list, she thought. Plan a little return trip to Ohio and kick his ass. If he had a wife or girlfriend, he wouldn't after she got finished with him. Who was she kidding?

So preoccupied in her own little tragic world, she almost missed Rocker slipping into his vehicle. She watched until he had driven out of sight. She strolled leisurely through the lobby and into the elevator. Thinking covert operation, she hummed *The Mission Impossible* television show theme song as she rode up to the fifth floor.

Behavior unbecoming a police officer, she quickly picked the door lock and entered his suite. She checked that desk drawer first but only found it occupied by a Gideon's Bible. She checked all other drawers, removing each and flipping them over just in case he had taped them underneath.

She checked the closet, his bags, under the mattress, under cushions, every where imaginable but found no photos. She sat on the love seat and pondered just where would he have hidden them if he did have them in the first place? He had them. She knew it.

She scanned the room and zeroed in on a couple of wall pictures. Removing them and flipping them over, nothing. Could he have taken them with him? She didn't remember seeing him with a brief case but he had already gotten in his car by the time she had seen him. Think...she willed herself.

"Now if I were Rocker, where would I hide those photos?" It hit her like a ton of bricks...of course! She returned to the desk and retrieved the Bible. "Eureka, a sinner like that bastard has no scruples."

She found a complete set tugged inside; matching those Sam had delivered to her. She was relieved to spot no unidentifiable stains on any of them. They were in cahoots, or head been. Did Rocker pull a double cross, or had Sam? Either way, something had gone wrong, so said her gut.

Continuing to mutter out loud she said, "Okay, so I have them and if I take them, surely he will know I'm the guilty party. So, *Miss Breaking and Entering*, what happens now?"

She figured he couldn't be so foolish as to confront me about stealing nude photos of myself, unless, he did kill Sam. It doesn't add up. What possible motive could he have had for killing her? She had to be alive somewhere and lying low, just waiting for the crap to hit the fan when he made them public. That had to be it.

What if I'm wrong and he is a murderer? I'm next. My hands are tied unless I expose myself in these pictures. Options, being caught up in a scandal that will most likely ruin my career or end up dead and still have my nude past splashed all over some seedy girlie magazine, paid for by the highest bidder.

"I'm screwed either way," she whispered.

All right, she surmised, I'll ride it out and see what happens. At least I have the pictures right now and Lance Rocker doesn't. Let's just see what he does when he discovers they are gone. To hedge my bet and against my better judgment, I better confide in Woody. I don't know how much Sam may have told Rocker. For all I know, he may already know Woody was involved in the counter blackmailing scheme. Best to CYA she decided.

She had one stop to make, the church, to pick through Jorge Cruz's things. She arrived twenty minutes later and met with Mrs. McCrery. Sadly she had no new information for the poor woman about her missing husband.

Mrs. McCrery gave her some breathing room in a small sitting room to rummage through the two medium sized boxes. Most of the possessions were church related bulletins, a couple of song books, a ragged bible and an assortment of receipts, none from any medical clinics. She found no more unpaid bills.

Striking out, she began placing the items back in the boxes. She held the bible in her hand thinking about how she had found the photos in the one in Rocker's room. She opened it then flipped through the pages but no such luck this time. She held it up and shook it but nothing dislodged. She did the same thing with the two Hymn Books with the same results.

Placing the books back into the second box something caught her eye protruding from the folded flap in the bottom. Trudy pushed back the flap and retrieved what appeared to be a business card. Printed at the top was The New Hope Clinic, Doctor Lincoln T. Hawthorne, address and phone number. Had she caught a break, she wondered. Trudy had never heard of this Doctor Hawthorne.

She started to call the number on the card but instead decided to check it out before going to the station. It would require only a slight detour. She may as well scope the place out before calling in the team. There was no need to sound alarm bells until she had evidence to support a possible warrant.

Trudy thanked the pastor's wife and promised her that she would call her if she had any news about the pastor. Instinct told her the pastor had most likely been murdered and body disposed of. She sensed the killers would not be sloppy with the cover-up.

Swamp Fox Hotel

After returning, Lance poured a Scotch on the rocks from the mini-bar. Sipping it, his thoughts returned to images of young Trudy Wager Pierce, those photos haunting him. They had shared quite a past, much of it extremely combative but he still couldn't visualize her as a murderer. It just wasn't her style but he would have never thought her a blackmailer either.

Sam had vanished and could be dead. If Pierce had not been responsible, then who had done this? It was time to retrieve the Gideon Bible from the desk drawer. Flipping to the scripture where he had stashed the photographs, he discovered they were gone. Pierce, she had watched him leave and had returned.

"Damn it. How did she know I had them?"

Now that she had them, what did that mean for him, he wondered? Could she be a kidnapper or worse? And would she do it again? He needed to tell somebody but who could he possibly tell? Who would believe him? She had his evidence. Hindsight, he should have made copies.

His cell phone rang. He almost dropped his Scotch. The display indicated it was Murray, his agent. "Yeah Murray," he answered.

"Ratings, we got the numbers big boy. So how do you plan to top it on the next program?"

"Definitely a follow up after that pawn shop shoot out, that's a given. And I've got something to tell you, before it hits the wire."

"Too late," replied Murray. "You're on the local news or haven't you had it on? What have you gotten yourself into with that missing ex-sheriff, Lance?"

"I'm innocent, I assure you."

"You, more than anyone, should know it has nothing to do with whether you're innocent or guilty, you're news. So how do we ride this and use it to boost our ratings?"

"You're asking me to air my dirty laundry on the show?"

"Your dirty laundry is already flapping in the breeze, my boy. You may as well capitalize on it. Fend off the accusers. Open your own investigation during the next show."

"I'll think about your suggestion, Murray.

"I'll call you tomorrow and, Lance, try not to get involved with more disappearances, even for ratings sake."

"I certainly don't plan on it, but then again, it wasn't my intent when I met with Sam."

Lance decided he could play this to his advantage. Exposing the case nationally would buy him some insurance against the detective. She would keep her distance and pose no threat. He knew just how he would ensure it.

The next show would blow the socks off the viewers and indeed live up to its reputation and rock their world. He decided to drop back by the hotel lounge. He had his eye on a hot little bartender that should be getting off duty about now. He needed some Rocker style relief. Just as quickly he decided against it. Sure as hell the bartender would turn up missing or dead."

The New Hope Clinic
Surfside Community

Detective Trudy Pierce pulled into the empty parking lot. She surveyed the clinic. It certainly didn't impress her as a place to be feared. The building was freshly painted and the grounds were landscaped and groomed. How could this be some sort of slaughter house? It had apparently been residential at some time. The back had a two car detached garage.

She stepped from her cruiser and walked the perimeter. Nothing appeared out of place. Stepping up onto the small porch and entrance way she spotted the CLOSED sign. She peered through the window and could make out a waiting room, very tastefully decorated. Again, this just didn't feel like a bad place. Her intuition rarely failed her.

She turned to see a white Lexus sedan pulling into the parking lot, circling then exiting. The angle didn't allow her to make the license plate. She shrugged, just someone turning around.

Lincoln had spotted the police car just as he made his turn into the parking lot. He saw the officer at the clinic's front entrance and decided it best not to do a meet and greet right now. Not panicking, he completed a maneuver of someone simply using the parking lot to turn around. He watched the officer from his side mirror, but she made no move to follow him. It worked flawlessly.

He wondered what had brought her to his clinic. He called Eugene. His brother agreed they should expedite their plans immediately following their sister's funeral. Time could be running out for them.

Lincoln spotted the three homeless men holding up signs, begging for food, but most likely preferring cash for wine or drugs. Two of them fit his needs. Their general build and size could pass for him and his brother. He pulled to a stop and watched them for awhile, biding his time. Cassandra had been much better at this than he.

Finally he pulled alongside, rolled down his window and introduced himself, giving them one of his business cards. He pointed in the general direction of the clinic several blocks away and encouraged them to meet him there. He offered them a free medical examination, fresh clothes and a hot meal. They smiled and eagerly accepted his offer, and before he could stop them, they clambered into the back seat of his Lexus. Accustomed to the smell of death and disease, their stench still overwhelmed him.

He watched them from the rearview mirror. He didn't trust them sitting behind him. One eyed him through the mirror then mumbled something to the one sitting next to him. Lincoln nervously approached the clinic in hopes that the police car had departed. It had.

He pulled around back and quickly exited the car, motioning for the three to follow him. Something didn't seem right. They weren't as helpless as he had perceived. The apparent leader of the three looked to be up to something. What he was doing alone with these three was probably an extremely stupid and risky thing to do. Eugene had already pointed out how he had become careless. Divide and conquer. He escorted each into separate examination rooms. He asked them to wait there, remove their clothes and he would bring them fresh ones.

He prepared three syringes with his secret serum and returned to the ring leader's room first. He wasn't there. Lincoln wheeled around to make sure he wasn't lying in ambush behind the door. He wasn't. Cautiously he checked the next room and his donor sat patiently on the edge of the table where he had instructed him to sit. Soiled clothes lay crumpled in a pile on the floor. The man's rib cage sported the signs of malnutrition.

He smiled at him as he passed behind, reaching for his stethoscope on the cabinet. He whirled and plunged the syringe into the man's neck. Seconds later he lay motionless slumped over on the table. One down and two to go thought Lincoln.

He entered the next examination room and found his prey. The man had his back to him, still fully clothed, squatting and rummaging through a cabinet. Moving swiftly he delivered his magic potion, leaving the second man crumpled on the floor. Now it was time to locate the third and finish this.

He moved as silently as possible, syringe ready, searching for the apparent ring leader of the trio. That one's eyes had spelled trouble. Lincoln cocked his head, listening for any noise that would indicate his prey's location. He heard nothing but his own nasally breathing.

He completed his search of all the examination rooms and restrooms. All were empty. He stood in the hallway near the entrance to his office and inhaled, hoping the man's body odor would reveal his presence. He did smell that familiar stench from the Lexus, unclean with a mixture of urine. The man bolted at him head on from his office and toppled him to the floor, jarring the syringe from his hand and spinning like a bottle on the tile.

He realized quickly he was no match for his assailant. Even undernourished he possessed phenomenal strength and he had a death grip around Lincoln's neck and shoulders. Lincoln stretched for the syringe but found it well out of his reach. The man's foul breath almost smothered him as effectively as the death grip he found himself in.

Twisting, he still could not gain any leverage with the man lying on top of him. The man had tightened the grip around Lincoln's throat, cutting off the air supply. Soon he would be unconscious or dead, if he didn't break the man's hold.

His foot touched the wall and he struggled until both feet were firmly against it. With his legs almost in a crouching position, he used the wall for a spring board, launching him and his attacker across the hallway slamming into the opposite wall. The impact was just enough for the man to relinquish his vise-like grip. Lincoln spun like a crocodile in one of those death role sequences and momentarily freed himself.

He half slid, half crawled, toward the syringe, inches from his finger tips. The man grabbed his ankle, flipped him onto his back, and then was on top of him again. The homeless man grinned, a yellow toothed disgusting smile. Now straddling

Lincoln's chest, pinning both arms underneath his legs, he held the syringe in his right hand like a dagger. "Looking for this, Doc?" All hope was lost.

Horry County Police Department

Lance Rocker stood in Woody's doorway holding a script for his next show. He handed it to Woody then had a seat, while the Sheriff perused the agenda.

He would open with the follow-up to the Brock Boudreaux-Scat Crowder murders, a proclaimed gangland assassination. Rocker would then make the tie to the Hispanic killing fields. After some file footage of both incidences and background about the MS-19 gang and IKL, he would move on to his personal involvement in the Samantha Burton case. Rocker had decided to tell his audience he planned to solve it and find the missing ex-sheriff.

Woody smiled, "You do have this knack for getting in over your head. More dead women, it just seems to be your MO."

"We don't know if Samantha Burton is dead now do we?" Lance returned the fire, remembering how he had blabbed the death talk to Georgetown police.

"Do you have her tied up somewhere, using her as your sex slave?"

"I should be asking you that," he blurted out.

"What the hell is that supposed to mean?"

Without thinking he played his first card. "Sam confided in me before she disappeared. I know about the explicit photos of your little CSI leader and your blackmail video of Sam and Pierce."

Woody, stunned by Rocker's revelation, leaned back in the leather chair and pondered carefully how he would respond. Clearly Rocker had the upper hand. Before he could muster up a response, Rocker spoke. "Here's what I want, to keep this between just us," bluffing, because he had no evidence to support what he knew as fact. He sensed Short Stuff didn't know that. Pierce must have kept him in the dark. She could be the killer indeed.

"I'm listening."

"One, I know Sam's case is out of your jurisdiction but you should still have some pull with Georgetown. I want them to go public, stating I am not a suspect in the case. I assure you I am not and that's a fact. I had nothing to do with her disappearance. You and Pierce on the other hand, have motive but that remains between us, right?"

"What else?"

"I film you exonerating me of any wrong doing in contributing to the Klansmen's deaths. I certainly don't need any gang members or the Klan targeting me for retaliation."

"You're just one poor little innocent son of a bitch, aren't you?"

"Of course, you keep me filled in, on all developments concerning your big Mexican murders."

"Is that it?"

"It will do for starters. And I want it in writing or on film, my insurance policy, you choose."

"It seems you're pretty damned good at blackmail too."

Lance smiled. "So where is our illustrious Detective Pierce? She should probably be part of this, don't you think?"

New Hope Clinic
Surfside Community

His attacker came crashing down on top of him; syringe pinged off the tile floor inches from his face. "Are you okay?" asked a voice.

Pushing the dead weight aside, he saw a young lady holding a revolver standing over him. He sat up and said, thank you. She offered him her hand and helped him to his feet. He recognized her. It was that police woman he had seen on his doorstep.

"Sorry, I whacked him a little harder than I intended. I didn't want to shoot him but he was about to plunge that needle into your chest."

"You did the right thing, dear. I feared he would do just that."

I dropped by earlier. I had seen the Lexus turn around in the parking lot. On my drive back to the station, I had spotted it again, heading back in this direction and decided to follow. Your driving just seemed a little too suspicious for a cop. I'm Detective Trudy Pierce."

Thinking fast, "Yes I suppose I can see why you would think that. I thought I had forgotten something back at my home but, stupid me, I had it all along. I returned to the clinic once I realized my error."

"What happened here?" she asked, pointing to the unconscious man at her feet.

"I'm not sure. I didn't lock the door. I wasn't expecting to be here very long. I suppose he entered undetected. Thank goodness for your arrival, Detective Pierce. The man asked for any valuables I might have, and then began attacking me with that syringe. I assume he is under the influence of some sort of narcotic to act in such a deranged manner. His eyes were quite dilated."

"I'll file a report and have the local blues haul him away then maybe we can chat."

"Anything specific, detective?"

"Yes. Do you know a Jorge Cruz?" She decided to see how he would react but he didn't flinch. He was either way too cool or innocent. She hadn't decided which yet.

"Name doesn't ring a bell, my dear, but we see so many people here of various nationalities. We can certainly check the files, if you would like. What has this gentleman done to deserve your attention?"

"He disappeared, then ended up dead. Let me call in the Calvary to pick up your intruder." And still his face remained expressionless and unaffected, interesting she thought.

"Very well," he replied. "And again, thank you."

She leaned down and cuffed the vagrant then stood saying this will take only a couple of minutes. Turning toward the door, she experienced what felt like a bee sting on her neck. She reached up and felt the doctor's hand and the syringe. Trying to turn and reach for her revolver to face him, her knees suddenly gave way and she crashed to the floor. How careless was her last fading thought.

After preparing an additional syringe and injecting his attacker, Lincoln called Eugene and told him to come to the clinic. Pronto, he urged. He now had four unconscious people scattered about and the female detective posed the biggest challenge. Department procedures, had she reported her current location to a dispatcher?

All had become so complicated. He should have heard her out instead of allowing his emotions to take over and put her down. Water under the bridge now, he would have to deal with the consequences.

He checked her ID. Detective, CSI unit, that settled it. He had made the right choice. She had been here to arrest him. He did remember the young pastor. He had been a tragic mistake. Pressured to meet orders he had instructed Cassandra to pluck the low hanging fruit. It had gone without a hitch, until that man and his son stumbled onto the gravesites.

Then that other pastor had shown up trying to be the Good Samaritan. How unfortunate, too smart for his own good. An ex-sheriff and now a Crime Scene Investigator, he thought, so much for culling the illegal population and staying low profile. Cassandra dead, he sighed, another tragic mistake after so many successful years.

One by one he dragged the detective, then the foul smelling homeless guy into one of the waiting rooms where another drugged body awaited. He only required two for their purposes. Eugene would have plenty of garbage to dispose of once he completed the dirty portion of the deed.

Lincoln decided it best to relocate the officer's squad car and fumbled through her pockets until he retrieved her keys. Using a keyboard, he entered the code to open the garage's double doors, then making sure no one saw him, he slid into the driver's side of the squad car and quickly pulled it inside.

Before he exited the car he noticed a folder on the passenger seat and scooped it up, just in case it might be pertinent to her being here. He activated the code after closing the door. Walking back to the office entrance he removed the contents of the envelope. Lincoln stopped in his tracks, when he realized the photographs exposed a younger version of the officer posed in extremely compromising and erotic positions.

He had second thoughts about disposing of the officer so quickly. His growing arousal indicated that the photographs were worthy of an explanation and further exploration. Trudy didn't know it yet but her photographs granted her a temporary reprieve. That might not necessarily be a good thing given what Lincoln Hawthorne had in store for her.

Trudy in her sedated and unconscious state dreamed a series of what-ifs and tried to solve life's mysteries. Surprisingly Brady had floated to the top of her priority list. She feared she would never see him again and he would never know how she had vanished from the planet.

She could almost hear voices, faint, but yes, they were voices. Did that mean she was coming out of it or was it just the way the drug worked? Yep, she heard voices all right, two voices, both male. She strained to try to decipher them but couldn't quite make out the actual dialogue.

Was Brady fondling her right breast? It sure felt like someone was fondling her breast or was she just imagining it? No. It wasn't Brady. It was much too hard and aggressive for Brady. It felt like someone was pinching her nipple. She wanted to yell out but couldn't.

Now someone had their hand in her panties and was pinching her there. Brady would never treat her like this. She attempted to resist, wanting to slap the hand, remove it from her panties but she couldn't will her hand to move. Was she just dreaming? She didn't think so.

How had she blundered again? She had this knack for getting herself into precarious predicaments. So confident of being invincible, she too often made bad choices. Why hadn't she called for back-up before coming here? She had made that same mistake with Mister Road Rage.

That wandering hand just wouldn't let up. It was groping her still and she found no pleasurable sensations from the deep exploration. This definitely wasn't foreplay, not by a long shot. At least she must still be alive but enough was enough. She wanted to scream *STOP IT*. She couldn't.

"Lincoln, what the hell are you doing?" yelled Eugene, observing his brother meticulously fondling the semi-nude female on the examination table.

Startled and red faced, Lincoln jerked his hand from the Detective's undergarments and turned to face his brother. Brother Eugene had not been aware of his sexual perversions, at least not until now, thought Lincoln. Cassandra would not have flinched seeing him explore the detective's anatomy, but he and she had shared a mutual fascination for this sort of thing. Playing with the toys was just part of their game.

Hers had led to the divorce from her husband. Cassandra's spouse had found her too many times in compromising positions. He didn't share her aspirations for sexual gratification. It went far beyond the husband-wife commitment, to honor and love one another and always be faithful. Theirs had been such a messy break-up, resulting in his brother-in-law eventually becoming an empty case. Mister Guy had fed the gators well. That one had remained a secret just between him and his sister.

"Eugene, what took you so long? I had to hide her car, drag her from the hallway, as well as move that other gentleman. You know how I despise all this manual labor. Perspiration is such a deplorable secretion. I was just examining her to determine if we might be able to use her as a donor."

"I thought we agreed we would fill no more shipments and get the hell out of here after we gave Cassandra a proper send off."

"Creature of habit, I suppose," explained Lincoln. "Always seeing the dollar signs. She is just an exquisite specimen, don't you concur?"

"She's a damn detective, L.T.," snapped Eugene, shaking his head in contempt for his brother's stupidity. "I must admit, I could not believe you had done this. I had hoped you were just pulling my leg when you phoned me."

"It couldn't be helped. How do they say it on those police television shows? *She was on to us.*"

"How do you know that, Lincoln?"

"Why else would she have come here my dear brother?"

Eugene just threw his hands up in disgust, searching the heavens for answers. He had a bad feeling that they were not going to escape this. "I'm surprised we've prospered this long!"

"You should be thanking our dear detective woman. She most likely saved my life. "

"You still haven't explained to me why you sedated three, when we only required two to mimic our deaths in the fire."

"Sorry Eugene, they came in a three pack and I couldn't break up the set."

"Don't try to be funny, L.T. This is coming out of your share. I demand a raise, compensation for your continual mishandling of these affairs."

"You forget, we have our deceased sister's portion, may she rest in peace, and we are the only heirs. Be assured you will be compensated handsomely for your efforts, Eugene."

"Two bodies expire in our fire, so that leaves me with two more to dispose of before we make our escape."

"Retirement sounds much better don't you think?"

"Whatever makes you happy Lincoln. When do you plan to euthanize them?"

"Anytime you wish. We should decapitate them and dispose of their heads. Dental records could foil our plans otherwise. I'll need your ring and watch. The family crest and those engravings will be a nice added touch, don't you think?"

"And what about you? Are you going to give up that diamond beauty on your finger?"

"That is my plan. A thirty thousand dollar ring should convince the crime scene investigators that Lincoln T. Hawthorne is no more."

"So what about the other two, what do you have planned for them?"

"Our third male is already dead. I didn't appreciate him attacking me like he did, so he has joined the homeless angels. I haven't decided about the detective yet."

"What do you mean you haven't decided?"

"Insurance policy possibly, just in case her cohorts are privy to her visit here. She could be our bargaining chip. We can dispose of her easily enough, if that proves to be incorrect." His real reason for keeping her alive, he had urges of his own to satisfy. Those photographs haunted him. He must revive her and complete his own interrogation, but not until Eugene had left the premises to dispose of the third vagrant. Brother didn't need to know everything.

Eugene nodded, "We still have her car in the garage."

"You will think of something, I'm sure. You always do."

"Tonight I will leave that guy out at Paradise City with the other homeless hopefuls. He'll be one less for that Street Reach program to feed."

"I'll restrain the others and ensure they remain in a sedated state. By tonight we should know if Conway Police are on to us and are missing their detective."

"Are you prepared, brother, if they pay you a visit or worse, if they storm the clinic?"

"God has a plan for all of us, Eugene, and what will happen, will happen and we can't alter our destiny. I'm prepared for the best or the worst consequences."

"I doubt that brother. I might survive but you wouldn't do well in prison."

Lincoln smiled, knowing his brother spoke the truth. Prison would not be kind to him. That's why he concealed the lethal injection in his trouser pocket. He had no intention of being arrested or incarcerated but hoped he never had to use his special syringe.

"I'll take our detective to the compound if you will be so kind as to help me place her in the Lexus."

"Sloppy, sloppy, sloppy," he muttered. "L. T., you're trying my patience."

"You stress yourself so needlessly, brother. Have you taken your blood pressure medicine today?"

"Let's just load her in your car and get this over with. Retirement can't come soon enough for my taste."

Young Lincoln T. Hawthorne and Siblings

Southern born and bred, the Hawthorne children had been raised spoiled and rotten to their cores. Born with a silver shovel in their mouths, rather than a spoon, they had wanted for nothing. Their ancestors, original rice plantation owners in Georgetown County and prominent figures in the rebuilding of the south after the civil war, had ensured their veins oozed southern heritage.

Their Daddy, William Hawthorne had been a prominent lawyer and eventually a judge, a hard but fair man, but one you best not cross. He had ruled the household with a stern hand and had pushed his children relentlessly, never accepting failure or anything short of perfection. At an early age, Eugene earned his daddy's respect but Lincoln and Cassandra had drawn pleasure in outwitting the fox in his own den.

Their school grades had always rivaled Eugene's, top of the class; however, neither Lincoln nor Cassandra earned theirs honestly. Preferring the lazy way out, they had lied, cheated, and falsified their way through high school and college. Money bought everything they required.

Both had become sexually active and promiscuous at very young ages, exploring and enjoying one another until college. Neither had experienced any outside sexual encounters, content to fulfill one another. Cassandra had been the first to break away and explore others.

Lincoln became quite jealous when he found his dear sister had been unfaithful to him with one of his college classmates. He had tricked Eugene into attacking the scoundrel telling him he had deflowered their sister. He had always been able to play Eugene like a puppet. Daddy Will had to pay a pretty penny to cover up the boy's almost fatal beating.

Mother Agnes Hawthorne, a hopeless drunk, had not served much as a mother or wife. Tired of her countless embarrassing moments, Daddy Will said he had discovered his wife's body, face down in the retention pond. He told his children and the community that she had stumbled, been knocked unconscious and had drowned. He professed he missed her terribly.

Lincoln and Cassandra had seen through their father's guilt. Both were certain he had murdered her but neither lost much sleep over the event. Eugene was devastated. He had definitely been the mama's boy. He had tidied up behind her for years, hiding the liquor bottles, helping her to bed, and cleaning up her vomit; a good son.

Daddy Will didn't hide his guilt for long, for he too succumbed to the bottle, and two short years later died of a liver pickled and preserved in Scotch. No tears were shed by any of the three children when he met his maker. Even Eugene had grown bitter of dear old Daddy Will. He had become an angry man, often slapping his kids around while in drunken rages. The slaps didn't faze Lincoln or Cassandra, pain and pleasure not a stranger in their lives. Eugene thought his father to be despicable.

The three young adults inherited everything. Cassandra squandered hers quickly, gone within the first year and a half. She married out of convenience to lay claim to her husband's fortune. If not for his successful medical practice, Lincoln could have suffered the same fate. Only Eugene had invested wisely while making a go as a prominent mortician.

Once he and his sister had eventually disposed of her ex-husband and his ex-brother-in-law, they briefly resumed their incestuous love affair. Lincoln's perversions had outgrown hers, and she soon severed their relationship but remained close just the same.

Lincoln began sedating his clients and taking liberties with them while they were under. Almost being caught in the act by one of his awakening patients, a distinguished citizen of the community, he decided to move his practice from Georgetown to Horry County before the community became more suspicious of his poor bedside manner.

He eventually founded The New Hope Clinic and suddenly found an endless crop of sexual toys in the Hispanic population. Eventually Sister Cassandra,broke and in need of income, joined him in his practice. Soon she too began partaking of the forbidden fruit. Eugene remained in the dark as always.

Sometime into the second year of operating the clinic, he and Cassandra had decided they should reward themselves with a long overdue vacation. Choosing an all inclusive resort in the Dominican Republic and leaving Eugene behind, they closed up shop and ventured to the island for a month long stay. There, they renewed their love affair, partaking of secret desires, rekindled it on an island known for having no sexual boundaries.

Haiti borders and shares the island with the Dominican Republic and it was while in a quant little seashore villa, pleasuring one another, that they met the ink black Haitian going only by the name of Walt. Soon there were three wallowing in the sheets, men on woman, man on man, woman on men, leaving no desire unexplored.

About a week later Walt had introduced them to a man only know to them as The Face, a deviously dark shadow, a self proclaimed entrepreneur, dressed in a white linen suit, a smile to die for and a master of the gift of gab. He quickly captured them in his web and seduced them into doing his bidding.

Organs and body parts, he had an endless demand for them, and they had the perfect venue and bottomless supply of illegal aliens. Naïve, the Hawthorne siblings partnered with The Face, figuring they could combine their pleasures and make a fortune to boot, the perfect enterprise for people in need of life saving transplants. Unfortunately and much too late into the venture, they discovered that this had been only a small part of it.

The Face had far too many clients, some of them only interested in certain human organs, parts and appendages for ritual purposes, potions, sexual aphrodisiacs, voodoo, and healing remedies. Worse still, his circle of friends was sinister, ruthless, devious and not willing to accept no for an answer. Too late they discovered their arrangement to be for life. Once in, there's no way out, an island version of the worst kind of Mafia.

While the money was good, as promised, there remained no margin for error. A missed shipment was not an option. The partnership only extended one way. Comply or die. When demand reached a peak, they had to lure Brother Eugene into the family business. He had the perfect mechanism, his mortuary, for disposing of the carcasses or empty cases as Lincoln would later dub them.

He agreed to provide that service on condition he committed no murders. Terms reached. He was in. Demand again peaked to uncontrollable levels. Eugene could not get rid of the bodies fast enough and eventually had to begin dumping them in the swamp and burying them in the secluded backwoods.

Eugene had once and only once, announced he was done, ready to quit, and was cutting his loses. Soon after his declaration, two gentlemen paid him a visit and proceeded to remove his left testicle, no anesthesia or sterilized surgical equipment had been used. Lincoln had stitched him. Eugene had never submitted his resignation again. He too was now in for life, no more questions.

Lincoln and Cassandra had used their little enterprise to fulfill their sexual desires, despite the other dangers looming from The Face. Closing one eye to everything else, they mixed business with pleasure, their distorted version of the circle of life. No longer maintaining any one on one contact with The Face or his cronies, shipments went out on time. Money was deposited in offshore accounts. Everyone prospered.

Now Cassandra was dead and getting out would spell their doom, too, unless they successfully scammed The Face and the authorities with their staged deaths in the fires. Lincoln, confident and proud of his plan, envisioned no further hiccups. Bury little sister, pleasure himself with the detective, burn down the clinic and the compound, then disappear into the sunset. It seemed so simple. Only one thing was missing from Lincoln's list; disposing of his sister's murderers. He hadn't worked out how he was going to accomplish that yet.

Why did Brother Eugene always have to be so pessimistic? Eugene didn't dream big. He ate the elephant in baby bites while Lincoln stuffed it down his throat, tusk and all. Lincoln was not beyond sacrificing his brother if he had to, but he needed him for now. Why couldn't it have been Eugene instead of Cassandra taken from him, he wondered? Cards are dealt. Hands are played. He still felt lucky.

251

Horry County Police Department

Sly and the others had arrived back at the station and had completed the task of comparing notes. Only six facilities remained on their combined list. The team had turned up nothing overly suspicious.

Lance Rocker had sealed the deal with Sheriff Woody Anderson. He had gotten their little agreement in writing and on his tape recorder. He had thoroughly enjoyed watching the look on Short Stuff's face, having been snookered again by a superior being. He paused in the hallway just outside the conference room, recognizing the computer geek's voice and expecting to hear Detective Pierce chiming in.

"Shouldn't she be here by now?" asked Tim Burroughs.

"If I know our faithful leader, she's probably still there consoling the pastor's wife," responded Sly.

So, thought Rocker, the little thief stopped by the dead pastor's church after lifting the photos. Maybe she's there and I can steal them back he contemplated as he treaded silently down the hallway.

"Any development on the Burton case down in Georgetown?" asked Captain Kirk.

"Still missing and Rocker continues to be a person of interest," replied Dallas.

"Something interesting I've being following over in Marion County," mentioned Tim. "The murder of one of our Horry County residents, a Cassandra Guy, sister to a Doctor Lincoln T. Hawthorne and a Eugene Hawthorne, a local mortician."

"So what intrigues you so?" asked Captain.

"Raped and sexually mutilated by Hispanic gang members. Her jeep stolen, she had been kidnapped and was dumped on the side of the road like litter."

"Was it the same gang that killed Scat and Brock?" asked Sly.

"Not sure, but they have two suspects in custody." answered Tim.

"Interesting," commented Dallas. "We seem to have quite an outbreak of this sort of behavior, don't we?"

"Too bad she wasn't driving a convertible sports car," stated Sly.

"Automobile was registered to one of her brothers, the doctor," added Tim.

"Run a check and see if she had any vehicles registered in her name," requested Sly.

"Are you not telling us something, Sly?" asked Captain.

"Probably nothing, but nothing is all we have so may as well play all the hunches. A dead, affluent woman, murdered by Hispanics, family connections to a doctor and a mortician, makes for a good plot. And sort of fits who we might be looking for, don't you think? If she owns a white sports car we could be on to something."

"An excellent deduction," commented Dallas.

"Shouldn't we try to contact Pierce?" asked Tim.

"I'm on it," responded Captain, just as Sheriff Woody Anderson strolled into the room.

Pentecostal Church

Lance Rocker had just finished questioning Preacher Raeford McCrery's wife. She had confirmed that Detective Pierce had indeed dropped by but had left almost two hours ago. When asked did she know where the detective had been heading, she told him about the business card she had found in Jorge Cruz's belongings. The New Hope Clinic would be his next stop.

Rocker's cell phone rang. The caller ID indicated it was his producer. He figured he probably wanted the final details of the script for tomorrow night's show. He almost didn't answer because he was still working last minute angles. What the hell he thought.

"You've got to be kidding me? Well, it at least gets us some free publicity. What do you mean you're planning to telecast a re-run of a previous show? Don't panic on me, now. We can work this out."

For the next thirty seconds Lance remained silent, absorbing an earful being delivered by his producer. Lunacy, he thought, absolutely unreal, this cannot be happening. The producer stuck to his guns and had pulled the plug on the next show.

Lance's final word, "I'm calling Murray. We can work this out without canceling the telecast. Re-runs just don't cut it while I'm on top of my game. We can blow the lid off the ratings this week, I'm telling you. This isn't over." The line went dead. "Nobody hangs up on Lance Rocker."

He could not believe the audacity of his spineless producer. Sponsors had been dropping like flies, too nervous about the implications of his involvement in Samantha Burton's disappearance and the heat the station had taken from the pawn shop slayings. The network feared he could instigate a Klan and Hispanic war that would most certainly deter tourists from visiting the Grand Strand.

The producer explained that the scenario had gotten out of control. He pointed out that there had been no arrests or convictions concerning the Hispanic murders. He didn't hold back about the Burton case and the pawn shop fiasco. The community was somewhere between trauma overload and going vigilante. Neither the station nor network had any intentions of being blamed or sued.

What were those stupid bastards thinking, he thought? This is national, award winning, over the top journalism, right up there with the Road Rage serial killings. Couldn't they see it? Sitting on this would only allow the competition to slip in and snatch it from them. He had to call Murray. His contract gave him creative control, but bets were off now that they had fired him.

Three blocks from The New Hope Clinic, he only managed to reach Murray's voice mail. The beep signaled he could now leave a message. "Don't be a damn wiseass, Murray. I know you're screening my calls. Those assholes are not putting me on re-runs and firing me. You better call me. I don't pay you to stick your head up your ass. You represent me. Pick up the damn phone Murray. You think you're the only agent out there."

Rocker, now furious, could hardly think straight. He wheeled into the parking lot of the New Hope Clinic, squealing the tires on his Z-28. The sound of rubber peeling from his tires shocked him back to reality. Luckily he didn't see any cars in the parking lot. He drove to the back portion of the lot and pulled to a stop.

Dusk approached, the street lights had begun to flicker, signaling darkness approached. Rocker visually surveyed the perimeter seeing two buildings, the clinic and what appeared to be a two vehicle detached garage.

He saw no interior lights, indicating it must be closed for the day. Pierce must be back at the station. The opportunity had been lost to reclaim the photos. He figured he may as well snoop about while here. He might get lucky and break this case wide open then the producer and network would be at his mercy.

Other than the front entrance, he could not see in any of the clinic's windows. He could only make out part of the lobby and the check in window from that vantage point. He walked to the back and jiggled a side entrance door to the garage but found it locked. The solid door offered no view inside. Walking the exterior walls he found only one window on the opposite side but blinds were pulled.

Sighing, Lance had decided this was getting him nowhere. He walked to the front. The double wide door contained a series of small glass transoms near the top. Standing on his tiptoes he peeped inside as daylight dwindled. He quickly dropped back flatfooted exclaiming, "Oh crap. This isn't good!"

He stretched a second time to verify what he thought he had seen. Lighting was poor but he had no doubt, it had to be Pierce's police car. Parked beside it was a white Mustang convertible. He had hit pay dirt.

He returned to the small window on the side, located a landscape stone the size of a brick and shattered the glass, hoping it would not set off an alarm. It didn't.

He reached inside, unlatched the window, and raised it slowly. It just barely offered enough wiggle room for him to snake inside. The cruiser was not locked. He sat in the driver's seat, and sure enough, Pierce's ID was clipped to the visor. He searched the interior for the photos but came up empty. They could possibly be in the trunk, but he didn't have the key and there was no trunk release.

Next he checked out the Mustang. Unlike the cruiser, it had been locked. Peering inside the driver's side window, it looked like anyone's car. He saw no blood stains, ropes or paraphernalia to indicate otherwise.

Against his better judgment, he decided he should call the pint sized sheriff. He wouldn't make the same mistake he had made in Tim Ford's garage. This time he stayed with the evidence.

With phone in hand, he pressed the first digit just as the side entrance door jiggled and began opening. Startled, Lance leapt for cover. His hand struck the police car's side mirror, launching his phone from his clutches, sliding underneath the cruiser. He managed to dive behind the front of the Mustang just as footfalls echoed on the concrete floor.

He lay belly down on the opposite side of the Mustang from where the cruiser was parked. He could see his phone just behind the right front tire. He watched as a pair of sandal clad feet dragged what looked like a body into the garage and deposited it into the back of the police vehicle. He sighed. Pierce had fallen victim to the murdering body snatchers.

The automatic garage door rumbled open. The cruiser thundered to life and began backing out of the garage. Lance watched helplessly as his cell phone crunched underneath the tire. He replayed that commercial in his head, *Can you hear me now?*

The door closed after the cruiser exited. Lance scurried to check the condition of his phone and discovered its condition critical. He peered out the garage door transoms and spotted Pierce's car cautiously advancing through the parking lot. A second set of tail lights followed. No phone, he had no choice but to follow them.

He exploded from the side door and ran for his Z-28 just as the second automobile pulled into the street and made a left turn, still following the cruiser. Keeping it in sight, he fired up his pursuit vehicle and shot across the parking lot. All the while he searched for something that might resemble a weapon, but Deputy Lance Rocker remained unarmed and not feeling very heroic. Actually he felt quite naked without his phone.

The motorcade of three abided the posted speed limit, maneuvering toward an unknown destination; at least unknown to the trailing car. Lance figured if he maintained a safe distance neither of the other two drivers would suspect his car for an undercover cop. After all he was still a deputy. Twenty agonizing minutes later the two cars came to a stop.

Lance recognized the area, Paradise City, residence for the ever-growing homeless population. Until just a few short years ago, only the big cities, like New York and LA, had to deal with this but, alas, Myrtle Beach had joined their ranks and now had to cope with the vast numbers of wandering nomads.

He had featured several stories while with the local television station. Why were they stopping here, he wondered.

The person in the trailing vehicle exited and joined the second person now opening the back door of the stolen cruiser. Damn, he realized they were dumping her body here where she may not be found for days or weeks. These homeless folks certainly wouldn't report finding her and would strip her of all possessions. Hell, they would probably conceal the corpse. Not a very fitting end for her he thought.

Lance wrestled with his choices. Do the right thing and retrieve her body or at least get to a phone and report this before the scavengers moved in, or follow them. Ratings won out. He couldn't do anything for the dead detective so he would instead follow her murderers. Hopefully her body could be recovered later.

The drivers quickly returned to their vehicles and pulled away at a normal speed. Rocker admired how cool they remained even after dumping her body. He was definitely dealing with professionals which intensified the danger level.

Being unarmed was not necessarily a good thing right now. Damn, he needed his phone. Worse still, he noticed his gas hand just a click above empty. He had intended to fill up earlier and now found his Z breathing fumes. Things were definitely not going his way.

The Hawthorne Compound

Still groggy, she cracked open one eye, slowly coming out of her *Sleeping Beauty* impersonation. She almost expected to see the seven dwarfs surrounding her, puckered and belting out that *Whistle While You Work* tune. Strange thoughts...this must be some good stuff flowing through her veins. While no longer completely in la-la land, she quickly discovered both her arms and feet were restrained. Obviously no *Prince Charming* had awoken her from her slumber with a magical kiss.

Taking an overdue deep breath, she blinked, trying to regain her focus and clear the crud weighing down her eyelids. Her surroundings looked like a bedroom, given the fact she could see her ankles spread eagled and tied to bed posts. Jogging the old memory cells, she recapped her last seconds before tumbling into sleepy town.

The good doctor had slipped her a loaded needle. Some thanks after she had just saved his life. Where had all the law abiding citizens gone? A thankless job, law enforcement had sunk to new levels.

Assessing her situation didn't take very long. Not only was she bound securely by all four limbs, her torso lay atop the bedding, naked as a Jaybird, and in a very un-lady like position. Nothing ached or hurt so she didn't think she had been violated; at least not yet. She still felt like the main course on the menu. Why else would she be naked? Unless, I've just become an organ donor, she thought. That should be consensual, but then again sexual exploitation should be too. Raping and pillaging, this wasn't the *Pirates of the Caribbean*.

Trudy gave each limb a good yank, searching for any signs of hope, an opportunity to escape. Nothing gave, snug as a bug. She would have to wait and see what the doctor had in mind. So far she had not been razzle-dazzled by his bedside manner.

She wondered why she was always the one that ends up naked and in the clutches of the bad guy. At least last time I was only missing my panties and Preston hadn't been interested in rape or organ mining, but I'm not so sure about the doctor.

Slowly but surely the fog bank lifted from her woozy brain. She raised her head like a terrapin, straining its neck from its painted shell. She knew no more than she did under fuzzier conditions. She lay tied to a bed, naked in a very decorative and plush bedroom fit for a queen, but she certainly didn't feel much like royalty.

She mustered up a faint whisper, "Brady, I'm so damn stupid. I hope you always remember I love you."

Approaching footsteps silenced her hopeless murmuring. The door opened, and in the doorway stood the man she had previously rescued from the syringe wielding vagrant. He smiled and looked quite harmless standing there dressed to the nines, as her mom used to say.

"Awake I see, Detective Pierce," he spoke in that same smooth manner that had been responsible for her being in this predicament. "I do apologize for not being more hospitable. I must say you do strike quite an outstanding pose, none the less."

"I suppose this is when I should shed a tear or two and ask what you plan to do with me. I'll cut to the chase; save us both some time. I'll ask you just what the hell your problem is. Killing illegal immigrants for monetary gains is one thing, but you've murdered a man of the cloth, two if you count the youth pastor, and it now appears you intend to do the same with an officer of the law. What next, steal the President's kidney?"

"A sense of humor under such tragic circumstances; you do surprise me, Detective."

"Kiss my ass you son of a bitch. I'm really not in a funny mood."

"My, now that wasn't so ladylike, and I might add, you're setting a poor example for your fellow officers. I would really regret having to gag that exquisite and wonderfully sensuous mouth God gave you. It would pleasure me tremendously to anoint those lips with semen from my magic wand."

"You stick that magic wand anywhere close to this sensuous mouth, and I promise you your new nick name will be stubby."

"How sad...I would have hoped you would prefer being conscious for our array of couplings but have it your way." He placed his hand palm down on her flat belly, then swirled his manicured thumb playfully inside her navel.

"You bastard," she shouted but refused to kick or squirm like she knew he wanted her to do.

Without warning he buried his thumbnail deeply into here exposed naval. She gritted her teeth, determined not to flinch, even though the pain was excruciating.

"A cavity sadly ignored and so misunderstood, but I promise you I'll ignore no orifice on your luscious body. We shall journey together to climatic oblivion."

This was worse than bad, she admitted. The doc was a loony, a total psycho and she really wasn't prepared to die, at least not like this. Pretending to like it sometimes turned off the sadistic type. They preferred resistance. If the doc sensed the game over he might just end it for good. Who was she kidding? Hog tied, she was at his mercy.

"Tell me about these photographs," he said, waving one in front of her face. You were quite young."

"How can I say it so you can understand it? FUCK YOU!"

"You were quite the exhibitionist in your youth, Detective Pierce. You've certainly maintained your girly figure. Do you still enjoy displaying it all for the lens?"

"And you're a pathetic little gutless bastard, probably a little mama's boy if I had to guess. Is this the only way you can have a woman? Did mommy treat you better?"

Lincoln laughed loudly, applauding her mockingly. "You really think you can get inside my head, Detective? Now who's the pathetic one? Sorry to disappoint you my dear but being traumatized or having a disastrous childhood has nothing to do with this. I simply enjoy it. It's so erotic and forbidden."

"Kiss my little bare ass."

"Who snapped these photos, a former lover?" He pinched her left nipple then the right one. "I must not show partiality."

"You do know I'm going to kill you the first chance I have?"

"You cause me to quake and shiver," he grinned. "But I'm tiring of these ridiculous games. Who took these photographs?"

"An old boyfriend...and he is also on my list too. There, are you happy?"

"His name," demanded Lincoln. "So I can send him a postcard from my island escape."

"His name is not important, you son of a bitch."

"My you have such a trashy attitude and vocabulary. You must have broken his heart to prompt possible blackmail, or do you just take these along for show and tell?"

"He's too spineless for blackmail."

"So, we still have a mystery, do we? You outsmarted the blackmailer and now you have the photographs. Did you kill the blackmailer? I apologize. You're a police officer. You're sworn to protect us, aren't you?"

"No...I didn't kill her, but I should have," she blurted out, realizing he had turned the game on her.

"Her...now I am hooked. You must share your little story with me and I might just spare you from some of my more bazaar wickedness. Who was she? What was her name? Where is she now?"

Figuring if she kept him entertained and talking, it bought her some precious time. "Her name, Samantha Burton, and she desired me as her sexual slave. I upped the ante and lured her into a little blackmail scheme of my own."

"Ah, Samantha Burton, the supposedly murdered and missing sheriff," he replied, showing her his perfect pearly whites.

"Missing, not necessarily murdered, and no, I had nothing to do with her disappearance, if that is your next question."

"You certainly didn't my dear, but she's dead just the same and no longer a threat to you."

"What is that supposed to mean?"

"It hasn't been so long ago that the good sheriff, and I do emphasize good, occupied this very same bed. Unfortunately she wasn't awake to enjoy the marvelous time we shared together."

"You abducted and murdered Sam?"

"On the contrary, she arrived here as my guest. Unfortunately, the cry for supply and demand influenced my decision, but not before I completed the world tour. I must commend you law enforcement females. You stay in excellent shape, but I base my opinion on a small sample size, just the two of you."

The bastard had murdered Sam. The Lord works in mysterious ways she thought, good riddance. A twist of fate, sadly she could be next unless she could turn the game.

"I can tell you are grief stricken by my confession but let's just keep it our little secret. We both escape winners. Well, in my case anyway, but sadly for you there will be no escape."

His cell phone rang. "Sorry, I must take this but I shall return. Don't start without me."

Trudy instinctively yanked at her restraints. They didn't budge. How was she going to survive this? She had no answers. She thought about Brady.

Highway 707

Rocker, still following the two vehicles had not yet come up with a plan to thwart them. Oddly, both vehicles took a left instead of a right that would have taken them back to New Hope Clinic. They were now traveling on 707. What were they up to, he wondered? He had no choice but to follow. He glanced at his fuel hand...not good.

Fifteen minutes later the driver parked Pierce's cruiser in front of a clinic in Socastee, the wrong clinic. Damn, thought Lance, they were staging her car at another clinic to throw off the investigators. The driver scampered into the passenger side door of the trailing vehicle. As before, they sped off at below the posted speed limit. Same choice, he followed them.

It didn't take Rocker long to figure this car wasn't returning to New Hope tonight. He followed, weapon-less and phone-less. Somehow he owed this to Pierce. He honestly regretted leaving her lifeless body dumped like yesterday's garbage, but the real story remained ahead.

Turn for turn he shadowed the remaining vehicle, confused about their destination but damned determined to see this to the end. What he wouldn't give for a cell phone or some gas in his tank.

The car slowed catching him by surprise. The brake lights almost illuminated the Z-28's interior. He had gotten just a little too close for comfort. No choice, he eased past and hoped he didn't raise their suspicions. Making the next left turn he pulled to a stop and exited the Z. Staying close to the shadows, he peeped back down the street.

The automobile was not in sight. Fighting off a panic attack he sprinted down the sidewalk, too loudly, the hard soles of his shoes thundering like horse hooves. He spotted the car in a parking lot. A different car was parked just past it, four spaces away. He wondered where this one had come from.

Rocker saw one figure standing on the opposite side of the third car. He was unable to identify the make. He must be talking with the driver of the one he had been following. He slinked closer, staying in the cover of a hedge. Just shy of the hedge's end he paused, remained crouched, hoping to blend in.

The man just stood there on the driver's side of the second car. Lance still couldn't make out what he was doing. He crawled on all fours. If he could reach the corner of the building he just might be able to hear what they were saying.

"Damn," he whispered, noticing the sign in front of the building "It's another clinic. What the hell are they up to now?"

The hedge's shadow moved. Still on all fours, Lance Rocker craned his neck to look up. Lights out, the hedge had clubbed him, game over.

Horry County Police Department

"Sheriff, I'm at the Pentecostal Holiness church and Mrs. McCrery, the preacher's wife, isn't here," radioed Detective Sylvester Stone. "A neighbor says she's gone to stay with her sister for a few days."

"Any sign of Pierce?" asked Woody.

"No, but the same neighbor said she saw her here earlier."

"I'll call Brady and see if she's there," stated Woody.

"One more thing...she's not answering her radio and I tried her cell. There's no answer on either."

"This isn't good. Something's bad wrong. The neighbor doesn't know where she's gone."

"She's a busybody but not psychic."

"I'm putting out an APB."

Woody called Brady's cell but ended up leaving a voice message. He didn't tell Brady she was missing. Instead Woody asked him to have her call him. Woody gathered the remaining crime scene investigators in his office and broke the news.

"What are we waiting for?" asked Tim Burroughs. "Let's find her."

"And we will," boasted Doctor Dallas Solomon.

"Good as found," chimed in Kirk Cardoon, the Captain.

Woody cheered them on but feared Trudy had gotten in over her head out there. He remembered Road Rage, and how she had tried to take him on by herself. She never radioed or tipped any of them off about her intentions. He had hoped she had learned her lesson with that close call...maybe not.

The Hawthorne Compound

Lance Rocker opened one eye then peeped from the second. His head ached worse than the mother of all hangovers. His vision momentarily blurred, he strained to focus. *Damn bushwhacking hedge...*

The light directly above added to his blindness. He attempted to wipe his eyes with his hand but found first one then the other bound tightly. So were his feet, like a bug in a spider's web. He waited to be spun in a cocoon.

"Ah Mister Rocker, I see you are awake," said a man's voice.

Lance strained to see the owner but the voice was somewhere behind him. He heard footsteps. He then saw a shadow and a figure standing by his side. "I've so enjoyed you for years. This is a first, *Mister Alive at Five* under my very roof. I had forgotten you have moved on to prime time. I commend you on the development of that marvelous syndicated show of yours. You're my first celebrity."

"Okay, so you know me. Who the hell are you?"

"How crude," the man answered. "Not a nice way to treat your host."

"Excuse me if I don't get up. I don't exactly feel like a guest. What's your damn name and what the hell do you want?"

A hand pinched and twisted his testicles extremely hard, bringing tears to his eyes. *Oh crap. I'm nude. The bastard has stripped me naked!*

"Crude and rude, you should be glad I'm not a network censor, Mister Rocker."

"You better be glad I'm tied up."

He received what felt like finger tips digging into the shaft of his penis and he let out a high pitched whine.

"Manners," the man ordered.

Rocker yanked, trying to pull himself free but all to no avail. *I don't like where this is headed.*

"My name is Doctor Lincoln T. Hawthorne, the lead story you were searching for and have now found."

"You're the Mexican killer."

"There you go again. I really don't appreciate that tone."

"And you're a cop killer!"

"You're so perceptive," he smiled, but he didn't divulge he had already murdered a sheriff.

"I saw you dump detective Trudy Pierce's body."

"Oh did you now?"

"I have photographs, and I've sent them to my agent."

"So tell me Sir Lancelot, where's your camera?"

"I used my cell phone!"

"This cell phone," said Lincoln, holding up Lance's crushed phone. "Found it at the clinic, in the garage. You should never play poker. You don't have the face for it. And just a little advice, don't leave such obvious evidence behind. Did you know breaking and entering is a criminal offense?"

"So if that wasn't her, where is she?"

Lincoln nodded and motioned to Rocker's left. Rocker craned his neck and sure enough, strapped to a bed next to his was the nude body of Trudy Wagner Pierce. He would recognize that body anywhere. She made eye contact but gagged; she couldn't speak.

"You're looking like a pin-up over there detective," said Lance.

She moaned something not so nice from the sounds of it. She gave him *the look.*

"So who did you ice?"

"No persons as important as you two, I assure you."

"You couldn't make enough money as a doctor?"

"My lifestyle requires much more. You should be able to relate."

"I've done some sleazy things, but I've never murdered anyone."

"What about that young lady they found in your very parking lot? She was our present sheriff's wife, if I remember correctly."

"You leave Janice Anderson out of this."

"So touchy..."

"What do you plan to do with us?"

"There are so many things that I don't know where to begin."

"Look, do me, but let her go."

"That is quite noble of you but actually, Detective Pierce is my favorite. You disrupted my plans. I so despise disruptions."

"Oh shit," Lance whispered, seeing the tray full of contraptions on the table.

Sister of Eternity Medical Clinic
Myrtle Beach

"Woody, we're at the Sister of Eternity Medical Clinic," radioed Sly. "Myrtle Beach city police found her cruiser."

Sly paused as he listened to Woody's response. "Pierce?"

"No, there's no sign of Pierce."

"The trunk..."

"Yes, we checked the trunk. It was empty and nothing is missing best we can tell."

"What about the clinic?"

"I have back up on the way. Captain and the Doc have the rear entrance covered. We're prepared to enter. We're just waiting on the search warrant."

Woody hesitated, "Yeah, best wait on it just in case we find something."

"Hold on. Tim and a city officer are motioning to me."

Sly walked around the block and spotted what had them so worked up. "Damn..."

"What's going on Sly? Talk to me."

"Rocker...we have his Z-28 here too, parked just around the block."

"Are you sure?"

"It has a ROCK YOUR WORLD plate on the front. It's Rocker's all right but no sign of him either."

"Doc found what looks like fresh blood inside, smeared on the head rest," stated Captain Kirk. "Not much, but she'll retrieve samples and contain the area."

"I'm heading there. I better try to reach Brady. Have Tim dig up what he can on this clinic."

"He heard you. He's on it," replied Sly.

"Damn it Pierce, what the hell have you done this time? And what's Rocker's role in it?"

The Hawthorne Compound

"I so hate it when you interrupt, Eugene. What is it?"

"A police officer and TV celebrity, this is getting just a tad out of hand, brother. It was bad enough you killing that ex-sheriff. This must end now."

"Witnesses," reminded Lincoln. "And I intend to end it."

"Harvesting illegals for the greater cause was bad enough. That got our dear sister murdered, and now this. You've lost it L.T!"

"You never really had the taste for this did you, Eugene?"

"Like you, I got caught up in the money and I convinced myself we were culling the Hispanic population, something the government wouldn't do."

"We were indeed doing our civic duty. They were here illegally, a burden on our healthcare system, taking American's jobs, fornicating, and gaining ground as the dominant race in the lower forty-eight. Yes, we were justified in our actions; most would agree."

"One hell of a speech, brother, but killing those two in there makes a mockery of it. We can't do this."

"Choices, so you really think we have choices here?"

"Damn right we have choices, L.T. We have all the money we could ever possibly need. We have new identities, a destination and plane tickets."

"But we must cover our tracks, Eugene. That was our original plan. Torch the clinic, the house, stage our deaths. The two at the clinic are already in place. We must tidy this mess up here."

"When I'm finished, you and your confidant can get rid of them like you always do, but then you must eliminate him too as a potential witness."

"Still so business like, even now. I'm not a cold-blooded murderer like you, L.T."

"But it is a business and your helper is jeopardizing our situation. You must get rid of the hired hand after I have done the same for those two meddlers."

"Might I remind you that the female detective and the newsman found us out easily? Others could be on their way here soon."

"And you're delaying the process, Eugene."

"No, I can't let you murder those two. It just isn't right."

"Hey Wagner, did you ever think we'd end up naked together?" asked Rocker.

Trudy responded, "Pierce" but it was muffled by the gag.

"So how do we get out of here? We're dead meat at the hands of the psycho surgeon if we stick around,"

Trudy Pierce, so frustrated that she could not respond, yanked and tugged at the restraints.

"Nice landing strip you have there. Those photos don't do you justice."

Growling now, she expressed her displeasure.

"Cold in here too, isn't it," he smiled, eyeing her erect nipples.

Lance became aroused and this wasn't the time or place for it, not with that wacky doctor just itching to dissect him. He couldn't really help it. Lance had always been skewed to the perverted side. His disgusting remarks and thoughts were typical, his way of dealing with situations beyond his control, even deadly ones.

Trudy noticed his growing erection and thought how disgusting this slime ball was, even in the face of death.

"I don't know if I've got the balls to bluff us out of this," commented Lance.

Instinctively, she glanced at him and mumbled something though the gag. He couldn't make out her words.

"Think, Lance, think," he muttered to himself.

She thought about Brady Pierce and how stupid she had been, again. Enough...time to get over the pity party she told herself. Assess the situation. Naked with Lance Rocker, both of them strapped to matching queen beds in a fancy bedroom in the Hawthorn mansion and time is running out like sand in an hour glass.

Leather straps, wrists and ankles, buckled in place; can't break them or slip out of them, she surmised. She was at a disadvantage; gagged. She wished Rocker was gagged instead.

She started rocking side to side, using her bound wrist and ankles for leverage. Could she flip the bed? She'd never know that answer because the bed was too heavy. It only ended up slipping slightly on the hardwood floor. What was she thinking? *I can't possibly flip a queen sized bed.*

"So that's it?"

A stranger entered the room. The resemblance was too uncanny. It had to be the mad doctor's brother, thought Lance. Trudy had him pegged for a brother too.

"I really don't wish to witness either of your deaths needlessly, but my little brother offers a good argument. You are witnesses. We have succeeded up until now operating our enterprise flawlessly. I sadly admit, you've compromised our position. I don't like this but I'm at a loss for an alternate plan."

"Killing a cop and a media star like me isn't going to be in your best interest. You're smart enough to know that already or you wouldn't be here. Could you remove the gag from Wagner, I mean Pierce, so we could get her input?"

"Plead her case you mean."

"You at least owe her that. By the way, where's the good doctor?"

"Let's just say he's cooling down right now."

"The gag," nodded Lance.

"Tell you what, I'll give you and the detective five minutes to mull this over, and then you get one shot at convincing me to persuade my brother to allow you to live. But don't hold your breath. This situation doesn't offer any viable choices as Lincoln has already pointed out to me."

Eugene slid the cloth rag from Trudy's mouth to below her chin. "You've got five minutes. Lincoln is not a patient man."

He closed the door and Trudy cut loose, "You bastard, you got those photos from that Burton bitch and you planned to do what...blackmail me?"

"And it's a pleasure to see you are still up to the task, Sweet Cheeks," Lance responded, eyeing her like a hungry dog.

"What are you doing here?"

"I thought they had iced you. I followed them. They clubbed me and stripped me down just like you. This wacko loves nudity, doesn't he? We've got about four and half minutes. Do you have any idea how we're going to save our bare asses?"

"They're not going to just let us go. They can't. They or should I say, he will kill us...eventually. It's what he's going to do to us first that worries the crap out of me."

Lance monitored the time on the mantle clock. "It's been four minutes, so what do we do?"

"Stall. Somehow we've got to distract him, offer up something more. Hell, I don't know...play along with him, maybe."

"I offered up me, but he prefers you. You heard him."

"Remind me to knight you later."

"A sword in your hands, fat chance... we're wasting valuable time and I'm not quite ready to be sliced and diced. Did anyone know where you were headed?"

"Not exactly..."

"You pull this horseshit all the time, don't you, Detective? Some damn cop you are? You got a death wish or something? Try asking for backup sometime, please."

"It's a gift. Besides, the situation didn't warrant backup."

"We have less than three minutes by the clock over there."

"The brother wants to do the right thing. I don't think he's a murderer, do you?"

"No, it sounds like he's just the damned undertaker. So you think we should pit one against the other?"

"I don't think so. They're too sharp for us to reel them into that scenario. I suspect it would only insult them and we don't want to piss them off."

"So what do we do then?"

"I'm thinking."

"Less than two minutes so you better think fast." "And best you do something more than just enjoy the view," she warned him. "And lose that erection, how about it?"

"We have no secrets now do we sweet cheeks? Do you like what you see?"

"I see it's only going to draw the doc to you like a magnet. Based on what we discovered from those poor souls we unearthed, he collects trophies like that and probably puts them in jars."

"Damn it, why did you have to say something like that? It's not like I can twitch it on and off at will."

The door opened.

Crime Scene
Socastee

"Have they found anything inside?" asked Woody, leaning against one of the squad cars.

"Not yet," replied Sly. "Place appears pretty damn clean."

"What about the automobiles?"

"They're finishing up dusting the exteriors then we'll have them towed to the garage where we'll have better light and equipment to check the interiors."

"I've sent Burroughs with a couple of city blues to bring in the owners and operators of this clinic for questioning," stated Woody.

"Something reeks here," commented Sly. "Lance Rocker's car parked down the street and hers here and both of them missing."

"What are you thinking?"

"It's too neatly arranged and convenient."

"Staged?" asked Woody.

"Yeah...my gut tells me we're being baited here. I don't think this is our clinic."

"What about Rocker and Pierce?"

"I believe one or both stumbled into something. They probably got caught off guard. Rocker has a nose for news and I bet the blood belongs to him or it's just staged too."

"So where are they now? You think they're still alive."

Sly didn't really want to answer that question. "They've murdered too many times. Two more would mean nothing to them. They've already killed one, possibly two men of the cloth so I would say the odds are not in their favor."

"You think this has anything to do with Sam Burton's disappearance?"

"Rocker is the common denominator."

"I would have never believed we would ever go though something like this again after the Preston Road Rage case, not here on the Grand Stand, not in Horry County."

"I wasn't here for that one, but I understand it was a hell of case."

"You could never imagine."

"I really thought this was going to blow up into the ultimate Hispanic gang and Klan war, but that sort of fizzled out."

Woody put his finger to his lips. "Don't say that too loud. That's all we need."

Hawthorne Compound

Lincoln stood in the doorway. He held a bloody scalpel. He looked angry.

"Did you just kill your brother?" asked Lance.

"Heavens no," smiled Lincoln. "I would never do that. His helper wasn't being very cooperative and obviously Eugene was being much too understanding. He really shouldn't have had him lock me in that meat locker like that even though I agree; I needed to cool off a bit."

Rockers erection retreated like a turtle's head disappearing inside its shell. Trudy almost laughed noting his reaction.

"So tell me, why should I allow you to live? Eugene gave you five minutes didn't he?"

"Four and half," replied Lance.

"I apologize. Please take another thirty seconds on me. Could I possibly assist you in your decision making?"

"What do you gain by killing us?" asked Trudy.

"My dear, I'm much like a cat with its prey. Toying with it brings me much pleasure. My sister so loved this part too. She would have thoroughly enjoyed you Mister Rocker."

"Take us with you," Trudy blurted out.

"Why would we do that?"

"Hostages," spoke up Lance.

"Not hostages," Trudy corrected him.

"You two should have done a better job collaborating on your story. After all, you did have four and half minutes.

"Four and half minutes sort of rushed us," quipped Lance.

"Please hear me out," she encouraged Lincoln.

Placing the scalpel on Rocker just above his flaccid appendage, Lincoln folded his hands just below his belt line and said, "I'm listening dear."

With the scalpel so close, Rocker's member shrank to boyish proportions but had nowhere to hide.

"Allow me to live and I will agree to be your sex toy. Do with me what you will, just don't kill me."

Placing his hand on the scalpel and his thumb touching the head of Rocker's penis he stated, "And I suppose you wish for me to consider the same fate for our Mister Rocker."

"I don't give a plug nickel what you do with him. This is about my own life."

"Wait a damn minute," babbled Lance, shocked by her all for her attitude.

"Gotcha," snickered Trudy.

Lincoln applauded her. "Well done my dear lady. I admire a sense of humor in such extraordinary circumstances."

"Lance Rocker is a journalist. What better than to bring him along and allow him to document your memoirs. Someday your autobiography will make one hell of a story. You'll be more famous than Hannibal Lector."

"I get dibs on the screenplay," spoke up Lance.

"What makes you think I desire to be famous? I've worked so vigorously to remain anonymous?

"A story like this deserves to be told, explained from your perspective. There's no case like yours in the history books." She winged it and poured it on.

"And this has absolutely nothing to do with your survival."

"Sure it does. I don't wish to die. I've made no bones about it and I'll do anything to prevent it."

"Even lie..."

"Even lie," she repeated.

"I really like you detective. You remind me so much of our dear departed sister, Cassandra. She possessed your tenacity."

"Crap," she blurted. "Your sister was killed by those gang members over in Marion, wasn't she?"

"What are you talking about?" asked Lance.

"My intentions were to possibly bail them out and avenge my sister's death. Sadly time is not on our side."

Playing along, Trudy said, "And they deserve just that fate. I have absolutely no use for their filthy kind."

"That's much too racial for a representative of the law my dear. You wouldn't be yanking my chain would you?"

"Hey, I'm spread eagle and naked and fighting for my life, I've got nothing to hide, you think?"

"What a pistol ball you are, Detective!"

"Call me Trudy."

"Free my hands and I'll play the violin," snapped Lance.

Lincoln jabbed the point of the scalpel into the shaft of Rocker's penis. Droplets of blood formed where he had pricked him."

"It would be my pleasure to document your rise and fall," said Lance in a much higher toned voice.

"As it would be mine to remove your manhood and roast it over an open fire," countered Lincoln, watching the color race from Rocker's increasingly ashen face. "Gotcha," laughed Lincoln.

"That was good, Doc," snickered Trudy.

Eugene entered. "So have they convinced you to spare their lives?"

"My dear Trudy has proposed an intriguing arrangement. Have you disposed of your hired hand?"

"You really didn't have to do that. He had just followed my orders. You needed a little chill time. Henry was a loyal employee."

"I do not blame you. You did what you thought was right, Eugene. Does she not remind you of Cassandra?"

"Not at all," replied Eugene.

"Not in looks...her temperament. Let's have a Brandy while I ponder her proposal. Stay put until we return."

"Regular comedian," commented Lance.

He waited until they were gone then lashed out at Trudy. "What the hell are you doing?"

"I'm trying to save our butts. Look, we've got to bargain with everything we've got to remain alive. I want to see Brady again."

"So you're willing to become his special little play toy for who knows how long."

"Work with me here, limp dick," she smiled, eyeing the incredible shrinking prick.

"Screw you," snapped Lance, unable to hide what once was.

"Closest you'll come to it is right here and now...so enjoy. Now cut the crap. Look, do you want to die or live?"

"I'm sorry. This is how I deal with stress. Do you think he bought it?"

"The fact that he's willing to ponder it has bought us some precious time."

"I must admit, it would be cool to document this."

"You'll do anything for the spotlight, right? I keep forgetting this is really all about you."

"It's my curse. I'm destined to be a star."

"Let's play this out. If he agrees, I don't think he's going to just allow us free reign, at least not for a while, if ever. We need to stay on guard at any opportunity to get the upper hand."

"I'm in. It's two against two. We should be able to take them."

"Remember, we're dealing with cold-blooded, ruthless killers and the doc has this thing for cutting off peckers. The dead Hispanics were missing theirs."

Lance swallowed and sighed, "But I think the Doc has the hots for you. It makes me wonder just what kind of relationship he had with that sister of his."

"That's the other card I'm trying to play. Get him to stick around and take out his revenge on his sister's murderers in the Marion jail."

"Anything I can do to help?"

"Stick to your game plan. Be your sarcastic smartass self. They'd smell a con if you became too agreeable. Just don't push him too far."

"I'm a master at playing the game," bragged Lance.

"Only with dumbass females," she cautioned him. "Don't push your luck. The good doctor is a murderer and shows no remorse."

"We'll get out of this, Sweet Cheeks. Hang tough, okay?"

Trudy nodded. "I'm not ready to die."

"It would certainly ruin my celebrity status too."

"We've got to work the brother, Eugene. He doesn't want to kill us."

"Something tells me the doctor rules the roost."

Trudy thought about Brady and how much she loved him. He needed her with what he was dealing with and she would find a way to beat this.

Horry County Police Department

"What the hell do you mean, she's missing?" ranted Brady Pierce.

"Have a seat, Brady," Woody encouraged him, noticing him trembling uncontrollably, obviously from his illness.

Brady eased into the seat at the end of Woody's desk, placing one hand on his knee, and the other hand on that hand to minimize the shaking. "Tell me what you know, Woody," he slurred slightly.

"We found her cruiser deserted at a clinic. We believe she may have been following a lead to those Hispanic murders."

"And..."

"And we did find blood near the scene. It is being analyzed as we speak. I don't think it's hers."

"What makes you think that?" Brady's head wobbled as he spoke.

"We found Lance Rocker's Z28 just around the corner and he's missing too. The blood could belong to him."

"What if he kidnapped her, Woody? You, for one, should know why with the blackmail going on."

"Thought about that too, Brady," Woody replied. "But why would he desert his car at the scene? I suspect whoever abducted Trudy, snatched Rocker, too."

"So you're telling me they both stumbled into the same hornet's nest?"

"It's just one theory.

"Do you have any others?"

"None that I am willing to share right now..."

"What can I do?"

"Pray and go home. Stay by the phone in case someone calls."

"Calls..."

"Could be a ransom demand..."

"You don't really think that do you?"

"We've got to play out all the angles. You know I think the world of that lady, too."

"I know you do and she loves you to death, Woody."

"I'll send an officer home with you."

"Find her Woody!" Brady propped on the edge of Woody's desk as he steadied himself. Woody figured the stress couldn't be helping his condition.

After Brady had left the premises, Woody stood with his back to the office door, pounding his head against the wall behind his desk. Tim Burroughs came sliding through the doorway, knocking on the door facing as he skidded to a stop just short of Woody's desk.

"You're not going to believe this," he shouted, waving a printout in his hands and grinning like a possum.

The Hawthorne Compound

Footsteps signaled the return and possible deliverance of the verdict from the brothers Hawthorne. Eugene and Lincoln entered, stone faced, neither indicating what had been decided of their fate.

"You have provided us with a most difficult situation," remarked Lincoln. Eugene remained silent, not making contact with either of them.

This couldn't be a good sign thought Trudy. She looked over a Rocker. She could tell he must be thinking the same thing. "Well, you have a captive audience."

"My dear brother and I have decided your fate. He is true to his convictions and wishes you no harm, however, Eugene doesn't always think wisely; what is best for us, not you."

Lance glanced over at Trudy, looking for any sign that he should step up his game but saw no such signal. He decided to take matters into his own hands. After all, his survival was at stake here too.

"Listen gentleman, I can make you rock stars if you don't jump to any hasty decisions. Once you have us all secluded in a secure country, I can work my magic and make you a legend."

"While I am absolutely intrigued by your proposition, I thought I explained to you that remaining anonymous is more important to us. We have worked vigorously for our legacy not to be associated with that of common murderers."

Oh this wasn't going as planned, thought Lance. He looked to Trudy for guidance but she still remained silent.

"We reached an impasse," continued Lincoln. "And finally we were able to compromise. While we both agree that having hostages could hedge our opportunity for achieving success, two are more difficult to manage than one."

Lance didn't like where this was heading and looked over at Trudy then back to Doctor Demento. Neither changed expressions.

"We'll be taking only one of you with us. The other unfortunately is dispensable. I can tell that the suspense is killing you; well, maybe just one of you," chuckled Lincoln, pleased with his dark humor.

"I am rather fond of Detective Pierce. She so reminds me of dear Cassandra. Sadly, my brother doesn't see this likeness."

Lincoln so enjoyed milking the moment. Lance Rocker sweated profusely while the detective continued to display absolutely no emotion.

"Eugene feels that you, Mister Rocker, would make a more difficult hostage, but I disagree. Surely, a trained police officer would be more of a liability."

"Oh just get on with this crock of shit," demanded Lance, tiring of the melodrama. "Which of us goes?"

Trudy said nothing. She just stared at the doctor and his brother.

"My affliction won out, I'm afraid," advised Lincoln, and as if finding his decision repulsive, Eugene exited the room.

Doctor Lincoln T. Hawthorne turned his back to his captors and removed something from his pocket.

"Screw both of you," snapped Lance Rock, not feeling so *alive at five* right now.

Horry County Police Department

"Spit it out Burroughs," demanded Sheriff Woodrow Anderson, tiring of Tim waving the paper and attempting to do an uncharacteristic moonwalk. He was no Michael Jackson.

"Under our nose all the time; we were so close," he chanted.

"Burroughs...spill it, please."

"All right all ready...I ran a check on Cassandra Guy and found it odd that she had no vehicles registered in her name. That just didn't seem right."

"Go on..."

"So next I ran a check on Eugene Hawthorne. He had numerous vehicles in his name; hearses, trucks, two Cadillac family cars, and three personal cars; nothing of real interest."

"Moss is growing underneath my feet, Burroughs."

"Then I ran the same check on one Lincoln T. Hawthorne and guess what?"

"I'm in no mood for guessing."

"Do you know how much you sound and act just like Sheriff Singleton?"

"He probably just turned over in his grave with that comment and you'll be joining him soon if you don't get to your damn point."

"He too, had an assortment of vehicles, way too many for one person to ever drive, I must say. He apparently has more money than sense. I suppose all rich people are like that."

"Burroughs," yelled Woody, now pounding both fists on his desk.

"He has a white vintage convertible Mustang registered in his name. It's got to be our car. She must have been driving it during most of the abductions."

"Sonofabitch, the heat was on so she swapped vehicles and chose the jeep," chimed in Woody.

"And maybe she barked up the wrong tree with those gang members."

"They turned the tables on her or maybe they just put two and two together and figured her out. Good work, Burroughs."

"Either way, we've got them. Her brothers, a doctor and a mortician, the perfect criminal cohorts for the Hispanic body parts murders and we now have the link. Here are the addresses for their homes, clinic and funeral home."

"Call the team and back-up, I'll request the search warrants," ordered Woody. "Again, fine bit of detective work, Tim."

He beamed with delight but his thoughts quickly turned to Detective Pierce. Had all this been too late?

The Hawthorne Compound

"Turn around and face us you spineless slug," shouted Rocker.

Lincoln turned slowly to face his accusers, a ghastly smile painted in ruby red lipstick. He puckered seductively and stated in an almost female sounding voice, "A kiss for the one we take with us."

"You," Trudy finally spoke. "It was your lipstick on those bodies."

Lincoln glided over to Rocker's bed, ran the back of his hand along his exposed thigh. Lance shuddered at his touch. Lincoln then seductively touched Rocker's flaccid penis with his forefinger then planted a kiss on his right cheek. "You'll be traveling with us my darling. And trust me, you will be my humble little journalist until I tire of you."

"Leave him alone you sick maniac," yelled Trudy.

"A woman scorned," sighed Lincoln. "I asked Cassandra to bring me a female the day she disappeared. She refused. She told me I preferred men just like her. She was right. Who was I fooling?"

"Take me," Trudy pleaded.

"Does it really matter, my dear detective?"

"Probably not, you're going to kill both of us so why torture him first?"

"For the sheer joy of it my dear. You should have figured that out by now. Yes, Cassandra had her way with them all, but she enjoyed giving them false hope. I, on the other hand, understand the real pleasures of eroticism."

"You tortured those poor bastards before you stole their organs, you worthless piece of dog crap."

"Yes, I so easily convinced my two siblings of the fortune to be made in the donor market, and then I reaped the full benefit, as was my intent all along. We didn't need the money, but it made it easier for them to justify our actions, especially Eugene, and oh how sis loved the amenities. The dangers were real. The Face is still a serious concern, but I won't bore you with those details. "

"All those poor souls senselessly killed, just to feed your fetish," stated Trudy in her no nonsense detective voice.

"Business and pleasure, my dear, perfect combination, don't you think?"

Lincoln turned to Rocker, mesmerized by the revelations and began kissing him with small affectionate pecks along his neck, working his way to Rocker's breast. Lance squirmed and shouted, "Stay away from me you sick psycho."

"Don't," screamed Trudy.

The Raids

Warrant in hand, Woody knocked and shouted a second time, but no one responded from inside. "Use the ram," he ordered.

The two uniformed officers did just that and on the third strike the door shattered. Sly and the Captain entered with weapons drawn. Cautiously they proceeded down the hallway conducting a room to room search.

This felt like the right place. Sly's gut told him so. He expected to come face to face with deranged killers at every turn. Captain Kirk had the same feeling. His finger rested on the trigger, ready to ask questions second.

"Sheriff, you better take a look at this," Sly called back to Woody.

Woody eased down the hallway and peeped into the room, his weapon drawn too. "Damn, check their vitals. Are they dead?"

"Both are still breathing," replied Sly, after checking the pulses of the two filthy derelicts strapped to adjacent examining tables.

"I wonder why they haven't killed them?" asked Captain.

"Maybe we interrupted their plans," answered Sly. "Look on their hands." He pointed to the rings they were wearing.

"A little pricey..." remarked Woody.

"The garage out back," radioed Tim Burroughs. "Dallas and I have found the Mustang. New Hope Clinic is our clinic, and this trio has to be responsible for the organ mining."

"Call an ambulance for those two homeless looking guys and let's check the rest of the rooms," ordered Woody. "Tim, you got a home address for any of these folks?"

"All three of them live at the same home, it appears. Third warrant is in my pocket. We can be there in less than fifteen minutes," answered Tim. "I'll have the blues secure the perimeter and we can be on the way, sir. By the way, the search of the mortuary turned up nothing. Neither of the Hawthorne brothers was there."

"Copy, we go as a unit," stated Woody, looking over at Sly and Captain Kirk. "That's the way Pierce would want it."

"Damn straight," answered Sly. "These sick bastards belong to us."

"Let's go kick some butt," shouted Tim.

The Hawthorne Compound

Too late, Lincoln had already clinched Rocker's right nipple between his teeth, leaving the impression of red lips round his breast. With razor incisors he snipped Rocker's nipple off, bringing a blood curdling scream from Lance.

"Up close and personal huh, *Mister Alive at Five*," stated Lincoln, spitting the severed nipple into the palm of his hand and then placing it on the bedside table. "We're going to have so much fun down below. Sorry, Detective, your vacation will be cut short."

"It was really you, not your sister doing all that biting on the Hispanics?" exclaimed Trudy a second time, not believing what she had just witnessed.

"Fine detective work," grinned Lincoln, lipstick slightly smeared now. "But so redundant, don't you think?"

Lance realized the consequences and so wished he could cup his hands over his privates. "Take Pierce," he blurted out.

"Spineless wimp," she snapped.

"You two really don't care for one another, do you?"

"Have Rocker tell you about his perversions," encouraged Trudy, pulling every trick she could to stall for time.

"Shut the hell up!" yelled Lance, in pain and no longer playing the game.

"Our famous newsman collected the panties of his conquests and used similar tactics as yours. He possibly drugged some of his unsuspecting victims, had his way with his lady friends, then photographed them and had quite a trophy room in his walk-in closet."

"I'm impressed Lance," smiled Lincoln, rubbing his hand down Rocker's chest stopping just short of his navel and forcefully sliding his pinky inside, "Tell me more, please."

"He screwed the reigning Sheriff's wife just before she was murdered by Preston, the Road Rage serial killer," she said, regretting she had gone there but she had his attention and intended to keep it.

"She's got plenty of skeletons in her closet. Don't let her con you. She's no damn saint."

"My, the gloves are coming off," exclaimed Lincoln, clapping his hands, cherishing the rivalry that had exploded.

"She had a sexual encounter with a defrocked Sheriff, a result of a double blackmail they had going on."

"Tell me, who was this gentleman?"

"You're going to love this. Not a gentleman...a woman. I had her myself just before she disappeared. Pierce probably murdered her."

"Saucy, we all have such common threads. Who was this female sheriff?" asked Lincoln, pretending not to know.

"Samantha Burton, and she is now missing in action."

"Small world," snickered Lincoln, again applauding. "I too, had Samantha Burton. We travel the same circuit, share the same toys."

"You," remarked Lance.

"I had my way with her right here, and then she assisted me in completing a vital order. One must keep the clientele happy. Yes we have a demanding customer; won't take no for an answer."

"You murdered Sam," remarked Lance.

"Right place, wrong time," he shrugged. "I had this hunger for a female. Sometimes I just have cravings for a good woman and she didn't disappoint, but you both already know that, don't you? She held my attention briefly."

"And Raeford McCrery," added Trudy.

"Ah, the good reverend," smiled Lincoln. "Honesty isn't always the best policy. He made good on the associate pastor's debt. He mistook himself for an amateur sleuth."

Eugene burst into the room. "Enough of all these dirty little secrets," he screamed. "I can't take any more. Let's end this now, L.T."

Lincoln turned, surprised by Brother Eugene's outburst. He made a swipe at his painted lips with the back of his hand but too late, Eugene had seen his red lips.

"What have you become, little brother? You and Cassandra, and you thought I was clueless, didn't you?"

"Leave her out of this, brother," warned Lincoln.

"You and her, I saw you, as kids, you and your filthy little secrets," he spouted, tears rolling freely. "How could you have sex with your very own sister?"

"Jealous," asked Lincoln. "You were such a wimp, a pathetic little loser. We've carried you forever because you were our blood, tainted as it appeared."

"You speak of tainted, L.T.," replied Eugene, shaking his head in disgust. "You had an incestuous relationship with our sister. You performed these sick acts on men. You have the gall to say my blood is tainted. You're a disgrace."

Trudy and Lance lay speechless. This could be the break they needed but only if Eugene came out on top. Trudy wasn't so sure the larger Eugene could take Lincoln, even in a fair fight, but she suspected no encounter with Lincoln would be on even ground.

"It ends now," repeated Eugene, pointing a finger toward Lincoln. "And clean that disgraceful paint off your lips."

Lincoln puckered and winked. "We're leaving as previously discussed, brother. Lance will be our hostage and the detective..."

Eugene cut him off. "Change of plans. We leave them both here. No more murders, L.T. We catch our prearranged ride. We start that new life. These murders gain us nothing. They're on to us. Staging the fires is pointless."

"Tidying loose ends, it must be done. They are witness to our carnage. They know too much and will report it to the news media. We can not chance *The Face* knowing we are still alive."

"Whose fault is that, L.T.?"

"It ends here, Eugene," he mocked his brother.

"Don't trust him, Eugene," yelled Trudy.

Eugene eyed the detective. "He's my flesh and blood. L.T. doesn't harm family."

"That is correct. Family means everything to me. With Cassandra gone, you are the last of my bloodline as weak and pathetic as you are, but you are my brother."

"Please clean that red smut off your face, L.T. and let's make our preparations."

"We will still torch the clinic and the compound."

"There's no time. I fear the clock does not tick in our favor now."

"Tick tock, tick tock, tick tock," mocked Lincoln, turning and smiling at Rocker, then like lighting, grasping Lance's penis in his mouth.

Lance felt the doctor's teeth close around his appendage. He would not be spared after all. Staring at a helpless Lance Rocker, Lincoln applied pressure. One quick snap and it would be severed. Lincoln still locked in the stare, now smiled then winked at Rocker. "Gotcha," he mouthed then released him and patted him on his tummy.

The caravan of patrol cars, marked and unmarked converged on the Hawthorne Compound, still five minutes away. Woody had phoned Brady, and told him to meet them there. Not typical police protocol, but Woody never acted like a typical lawman; at least not since meeting Trudy Wagner.

He just hoped it wasn't too late. He thought about how he missed Janice, and how Brady didn't deserve the same fate. Rocker on the other hand did. A part of him wished nothing but the worst for Lance Rocker. An officer of the law should not think this way but he had participated in blackmail, withheld evidence, made radical and unethical decisions, and so wishing this on Rocker seemed mild in comparison.

One thing for sure, he had no interest in remaining Sheriff. He would not toss his name in the hat come next election. Woody wasn't even sure he still had the desire to remain in law enforcement. He looked over at Tim Burroughs driving, and he beamed with pride how far the geeky policeman had come. The kid had become a man under his watch.

He hadn't gotten to know the others as well. Sly, Captain and Dallas were outstanding picks by Pierce. Somewhere up there he was sure that Hank Singleton looked over them, basking as only Hank could.

Judgment time approached. His heart told him that his partner had survived far worse things for it to end like this. She had a purpose, a destiny. It couldn't be over. He refused to allow it. "Put some lead in that foot, Burroughs."

The Hawthorne Compound

"Glad you came to your senses, L.T.," remarked Eugene, leading the way to the already packed Lexus SUV.

Lincoln hesitated at the garage doorway. "I will be with you in a second, brother. I forgot something."

"Quickly," Eugene urged. A mere minute later he returned and they were on their way.

The Calvary closed in. Woody spotted their final destination half a block ahead. The Lexus cruised past them, abiding by the posted speed limit, going in the opposite direction. The officers poured from the vehicles like ants, quickly surrounding the compound, cutting off any possibility of escape.

Woody took a sniff then looked at Sly. "I smell it too," remarked Sly. "Smoke."

"No...Fire," yelled Tim Burroughs, pointing toward the flames now visible through a first floor window.

"Oh crap," shouted Captain Kirk.

"I'm calling the fire department, go," screamed Dallas.

Woody checked the main entrance door, locked. He grabbed a metal chase lounger off the porch and tossed it through one of the two story high windows, shattering it on impact. Followed by Sly, Tim, Captain and three uniforms, they scattered and began searching the first floor of the massive complex.

"Wagner," screamed Woody over and over but no answer then he yelled, "Pierce."

The fire spread rapidly, now consuming three rooms on the first floor. Woody spotted the stairway. The fire roared just beyond the hallway leading to the steps.

"I'm going up," he yelled.

"I'm right behind you," yelled back the Captain, Detective Kirk Cardoon.

Room to room searches resumed on the second floor. Woody yelled, "Wagner, Pierce, Trudy..." over and over as he crashed through door after door.

"Here," yelled the Captain from the opposite end of the hallway, vanishing through a doorway.

Smoke now burned Woody's eyes. It had begun forming like fog hugging the floor and rising. Woody entered the doorway where Captain Kirk had disappeared. He bounded past the first bed containing a restrained and bloody Lance Rocker.

He stared at the nude body of Trudy-Wagner-Pierce. "What took you so damn long, partner?" she said between coughs.

"Due process of the law is such a bitch," Woody responded, releasing her from her restraints.

Captain had already freed Lance Rocker. His blooded scalp was not bleeding but his breast showed signs of a fresh wound. "My nipple," mumbled Lance. "Find my nipple."

Captain confused by that statement instinctively looked at both of Rocker's breast. Sure enough, one nipple was missing from a breast.

"On the floor," shouted Rocker.

Captain now understanding his concern began searching the floor around the bed. Windows exploding below them reminded them that the fire still raged out of control.

Woody had wrapped Trudy in a sheet and led her toward the doorway. "We've got to get the hell out of here now."

"Sorry man," exclaimed Captain. "I don't see it anywhere. We've got to go."

Lance got down on all fours, scrambling and trying to find his severed nipple but the smoke was so thick now that he could hardly see the floor. He pulled the bedspread down on top of him and around his mouth and nose.

"Now," yelled Captain, trying to cover his mouth with his shirt.

Woody and Trudy stood at the doorway yelling for them to follow, and then turned to backtrack toward the stairs. Captain yanked Rocker to his feet and pushed him toward the open door. He could feel the heat from the floor beneath him. The room seemed to almost be smoldering.

Lance made it to the bedroom door and turned to check the progress of the detective. Captain yelled "Go, I'm right behind. Hey look what I found! It was on the table." He held Rocker's severed nipple in the palm of his hand.

Lance made a step towards him, "Thank the Lord," he spoke as the floor collapsed into a wall flames.

Captain Kirk dropped out of sight; was gone just like that and so was Lance Rocker's nipple. The towering flames reached the bedroom's ceiling and followed the contour toward the doorway. Lance exited, pulling the door closed behind him, hoping by doing so, it would buy them some valuable time.

Woody and Trudy stood at the stairway. The steps and railing had been overtaken by the ever expanding fire. There would be no escape the way they came up.

"Is there another way out?" asked Woody, his eyes and nose burning from the heavy smoke.

"I don't know. I was drugged when they brought me here." She coughed and could barely see.

"Got to be another set of stairs somewhere," yelled Woody over the deafening explosions of more windows below and to their right.

Lance had caught up with them but he was fading fast from the thickening smoke. "We can't last much longer in this," he coughed.

"Where's the Captain?" asked Woody.

Lance bowed his head then shook it back and forth.

"What's that supposed to mean?"

"Dead, the floor gave way in the bedroom," yelled Rocker. "He found my nipple. It's gone too."

"This way," screamed Trudy, heading toward the farthest end of the corridor.

They moved as one, each touching the shoulder of the one ahead of them. "Here," she said, sliding up the door.

"What?" asked Woody.

"Dumb waiter," she shouted, pointing to the rope and platform inside.

"You want us to get in there?" asked Lance.

"Not all at once," she answered. "One at a time, we lower each other down."

"What if it leads to the mouth of hell?" asked Lance.

"Well we're sure to feel hell's fury if we stay here," coughed Woody.

"No smoke coming up and I don't feel any heat. The draft feels cool. It probably goes to the basement."

"Then you go first," pointed Lance, sensing no reason to be a dead guinea pig.

She climbed inside, and like Santa going down a chimney, she began lowering herself out of sight. Less than two minutes later she yanked on the rope and yelled for them to pull it back up. She was indeed in the basement. It felt cool and damp and wonderful.

Once the dumb waiter had been hoisted back to the second floor Lance, feeling safe, yelled, "I'll go next."

"You're such a dick," shouted Woody.

The heat was almost unbearable now. The smoke was sucking the breath out of them. Lance was in and heading down. He reached the bottom unscathed and signaled for Woody to pull it back up. The rope didn't move. Smoke was now filtering down the shaft.

Trudy crooked her head and yelled up the shaft but received no answer. Suddenly a flash of flames poured through the dumb waiter's door on the second floor. "Woody..." she screamed.

"This way,' yelled Lance. "It looks like some sort of delivery entrance."

Trudy ignored him, still holding out that Woody would appear in the shaft, but he didn't. She could now feel the heat snaking down from the inferno above.

"Pierce, you coming? You can't save him. He's dead."

"Shut the hell up Rocker before I rip off your second tit."

"Seriously, we need to go before this whole house comes crashing down on us."

One last look and a long sigh, she then followed him. Her heart ached. She could not believe he was gone. Plunging through the delivery door, they were instantly blinded by all the flashing rescue lights.

Dallas spotted them first and waved others in their direction. Sly and Tim and a stampede of firemen sprinted towards them.

Their joy was short lived when they realized neither the Sheriff nor Captain Kirk was anywhere to be seen.

Medics tended to Lance Rocker's wounds. Trudy waved them off, still watching the burning mansion, heart heavy over the loss of her fallen comrades. Fire fighters from several stations fought bravely to extinguish the blaze but it was futile at best.

"The Hawthorne brothers," asked Trudy.

"We're setting up road blocks and are still searching for them," answered Sly.

"The airports...check all the airports. They were leaving the country tonight."

"I'm on it," replied Burroughs.

Dallas placed her hand on Trudy's shoulder, sheet still draped around her as if she had just returned from a toga party. "The Sheriff, he'll be sadly missed."

"This shouldn't have happened," mumbled Trudy. "Stupid, carelessness on my part. He's dead because of me."

"Don't bury me just yet."

Trudy whirled, dropped her sheet and stood there in the buff, grinning at Woody less than ten feet away.

"You've got this thing for flaunting your assets tonight, don't you," said Woody nodding to her and the sheet at her feet.

"That's my wife, a damn exhibitionist."

"Both of you get your asses over here," shouted Trudy.

"Reckon that's the only way we're going to keep you from being arrested for indecent exposure," answered Brady, embracing and covering her with his arms and torso.

She pressed her womanly nakedness against Brady and Woody, sandwiched between them.

"This is carrying this partner stuff a tad too far don't you think?" stated Brady, breaking into a laugh.

"How did you get out?" asked Trudy.

"Well, I haven't climbed down a tree in forever but found one close enough to one of those back bedroom windows. I shimmied down when the fire let me know I wouldn't be joining you two down that chute."

Trudy noticed the burns on his neck and back of his arms. His hair was singed. "Medic," she yelled.

"Did they catch them?" asked Woody.

"Not yet," she replied.

Lance, sporting bandages on his head and chest, walked over with the bedspread still wrapped around his waist. "Glad to see you made it short stuff."

"Wish I could say the same for you, asshole," answered Woody.

"Woodrow," scolded Trudy.

"Sorry, old habits and deep wounds," he replied. "You look like dog crap, Rocker."

"That's better Sheriff. Sorry about Detective Cardoon. I didn't know him very well but he did find my nipple. Unfortunately..."

"Stifle it, Rocker," ordered Trudy.

"So does anyone care to fill me in?" asked Brady.

"Get her home and cleaned up and clothed," motioned Woody. "She's got a lifetime to catch you up to speed."

"What about me?" asked Lance.

"Take him to his hotel, Tim."

"I will but I'm sure not going to bathe and dress him," replied Tim Burroughs.

"That cuts so deeply," replied Lance, pinching him on the cheek as he passed.

"Get him out of here," snapped Woody. "Let's go catch us those murdering bastards."

"Not until they see to those burns," said Dallas.

"All right, but keep me posted on the progress, and don't let them out of Horry County."

Horry County Police Department
One Week Later

"I still can't believe we lost the Captain," stated Trudy. "And how are those burns."

"A good man," answered Woody. "I'll mend just fine."

"Still nothing?"

"Nope, they dropped off the face of the earth."

"You still think they were on that charter to the Bahamas?"

"It seems likely. The plane stayed below radar and no one can tell us exactly where it landed."

"We'll probably never see them again will we?" "Unless we believe in the theory that they always return to the scene of the crime or we go bounty hunter and drag their butts back here."

"It worked for Road Rage. Preston came back to roost."

"These are different circumstances. Where's Rocker?"

"Getting his boob job probably," snickered Trudy.

"I wish the doctor would have aimed lower."

"Actually he did, but he didn't pull the trigger," recapped Trudy. "He was one sick individual."

"I can't help it. I hate that bastard, Rocker."

"And you have just cause, Woody," she said, placing her hand on top of his.

"How's Brady?"

"He's about the same. He's determined to be the ultimate human guinea pig. He believes there's a cure out there somewhere. I've got to believe too."

"You have to admire him. He's a fighter."

Tim knocked at Woody's office door. "You're not going to believe this?"

Woody rolled his eyes. That was always Tim Burroughs's leading sentence. "Spill it."

"You know those two gang members over in Marion, the ones accused of killing the doctor's sister. It seems that they made bail yesterday."

"Bail," stated Woody, shocked by the news. "I thought that bail had been set at half million a piece, because they were illegal and a flight risk."

"Son of a gun," exclaimed Trudy. "They're still here."

"Come on Pierce, you can't possibly believe they're still in the country. That would be just plain stupid. I bet they have high-tailed it for sure."

"Not the Hispanics," clarified Trudy. "The Hawthorne brothers are still here. The doc had a grudge to settle with his sister's murderers. We locate the two released on bail and find the doc and his brother, guarantee it."

"I'll call the sheriff over in Marion and see if he has any information on their whereabouts."

"Don't hold you breathe. They've got a day's jump on us."

"We owe Captain Kirk," Woody reminded her.

"I've got a little score to settle, too," she reminded him.

"That you have," nodded Woody.

Conway Medical Center
Several Days Later

"How's Brady doing?' asked Woody.

"Not bad I suppose for a man with pneumonia and one collapsed lung," responded Trudy with a forced smile.

"How are you holding up?"

"Like a wife with a husband with pneumonia and one collapsed lung..."

"You may want to have a seat," advised Woody.

Without questioning why, Trudy collapsed into one of the *oh so comfy* waiting room chairs. She gave Woody a look that said get on with it. You have my attention.

"I got a call from Marion County law enforcement about an hour ago. They think they may have found those gang members that were bailed out."

Trudy sat on the edge of her seat. She had been hooked. She eyed Woody and said, "And."

"They're still sorting through the pieces...literally. They had been brutally dismembered and scattered about the area where Cassandra Guy's body had been discovered."

"That's it."

"Not exactly, a sedan was parked nearby, stolen of course. It was covered with graffiti and what appears to be blood, probably belonging to the two Hispanics."

"Graffiti..."

"Yeah, it said *In Her Memory,* and a bible rested on the hood next to the bloody message. It belonged to that Preacher, Raeford McCrery."

"They went further than I would have anticipated. Is that it?"

"Not hardly. There was also a crushed telephone belonging to Lance Rocker and a Franklin Planner, Samantha Burton's, with yours and Rocker's names written inside it. Your photographs, you know the ones, were tucked inside the pages."

"What did you say to the Marion police?"

"I didn't. What could I say? The blackmail photos were the ones lifted from your cruiser, and now they are evidence in the case. And underneath one of he photos, scrawled in blood, it said GOT'CHA."

Trudy slammed her hand on the chair cushion. "The sick bastard..."

"Looks like he decided to muddy the water with all the crap and totally screw up the investigation. He posed more questions than answers."

"This is so screwed up," sighed Trudy. "So what is your counterpart over in Marion County having to say about all this?"

"He said he would consider giving the photographs back to you once you came by and did some explaining and filled in the gaps, so to speak. He's not stupid. He saw what Lincoln Hawthorne was trying to do, and he's not buying it."

"Thank goodness for small miracles, I suppose. Are there any leads on Lincoln and Eugene Hawthorne?"

"Not yet..."

"How about staying here with Brady while I tidy things up?" She asked, hankering to play a hunch she had.

It hit her like a run away freight train. She had walked out on her Mom, just like this, while putting duty first. Trudy had selfishly asked Brady to stay with her. That was the last time she had seen her mom alive. Now she was about to do it all over again and to Brady, asking the same favor of Woody.

"Never mind," she told Woody. "Ask that sheriff over in Marion if I can settle some family matters first."

"I'm sure he'll be okay with that, but there's something else isn't there?"

She nodded.

"You want to share it with me?"

"I know where we can catch them, but I can't be there and here too. "I'm going to burn in hell if I do this."

"Then let me handle it, partner. You're not the only one that can do this. Let us take care of it. Stay here with your husband where you belong."

"I owe them. Don't you see," she said, now standing and clinching her fists. "You saw what that sick bastard did to me, but Brady needs me. You see just how messed up this really is. I've got Brady and them on opposite sides of the scales, and I shouldn't be treating them the same, but I can't help it. I've never been able to help it, damn it."

Woody said nothing. What could he say?

"Choices, I can't make them like a sane person. I'm obsessed with my work, duty first, and family always last. I should have been there for her, Woody, don't you get it? I should have been there." Even now the tears wouldn't flow. The obscenities did. Woody let her get it out of her system. What else could he do?

****

The glass pane shattered. A jiggling of the lock indicated that entry had been breached. The door creaked slowly open. Footfalls echoed on the tile floor, illuminated by a penlight. A search, room by room ensued. Frustration overcame caution. Items began breaking. "Where is it?" whispered an angered voice. "It must be here somewhere!"

The mortuary lit up like a theater stage, startling the searcher, stopping him in his tracks, blinded by the light.

"Is this what you're looking for, you son of a bitch," proclaimed Lance Rocker, holding the urn that contained Cassandra Guy's ashes.

Lincoln T. Hawthorne smirked, "I underestimated you, Mister Rocker. Did you return for seconds?"

"You underestimated all of us," spoke up Woody, now stepping from the open doorway, revolver drawn.

All Lincoln could say was, "Sheriff." He pretended to tip a hat.

A voice crackled over the walkie-talkie, "We've got the brother outside," announced Sly. "He offered no resistance."

"So where's that sweet Detective Pierce?" asked Lincoln, "Or is she still trying to explain to the authorities her involvement?"

"With her husband, where she should be, but just so you know, she's the one that figured where you would be coming next," clarified Woody.

"A force to be reckoned with, that detective, and as I have pointed out, she so reminds me of Cassandra," acknowledged Lincoln. "She and you, Mister Rocker, should have perished in that fire. That was a grave mistake on my part for not finishing what I had started. Loose ends, I knew better."

"You give yourself too much credit," replied Rocker. "Good always wins out over evil. It says so right here in Raeford McCrery's bible." Rocker smiled, waving the bible in Lincoln's direction.

"I'm glad you're such a religious man. Can I hold my dear sister now?"

"Sure," answered Lance, pretending like he almost dropped the urn. "Gotcha..."

"Please be careful with her."

"With this," replied Woody, taking the urn from Rocker. "I don't think so." He slammed it to the tile floor, shattering it and spreading its contents.

"Nooooooo..." screamed Lincoln Hawthorne.

"Gotcha good that time," grinned Woody. "That's not you sister; just fire place ashes. Pierce owed you that one. Burroughs, read him his rights and get him the hell out of my sight before I forget I'm Sheriff."

Tim Burroughs cuffed him as instructed. He secured the doctor's arms behind his back then faced him nose to nose. Shaking his head in disgust he delivered a head butt, sending him to his knees. "That was for Captain Kirk Cardoon, forensics, and my friend."

Sly jerked Lincoln back to his feet but Doctor Dallas Solomon sent him back down for the count with a well placed kick to the groin. "That's for all those young men that you murdered and just because I felt like it."

"This is police brutality," moaned Lincoln, as he rolled around on the floor. "I'll have your entire department brought up on charges, Sheriff."

"Didn't see a thing," announced Detective Sylvester Stone, grinding his heel into Lincoln's crotch.

"No witnesses that I can identify," added Dallas.

"Witnesses to what?" asked Tim.

Lance walked over and spat on him. "No cameras running, I'm afraid." He squatted beside the doctor and pinched him on the nipple. "Be glad you get to keep both."

"Like I said, Tim, get this worthless piece of crap out of my sight. You're lucky you live north of the border, Doc. I don't think our friends down south would have treated you quite so well."

"Possibly after you are imprisoned, you can apologize to the Hispanic population. I'm sure they will forgive you for your sins, or maybe they will just rock your world."

Woody turned to face Rocker. No words were passed between them but both understood without a doubt, it stopped here. They'd never be friends but that was okay too.

Conway Medical Center

"Who was that on the phone?"

"Woody...they've got them," smiled Trudy.

"And I've got you," replied Brady, reaching over to hold her hand.

"And I love you too, Circus Boy," she said, climbing into the hospital bed with him.

"I must be feeling better."

"Indeed you are," Trudy answered, sliding her hand under the covers. "Indeed you are."

"Parkinson, it makes me rigid," laughed Brady.

"A wonderful disease then," she laughed.

"We're going to be all right," Brady assured her.

"Yes we are," Trudy agreed, "A lifetime of forever ahead."

Epilogue

"Woody, are you sure about not running for Sheriff," inquired Trudy.

"Sure as I'm standing here, and I'm officially done with policing, partner. I handed in my resignation yesterday, effective immediately. I have enough comp time built up to take a long paid vacation with the kids, probably to Disney World, and I plan to treat them to all those other attractions in Florida."

"You quit? You didn't tell me you were going to just up and quit."

"I've been thinking about this for several months. It's the right thing for me to do. It's not what I originally signed up for, all these senseless murders and us not exactly playing it by the book."

"So what you're really saying is you were an honest cop before you met me."

"You said it, not me."

"You just tossed away your retirement pension just like that."

"I was never in it for the money. I have savings, enough to get by."

"What's next for you, Woodrow?"

"I'm not sure. I've got a few ideas but I'm not ready to say yet."

"You'll be back. I know you, partner. You're more cop than you want to let on. I'll be here when you come to your senses."

"Did I tell you I had an email from Janice's cousin Marian, you remember her, right? She's thinking about moving to the beach of all places."

"Is that why you're hauling ass?"

"How's Brady?"

"Right," Trudy gave Woody a little wink. "He's sucking it up, but those experimental drugs aren't working any miracles yet. Your phone is ringing. You're not going to answer it?"

Woody eyed the phone on his desk. "Officially it isn't my phone. I'm off the clock, remember." The dispatcher paged him, stating urgent call on line three. Woody bit the bullet, saying what the hell, one last time.

Woody listened to the caller and crashed back into the leather desk chair. The color had drained from his face. He shook his head backwards and forth. He thanked the caller then ended the call.

"You look rattled. What was that all about?"

"You do remember Detective Shannon Chestnut's Aunt, District Attorney Claudia Livingston."

"Indeed I do. She made sure we nailed Ford."

"She's dead."

"Dead, what happened?"

"They suspect suicide, but the coroner hasn't completed his investigation yet."

"That makes no sense, Woody. She didn't seem to be the type to do something like that."

"Maybe Shannon's death took more of a toll on her that anyone suspected. Or maybe it was brought on by the pressures of being a D.A. Who knows what makes people hit their breaking point."

"Are they sure it was a suicide?"

"Like I said, her death is still under investigation. She was found hanged in her garage."

"Hanged, she just didn't seem the type to do that, to me. It smells fishy."

"Partner, let it go. This isn't your case. She had moved to Wilmington. The call came from an old buddy of mine in the police department up there. He seemed to think it was just what I said."

"I don't know. My gut tells me there's more to this."

"It's not my problem, and you don't have a dog in the hunt either. You should know by now that Horry County is a damn handful, so there's no need to cross state lines. We seem to be a melting pot for big time cases so just bide your time until the next big one comes along. As for me, it's fun in the sun with the kids."

"I get it. I'm going to miss you, Woody."

"Hell, I didn't say I was leaving for good; just a little vacation. You'll see enough of me after I get back. For now, I'm going to Disney World." Woody imitated one of those quarterbacks that had just won the Super Bowl.

"That was too cheesy even for you, Woody. See you when you get back. Please try not to stumble into the Disney character serial killer, okay?"

"I'm not *goofy*, just yet." Woody winked, then gave her a squeeze on her shoulder.

Trudy watched him exit and then shook her head. She just didn't buy this suicide assumption but like Woody had pointed out, she had no jurisdiction in North Carolina, but there was no harm in following the case. She owed that much to Shannon Chestnut. Her first priority right now was to go check on Brady, and then she should probably call her sister. The criminals would be there tomorrow. Family first, she was indeed a reformed southern belle.